Edward H. Cooper

# Resolved to be Rich

A novel

Edward H. Cooper

**Resolved to be Rich**
*A novel*

ISBN/EAN: 9783337027148

Printed in Europe, USA, Canada, Australia, Japan

Cover: Foto ©Andreas Hilbeck / pixelio.de

More available books at **www.hansebooks.com**

# Resolved to be Rich

## A NOVEL

BY

## E. H. COOPER

AUTHOR OF

*"The Marchioness Against the County," "Children, Race-horses, and Ghosts," etc.*

HERBERT S. STONE AND COMPANY
CHICAGO AND NEW YORK
MDCCCXCIX

# Resolved to be Rich

## CHAPTER I

"On the Corniche Road, near to the little village of Eze, where the plash of Mediterranean waves is the only sound heard, one may see an old tombstone inscribed with the strange words: 'HERE LIES THE SOUL OF COUNT LOUIS ESTERFELD.'   Wanderers along this road had passed by the stone year after year repeating the words: 'Here lies the soul of Count Louis Esterfeld' with a light laugh, and muttering to themselves 'a madman!' till one day there came by a man with thoughts in his mind of which these words were a curious echo.   He paused in front of the stone considering, and at last began to dig.   Working for some time with his hands he came at last upon a metal box, and opening it found it full of gold and jewels.   Among them was a paper containing these words: 'You are my heir: to you I bequeath this wealth, to you who have understood.    In this box is my soul—the money without which man is but a machine and his life but a long procession of weary empty years.    .   .   .' ''

A boy who was reading this queer legend dropped the newspaper and stared round him with hungry eyes and parted lips.  He looked like a youngster of eleven or twelve, though he was in fact fourteen, and had a face differing in no respect from that of a hundred of his contemporaries.  Freckled cheeks, small turned-up nose, broad forehead and indeterminate mouth—this is a combination of feature which Nature seems to turn out by the hundred thousand for the confusion of parents who want to discover some indication of a special talent in their sons: the good dame giving no indication of the iron will, reckless courage, calculating energy or grubbing greed which is hidden behind it.  Perhaps she is right, and the humour and interest of a study of life would be perceptibly lessened if we could not now and then see men with noble countenances do great deeds for love of gold; and cowards with receding foreheads and timid eyes sacrifice ease, reputation, life itself, for a sudden whimsical notion of honour; and an idle vagabond suddenly grow upright and industrious while his once reproachful and irreproachable neighbour forges a cheque and goes to Spain with the proceeds, and his neighbour's wife to help him spend them. But this sketch (or part of it—never mind which part) is anticipating the career of Master Gerald Franklin.

The young gentleman sat in a deep and comfortable arm-chair with his legs crossed, his feet (or, to be exact, as he invariably was himself, with one foot) on a foot-stool, and a Manchester weekly paper in his hands. He had read every word of it, foreign intelligence, money-market news, local gossip and leading articles, not because he was interested in a quarter of what he read but because it was his principle and practice to collect every morsel of information available on every business subject. For general literature he had the profoundest scorn. Latin and Greek poets he not only loathed as his contemporaries loathed them because they meant work and pain and tears, but above all despised because they were useless. He worked at these idiotic tasks, as he called them, just as much as was necessary to avoid the fate of other young gentlemen with strong (though, perhaps, less debatable) views as to the value of their tasks, but he never gained or aspired to high marks for Latin verses or brilliant construing. The classical master thought Franklin a dullard and the youth thought the classical master a bore: that was the extent of their concern about one another. But when Gerald found himself in a class where arithmetic, geography, or other modern useful knowledge was being imparted, or even where a German or French master was doing battle with giggling and scornful young Britons, there was another story to be told. Many a man looked anxious when Franklin began to ask him questions: most of them had to think before answering him, and to realise sometimes how slight a hold they had on their subject. The masters at Gerald's school were young men from high schools and training colleges who had studied science not to know but to pass examinations, and outraged science had avenged herself: they did pass and they did not know.

The purely imaginative side of life did not often present itself to young Franklin, and since it mostly concerned itself with love, self-sacrifice and such-like unprofitable subjects, he did not go in search of it. Books of adventure interested him when a treasure-hunt was the point of the story, but otherwise he despised them and their readers. In any case he considered that to read them was a waste of time, since, as he justly observed, the story could have been told in a page if the writer had left out all the scenery, character-description, lion-shooting, snake-bites, and other superfluous matter. Never before to-day had he come across a story like this one in the *Manchester Weekly Sun* which combined interest and brevity in such a high degree. The fact that it was an advertisement of some one's pills (a five-years' sufferer from dyspepsia, discovering the pills later on in the article, even as the young man discovered diamonds) affected him not at all, or even gratified him further as evidence of a business-like mind. For one single moment the story forced him into a day-dream, filling him with a vague desire to visit foreign countries and dig there. Then he shook himself together, read to the end of the advertisement, and came to the conclusion that it would be better to make pills. Just as he had arrived at this sensible decision the door of the room opened and his sister came in. The child approached him hesitatingly and stood looking at him with troubled eyes.

"Well, old girl?"

"Don't you think, Gerald, that you could come and see Aunt Marian? She has asked for you twice."

"I've got to go to school. It's past eight already."

Monica Franklin looked at the arm-chair, foot-stool and newspaper, without any verbal answer.

"I suppose I must come in for a bit," said the boy vexedly, "though it will probably make me late again. If she's worse I mustn't stay long, I suppose?"

"She is much worse," said his sister gravely, yet unable to repress a smile at the consideration shown in this remark, and the speaker's obvious satisfaction at his own thoughtfulness.

The woman by whose bedside the children were presently standing was white and motionless. As the boy came in she tried to raise her hand, but could not move it and lay in silence looking at the young pair with eyes which already knew the last great secret. A grey shadow was even now stealing across her face; her breathing seemed almost at an end, though now and again with a great struggle she would win one more deep breath from the enemy which had already conquered her. The thought that her time for speech was probably now an affair of minutes made her set her teeth in a last desperate effort, and raising her head she beckoned the boy nearer to her. He bent unwillingly and nervously over the bed.

"Monica . . . you will take care of her?"

The lad looked helplessly across at his sister, not understanding.

"I am dying," said the woman; "don't you know? don't you see?" Through the mists which hung round her Marian Franklin caught sight of the sudden blaze of terror which started up in her young nephew's face. "Dr. Hare should have told you. Answer me: will you take care of Monica?"

Gerald spoke no word; he hardly heard the question; his mind was trying to adjust itself to the reality of death as presented to him in this room. Hitherto it had appeared to him only as a last refuge of people who could not do any more business; it had not entered into his range of actual vision. Sickness he knew (by reputation) and weakness and pain, because his aunt had often been ill, but the idea of death could not immediately reach his understanding. He stood in continued silence bringing his intellect to bear on the problem as he would have brought it to bear on a new rule of arithmetic which was presented to him, without sympathy, fear, anxiety, or any other emotion, but merely with resolution to understand it.

"You shall answer me," said the woman with a sudden access of strength; "you shall promise!"

"What do you want me to promise?" he asked cautiously.

"That you will keep Monica with you . . provide for her . . . she has nothing except what you will share with her."

"Say yes; please do say yes, Gerald," whispered the sobbing child who was standing by his side; "only just to please her now; I will not hold you to it."

"But I will," said the dying woman in a low clear voice which thrilled through the room like the whisper of some great tragic actress, so that the two children turned to her with startled faces. "Wherever I am I shall know, and if you break your word . . ."

There was a long silence during which she lay with her eyes fixed on the boy, as though she were reading every thought which was passing through his mind and foreseeing every future thought which would pass through it. A great wave of fear suddenly swept over his soul as the eyes with that dread knowledge in them held his own and would not let them go. He stammered out some words; he did not know what. She did not understand them and spoke again in an impatient whisper:—

"Do you promise? Yes or no?"

"Yes."

"Louder."

"Yes."

"I hear. I will remember."

There was another long silence broken only by an occasional sob from Monica, and then Dr. Hare came quietly and quickly into the room. He looked in startled fear at the unconscious figure on the bed and then at the children standing in frightened helplessness by its side.

"I couldn't get here a minute sooner," he muttered, seeming rather to be offering excuses to himself than to them, and began hastily to apply remedies. "One of you had better run to the Vicarage and ask Mr. Lowe to come; or stay—don't—it is too late, I am afraid."

For even while he was speaking Miss Marian Franklin died.

# CHAPTER II

In the little study of Oakhill Vicarage the Reverend James Lowe sat in a desk-chair with his arms folded and brow puckered, while opposite to him in an exactly similar attitude sat Gerald Franklin. It was the day after Miss Franklin's funeral, and the Vicar of Oakhill had taken upon himself the task of explaining to the boy the financial position of himself and his sister.

"You have no other relatives, I think, and I don't know who will be the new trustee of your money. This is a sum of £3000 left you by your father, and it brings in £120 a year. Your aunt had an annuity of a similar amount which died with her, but she had insured her life for £200, and has left this sum to your sister. This and your income of £120 is what you both have to live on."

The Vicar felt that it was ridiculous to be speaking of such matters to a boy of this age, but talked on in the perfunctory manner of a lawyer reciting to some young spendthrift the terms and conditions of a mortgage.

"Whom does the furniture belong to?" asked his companion, in business-like fashion.

"Eh? The furniture? Oh, that is Monica's," said Lowe, in some surprise.

"Is there any money in the bank, or any other money at—all?"

"Money in the bank? Oh—er—yes; about £15, I believe."

"My aunt ought to have saved something out of my £120 a year," said Gerald.

The Vicar stared at the young gentleman before him with the look which one might bestow on a monkey who became suddenly endowed with speech and offered opinions on the subject of house-keeping.

"Your education cost her a considerable sum," he said, with mild severity, "and she thought herself justified in spending some of the money on your sister."

"Women are certainly pretty cool hands in dealing with money," said the boy.

Mr. Lowe sat silent for the space of a minute, trying to realise the fact that instead of consoling a puzzled and unhappy little boy he had to discuss business with a sharp man of the world. He was the mildest and gentlest of men, who, when he said to a parishioner, "You grieve me greatly," imagined that he had administered a stern rebuke, but he thought that this boy certainly wanted whipping. Moreover the good man felt somewhat nervous about himself: he had agreed and sympathised with Miss Franklin as to the impossibility of saving money out of her narrow income except by giving to the two children an inferior education, and had advised that the money should be spent as Miss Franklin had spent it. She had, he argued, taken the children out of pure kindness: their arrival compelled her in any case to go without many of the small comforts to which she was accustomed, since the children's income was insufficient for their life as she had planned it, and there was no actual necessity to save money. In the event of Miss Franklin's death the two children could, he supposed, be sent to school on the interest of Gerald's £3000: the idea of this being unjust or of Gerald objecting to it really never occurred to the Vicar. Now that Gerald mentioned it (and not till now), he understood that Miss Franklin's arrangement had in fact been a trifle unbusinesslike—"cool" as Gerald had called it—and apparently he was going to be called to account for it by this boy. The Vicar stroked his beard and wished devoutly that he had left this task to Dr. Hare. Gerald, on his side, sat pondering with folded arms and vexed frown. He knew most things about house-keeping from house-rent down to the price of Malaga raisins—which latter he bought in a falling market to retail to his school-companions at a price which showed himself clearly the folly of dealing with middle-men instead of directly with the producer. He had remarked more than once to his sister that the household was conducted on very wasteful principles, and now his opinion had received confirmation. I do not wish, you will understand, to suggest that my young friend Gerald was a very agreeable boy, but I must do him the justice to point out that what he knew he knew thoroughly. There were many persons who, both at his present age and in after years, would have done well to take his advice. Unfortunately no one could ever get beyond a vehement desire to box his ears.

"I do not think," said the Vicar, "that it would be kind or profitable" (he put a slightly sarcastic emphasis on the word profitable which he hoped would rebuke the boy, whereas Gerald merely viewed him with good-humoured contempt at the word "kind" and with surprised approbation at the word "profitable") "to discuss now what she did. It was done for the best after long consideration. What I wished to talk about was the future. Miss Franklin has appointed Dr. Hare and myself executors under her will and has asked her cousin, Miss Christina Bertram, to be Monica's guardian.   I think it would be best, if possible, to place you both under the same guardian, and for you both to live with Miss Bertram. Should you be willing to agree to this if it can be arranged?"

"I couldn't answer just yet," said Gerald cautiously.

"For us to ask your consent to our arrangement," said the Vicar drily, "is rather a matter of politeness than necessity, you know."

'I know that," was the quiet reply, "but I think it would be more pleasant and easy-going for all parties if I did happen to like your arrangement."

Mr. Lowe lay back in his chair and stared at his companion with absolute dismay.   What on earth had he done in thrusting himself into such a post as adviser to these children and trustee to one of them?   Why had he offered to undertake such a task?   He had rarely seen this boy and knew nothing whatever of him except what Miss Franklin had told him—that Gerald was "a little precocious in business-matters."   A little precocious!   The creature was a full-fledged business-man fit to go on the Stock-Exchange or set up a money-lending establishment this afternoon!   Miss Franklin had expressed her fears lest Mr. Lowe should find the post a tiresome one—"full of small worries" was her exact expression—and he thought now that she was very likely to prove right. Her words, he said to himself, were a euphonious description of the situation of a man in a hornets' nest without his clothes on.

"Do you know Miss Bertram?" he asked.

"Oh yes," said Gerald. "She used to come and see Aunt Marian pretty often. There is really nothing particular against her being guardian, but—are you sure we have no other relations?"

"Miss Franklin spoke once of a relative—an uncle, I think—who went out to South Africa many years ago. I gathered in fact that she was a favourite of his, that they were very great friends once, but nothing has been heard of him for many years. I believe he is supposed to have been killed in the last Zulu War. You probably have some other relations somewhere, but I don't know who they are."

"Well, that's a mercy," said Gerald, "there'll be nobody to lend money to."

Mrs. Lowe came into the room at this point. She had intended to allow her husband a reasonable time in which to explain money-matters to Gerald, and then come in with motherly pity and consolation. She had also

prepared a large tea—knowing something about
the nature of boys in general—with abundance
of cake, and meant to proffer first pity and
then cake as consolation.  As a preliminary to
both she put a hand on the boy's shoulder and
kissed him, at which her husband looked
shocked and amazed, and Gerald murmured,
"Oh, Lord!"

"Has Mr. Lowe finished talking to you, my
dear," she asked, noticing nothing; "it must
have been so sad for you listening to the story
of all that your dear aunt has done, and the
arrangements which she has made for you.  I
do so hope that you and Monica will be very
happy.  Have you finished talking to Gerald,
my dear?"

"Yes," said her husband, looking round him
rather doubtfully.  He had an impression that
it was Gerald who had done most of the talking, and that he himself had come rather dis-
creditably than otherwise out of the interview.
However, it was over, which was a great
point, and he was relieved to see Mrs. Lowe
leading the youth away, though he could have
wished that her arm was not round Gerald's
neck.  The young scamp just gave the Vicar a
little look out of the corner of his eye as he
passed, which said: "This must be a very dis-
tressing affair for you to witness, but I pledge

my word that I have given her no encouragement."

Being seated at tea he became affably con-
versational, as though recognising that Mr.
Lowe had meant to do well, and had failed
through no fault of his own. He spoke of the
poor of the parish, lamenting their improvi-
dence, drunkenness and general incapacity.
His friend Mr. Muirhead had explained to him
a system by which a man might, by paying a
very small yearly sum from the time he was
twenty, receive a regular pension at sixty, or
even before if he increased the earlier pay-
ments. Every one ought to insure themselves
against old age in this manner. . . . Even
Mrs. Lowe became a trifle puzzled and suspicious as the boy talked on. She had heard
persons by the dozen talk like that before, but
she had never gone into tea with her arm
round their neck. The poor woman got quite
hot at the recollection.

Towards the end of the meal Mr. Lowe made
a resolute effort to get back to the question of
guardianship. He was sorry for Miss Christina Bertram, but he supposed that in appoint-
ing her to be guardian to one child, and asking
her to be guardian to the other, Miss Franklin
had known what she was doing. He could not
of course be aware of the truth—that Miss

Franklin knew as much or as little about the boy's character as he did himself.

"I suppose then," he said, trying to speak lightly and cheerfully, "we may take it for granted that you will be content to live with Miss Bertram?"

"I cannot answer now," was the politely resolute reply. "I must talk to my friend, Mr. Muirhead."

# CHAPTER III

In introducing the villain of his piece the dramatist has a great advantage over the novelist. If a man comes on to the stage with black whiskers, rolling eyes, a terrific frown, immaculate trousers and a hoarse whisper, you see the villain before you, you hear his dark innuendoes, watch his blighting though loving glances at the heroine, and you know without further words or elaborate introduction that the man is ready for forgery, abduction, highway robbery or murder, as circumstances shall dictate. Even if his actions are dull he can always loll about and look picturesquely rascally. Like the young lady who, consulting a manager as to whether she could play Juliet, was told that she would look very nice in the tomb, so any man aided by burnt cork can make something on the stage of a villain's part.

But the novelist's introduction of this character is much less effective. How laborious is the written catalogue of his points—the sinister frown, the shifty eye, the stealthy tread!

How dull the fellow is except when he is moving briskly about with his knife or pen and book of (somebody else's) cheques!

I beg therefore for the kind toleration of the reader while Gerald's friend Mr. Sampson Muirhead is clothed with such flesh and blood and raiment as my poor pen can depict. Frankly he would have made but a poor figure on the stage and is not worth, so far as externals are concerned, a very elaborate description. Figure to yourself, please, a thin, starved-looking man of medium height and some thirty summers—though he did not look as if anything so wholesome and warm as summer had ever been near him—with grey, rather pleasing eyes, straight, narrow pointed nose, a wide mouth and an expression of absolute vacuity. That was his ordinary appearance, without interest to any man. There were persons, however, who had seen the thin lips set, and eyes grow hard and keen, and nose twitch like that of a cat with a bird under its foot, and these persons said that if they ever had to do business with Mr. Muirhead they would choose the morning, before lunch, on a day when their wits were sharpest, for its transaction. Probably they were right, for the gentleman had been meddling, ever since he was eighteen, with various bits of business in which one side or the other had mostly got to burn its fingers, and if any fingers had been burnt during these years they had not been those of Mr. Muirhead.

Sampson was just now in a position which seemed sufficiently harmless so far as financial operations were concerned. He was master in a high school in Stoke-on-Trent, and though he might have presented Stock-Exchange problems to his arithmetic classes, could not, one would imagine, have had any serious influence for good or ill on the neighbourhood. But the fact is that in money matters people will take any advice, so long as it is risky enough, and the adviser is not a broker, lawyer or other person whose business it is to give it. A schoolmaster thus has many advantages as a financial councillor. He knows no more and no less about such matters than the parson, the friendly post-master, or other persons who are usually consulted, but from mere habit he speaks with more authority. He is so accustomed to stating in a masterful voice that seven times one are seven to an audience who dared not if they could dispute the fact, that he talks about gold-mines, railways and building-societies, in the same way; and finds too that men are but long-legged boys, and will listen with similar docility to any one who speaks with decision. Muirhead besides had

the jargon of the money-market at command,
an accomplishment which would impress no one
nowadays, when your baby, if it could speak,
would ask for "Chartered" shares as a chris-
tening present, but was a matter for local
wonder then.　He was a clever man, too, as
evidenced by the position to which he had
attained at the age of thirty, and could make a
little knowledge go further than most people,
besides being possessed of a discrimination
amounting to an instinct as to the company in
which it was and was not safe to show it off.
Soon after his arrival at Stoke he made a little
money for himself and his friends by a small
speculation in Mexican Rails; the friends
talked far and wide about the author of their
success; people begged for an introduction to
this magician who could bring gold from the
clouds.　In short Muirhead had not been in his
position for a year before he became known as
a man who could influence capital to a quite
appreciable extent, and such a reputation flies
nearly as far and fast as a reputation for having the capital itself in your bank.

· To a casual observer of men and things—to a
person going about the world, so to speak, with
a rough note-book and jotting down mere
results of superficial observation, without caring to consider their connection or results, it

must seem sometimes as if Providence, having put a raw rather helpless person on a hedge between good and evil, occasionally heaped up to an unnecessary extent the influences which should make him come down on the wrong side. Gerald Franklin had his good points. All men have. Even Turkish Paschas and Belgian Colonial officials and American railway speculators are not as black as they are painted —though they have so many other points of resemblance to the devil that one feels no desire for closer intimacy with them. Gerald was quick, industrious, accurate, patient and scrupulously just, and there was nobody among all his elders who could appreciate or recognise these qualities in him or help him to develop them aright. On the other hand he was conceited, avaricious, and not very scrupulously honest (a failing which is not incompatible with being just), and by mere chance Sampson Muirhead had become his most intimate friend and counsellor. This, I maintain, was hard luck on Gerald, who was running the race of life with an amount of over-weight which handicapped him quite out of the contest. The odds were 1,000 to 1 against him.

Gerald spent the evening thinking over Mr. Lowe's statement and by bedtime had decided on which points he meant to ask Muirhead's

advice, and on which other points he had
already made up his own mind and wanted no
advice.  The youth had method.  In the morning at school he went through a Virgil lesson
with his accustomed air of good-humoured
contempt, wrote a short essay on the Spanish
Colonies, the information in which was so
much fuller and more accurate than that in the
geography, book out of which he was supposed
to have obtained it that the master could not
make up his mind how to mark it; and at last
the boy found himself free and by Mr. Muirhead's side.

"Well, Franklin, have you made any plans
yet?"

"I have been thinking over some, sir, and
wanted your advice if you could spare me half-
an-hour."

"Certainly."  The man eyed his little companion for a moment, and again on his face
was the look of a cat with a bird in its claws.

Gerald briefly recapitulated what Mr. Lowe
had told him, and went on: "This Miss Bertram lives only just a little further off from
here than my aunt did, so I should come here
just the same.  It is a choice between my
going to school as a boarder somewhere else at
a cheaper place or staying here and living with
her."

"Stay here," said the man decisively—rather eagerly in fact.  "The education is very good; you could hardly get anything better for the money anywhere;  and I think I may say that you will find me of some use to you.  From here you will easily pass on to some business post in the mines or potteries, or if you liked it better you could get into one of the banks or lawyer's offices.  I will tell you something about myself if you won't repeat it."

"I promise not to, sir."

"In a year's time, when my engagement here is at an end, I am going to set up a little business of my own.  I shall begin, I hope, with an agency for the Merton Insurance Company and one or two little things will follow. In two years' time when you are thinking of leaving school you may find it worth while to come and join me.  I advise you to stay on here."

"What capital would your business want?" asked the boy cautiously.

"None, my dear fellow; only brains and push, and a few matters like book-keeping, which you could  pick  up  in  a · month  or two."

"Will you undertake to teach me that while I am here?"

Gerald was perfectly aware that a bargain

was being driven, and meant to have the terms of it clear.

"Certainly. We will begin directly you have settled down at Miss Bertram's," said the other, who was accustomed to his pupil's style of doing business, and admired it. He had himself given nothing for nothing all his life, having indeed made but one present in the course of his thirty years, and that was merely to give his deceased mother's false teeth to his landlady.

"I will join you," said Gerald deliberately, "if you have got that agency when I leave here. There would be work for two even in that; and of course we should get plenty more work of that kind."

"Yes, I could command plenty," said the other, with a dry emphasis on the personal pronoun.

Gerald looked at his master out of the corner of his eyes, and a very faint smile twitched his face. No respect for Muirhead kept him silent, yet he said nothing. It was odd that in this little personal altercation the boy was the first to drop into contemptuous silence.

# CHAPTER IV

There are old maids and old maids.  Some
have the recognised habits of the species
encrusted on them too thickly and fast to allow
of any alteration by any accident; others for
some imperceptible reason slough these habits
like a snake his skin (only that they really
renew them), and astonish and occasionally
terrify their relations into fits.  I knew a
maiden lady of fifty who was so much struck
by the effect wrought on a lively contemporary
by a little rouge that she bought some herself,
moved from a respectable Sussex village into
the giddy frivolity of Brighton, and went to
every ball for five miles round (in a white dress
with blue ribbons) till she died.  I knew
another who, having spent a long and virtuous
life in cultivating poetry and selling eggs, suddenly lost her head at the sight of a bicycle,
invested all her egg-savings in a "Humber"
with the latest improvements, and was
arrested by the police three times in five
weeks for scorching.  Such reminiscences are
not, however, in any way (except by the
law of contraries) suggested by Miss Christina

Bertram, the lady to whom Fate, in unkind caprice, had assigned the charge of Gerald Franklin and his sister.

Miss Bertram was a queen among old maids, a precision compared to whom Greenwich Observatory clock was a disorderly and rowdy piece of mechanism. She never broke, upset, spoilt, or changed anything; she did everything at the same hour every day every week, and had detested all hurry and unrest from the days when she screamed at her cradle being rocked to this very morning when she had reproved Jane for telling Bridget to "hurry up with getting those children's bedrooms ready." She lived in the little suburb of Stoke called Hartshill, near to the Infirmary, of which she was a pillar of support. The house had at first been taken to accommodate Miss Bertram's brother, who had also supported the Infirmary (as Secretary) for some time, but was found at length to be rather in the nature of a flying buttress, since he had absconded to Spain with most of the current funds. Miss Bertram had paid the greater part of the money and no more was heard from or about her brother by any human being in England except a certain Stoke lawyer who twice a year paid a certain sum of money on Miss Bertram's behalf into a bank at Madrid, and after an interval of varying length got receipts from Madrid, Rio Janeiro, Buenos Ayres, and other places resorted to by gentlemen for whom the police have made other (though futile) arrangements. This little incident happened eleven years ago, and Miss Bertram still occupied the house on Hartshill, looking down through a cloud of blue smoke into the valley where men and women worked in their small companies—flat-pressers, hollowware pressers, "jolly women," casters and squeezers—and the great crates of dishes, plates, jugs, basins, jam-pots, cups and vases, were packed and swung into barges, for a reality of 30s. a week and a vision of heaven knows what wealth and fame. In the blue smoke-clouds Fortune hovered, sometimes out of sight and sometimes in: you could hear the rustle of her wings in those halcyon days as she made a swoop, now on some young inventor, now on some lucky speculator, and lifted him up into the sunshine. During the daytime the smoke-cloud hung motionless or in a high wind rocked slowly to and fro, floating past the tall chimneys out of which it had come: while at night the orange-red light of colliery and iron-work furnaces throbbed through it and played over it like the rays of a flashing light-ship over a heaving sea-swell.

Miss Bertram was expecting the arrival of the two children one Wednesday afternoon in May. She had thought of going to fetch them, but considered that they would prefer to go through their home-partings alone, and she sat now at her sitting-room window watching for a luggage-laden cab. It came into view presently, crawling up the steep hill and stopping opposite her low green gate. The children got out and walked soberly and a little shyly up the front to the doorstep on which she was standing.

"How do you do, Aunt Christina?" said Monica; "we are so glad to be here."

"It is very kind of you to take us, Aunt Christina," said Gerald.

Miss Bertram had asked the children to call her Aunt Christina and they did so obediently. Gerald always conceded these small unimportant points, maintaining that to do so surprised people into conceding him large and important ones. Miss Bertram, watching him, saw with satisfaction that he wiped his boots on the door-mat, hung his hat and coat in their proper place in the hall, and walked twice across the drawing-room, entered the dining-room, and finished his tea without breaking anything or even treading on the cat's tail. She said to herself—rashly—that he was a model boy, and having had no expectation of finding him more than tolerable she made up her mind that she could tolerate him, and so turned her attention to Monica.

And now, the villain of the piece having been presented, we will if you please look at the person who (if it is not premature to make such an announcement) is to be the heroine.

Once upon a time, when Monica Franklin was half-way between her seventh and eighth birthdays, there arose some trifling occasion when one of the children—only one because money had to be carefully guarded—was to accompany their aunt on a visit to a certain relative where strawberries, sponge-cakes, "tips," and other matters dear to the seven-year-old heart, would certainly be plentiful. Monica was first invited to go, but declined: "Cousin Alison would like to see me best," she said; "but Gerald would like to go best. Take Gerald." And Gerald went. Written on the child's face as she made her decision you might see even then the proud little knowledge of her own value in the world, the certainty that people whose love and respect were worth having loved and respected her, and also the quietly resolute unselfishness whose existence is a long wonder to those who possess only the saving grace of being able to admire it. Now at the age of fifteen Monica was for a time inclined to exaggerate this self-renunciation, to give up things needlessly, to fling self and the world too far on one side, and yet to guard a very high—rather conceited perhaps—idea of her own importance in the world. As you may sometimes see a little child throw away all its toys and fall upon a chair in an apparently complete abandonment of woe, while all the time it has one eye on its nurse or mother to see that its sorrow is being watched and to hint mutely that it is still open to be consoled by kisses and chocolate: so their elders may be noticed sometimes doing their good works not for men to see but with the too evident knowledge that men do see, and too high an estimate of what is being done. And for Miss Monica's personal appearance? Was she lovely as an old-fashioned heroine or ugly as a new-fashioned one should be? I know not yet. I am blind as regards little children, seeing only something which is small and innocent and fresh and therefore fair, and being myself content at any moment to exchange a room full of the most lovely women in London for the company of one little maiden with a brain full of fairy-stories and eyes which ask questions about all things, of all men, and believe all the answers. What indeed is the

pleasure of raven locks and flowing tresses if
you may not stroke them? of rose-petal cheeks
if they are not to be kissed?  And would you
choose to listen to the talk of balls and fash-
ions, of theatres, scandal and theology, to stale
cynicism and staler philosophy—oh! the weariness of it!—when you can have my little lady's
company with her whispers from the dawn of
life, with her breath of hope, and youth and
novelty, and faith?  Miss Bertram at any rate
fell in love with her young charge from that
Wednesday evening, and watched over her and
puzzled over her as maiden ladies sometimes
will over such living problems, making little
advances, proffering timid bits of help, holding out experienced hands and showing the
stepping-stones at life's most dangerous cross-
ings.  The two, woman and child, understood
and loved one another from the first.  "She is
worth all our care; we shall all be proud of her
one day," said Miss Christina to her chief
crony, the Vicar of Hartshill.

"And the boy?" asked Mr. Lowe, curiously.

"He is very nice too.  A quiet, well-mannered, harmless little fellow.  I like him very
much, though he has not got anything like his
sister's brains, or cleverness, or industry.  He
has asked leave to bring his friend Mr. Muirhead to tea here this afternoon—one of the

masters at his school, you know, and a great friend of Gerald's. It is a good sign when a boy and his master are friends, isn't it?"

Mr. Lowe looked round him doubtfully; he hardly liked to express the deep suspicion with which he himself regarded Gerald and all his friends.

"Here they come," went on Miss Bertram, as the boy and his master walked up the front. "You will stay and have tea with us, Mr. Lowe, won't you? Have you ever met Mr. Muirhead?"

"Yes, oh yes," said the parson. He had risen as if to go, and now stood hesitating, realising with a shock of surprise that he regarded this boy with something absolutely like fear. "It is too absurd," he muttered to himself, and accepting Miss Bertram's invitation he went and stood by the mantel-piece with his eyes on the door.

Muirhead was very soon on a friendly footing with the company, talking of Infirmary business, of the last big order received by Messrs. Wedgewood, and other local matters with the detailed accuracy and decision which always marked his gossip. At tea he sat next to Monica, who had a child's instinctive dislike of him, but as the man was Gerald's friend did not care to show it or speak of it. He asked her if she had yet made friends with Mary Carton, who lived near by.  The child said no: her aunt only knew the Cartons very slightly.

"Mr. Carton goes to races and bets and speculates," said Miss Bertram, shaking a big knife at a loaf of bread as if the loaf were Tattersal's Ring, and she were about to hack it in pieces. "He made all his money by speculation.  I should not like Gerald to be intimate with him or his sons.  I am sure indeed that Gerald would not care for such people."

Mr. Lowe glanced at Gerald, but the boy was eating his bread and butter steadily without paying any apparent attention.  He scarcely seemed to hear his aunt's remarks or Muirhead's reply.

"I think," said the latter, "you can hardly say that he got his money by speculation.  He joined with some other friends in buying some shares in a company to make a railway in Argentine.  The railway was built and was very successful.  Is that speculation?"

"No one has any business to want more than three per cent. for their money," said Miss Bertram dogmatically.  "Don't you think so, too, Mr. Lowe?"

"I must confess that I am getting three and a half for the £4,000 which poor Mrs. Monckton left me," said the parson with a smile, "but I think that is quite enough."

"You would get just double—seven per cent.—in the East Argentine Railway," said Gerald quietly. "That would be £280 a year, and it would be quite safe."

Miss Bertram looked at the boy with suspicion, Mr. Lowe with a sudden renewal of vague fear. He had then been listening to and taking in everything. Of course there had been no harm in the conversation, but how should this lad know that the East Argentine Railway paid seven per cent., and how had he been able to calculate in ten seconds that £4,000 at seven per cent. would produce £280 a year? Mr. Lowe would have required a pencil and paper and five minutes to do the sum.

"I know more than one sound business where you can get eight per cent. nowadays," added Muirhead.

"I would rather buy tickets in a lottery!" said Miss Bertram angrily.

Seeing that she was really annoyed, Muirhead turned the conversation skilfully.

"I am surprised at the number of lotteries which exist in this neighbourhood," he said. "Harper has one at the Red Lion; Grenfell had two last Christmas at his house; Roberts had one every Christmas, with prizes of geese, turkeys and plum-puddings, but he will never have another.  He used to win several—sometimes half—of the prizes himself, and people talked of his good luck.  The lottery was managed like this: small pieces of tin were numbered and put into a bag and one was drawn out by the man's little seven-year-old daughter.  Last Christmas when the drawing was going on there was a long pause, the child holding her hand in the bag for an unusually long time.  Her father told her to be quick, to which the child answered: 'I can't find the hot one, father'!  There won't be any more lotteries at the Old Canal Inn at Tunstall!"

"To make his innocent child a party to such wickedness!" said Miss Bertram, who always made the inevitable comment on a story. "That Roberts was one of your parishioners, Mr. Lowe, wasn't he?"

The Vicar answered yes without further comment.  He had been watching Gerald's face again.  At the point of Muirhead's story the boy's lips had turned down and his eyes had lit up with the beginning of a good laugh. Then at Miss Bertram's words every symptom of amusement had disappeared and he had gone on eating quite gravely, so that a casual observer would have judged that he saw as little point in the story as Monica did.  It was a curiously clever bit of acting, as Mr. Lowe admitted to himself, with a mental addition of "the wretched little hypocrite!"

Tea being over, Miss Bertram led the way back to the drawing-room, and began a conversation with Muirhead, who feeling that he had not yet made a very favourable impression talked more seriously while Mr. Lowe sat down by Gerald.

"You are happy here?" he asked in a kindly voice, resolute to overcome his antipathy to his young charge.

"Yes, thank you."

"And has your aunt made any plans for you, or"—Gerald's face had remained absolutely expressionless, and yet something compelled the Vicar to add—"have you made any for yourself?"

"Oh no, none."

"Yet it is time to begin to think of this, isn't it?"

"Yes, perhaps it is." There was an air of polite resignation on Gerald's face which would have enchanted a cynical spectator. He was evidently saying to himself: "Parsons and platitudes happen to all men sometimes. I will not even yawn in this worthy man's face if I can help it." So he sat giving gentle assenting answers to everything said by Mr. Lowe, while he listened anxiously to the conversation between his relation and Mr. Muirhead. He was nervous about it: vexed at his master's failure at tea-time: anxious that they should make friends now if it was not too late. It mattered much both to man and boy for certain reasons that this should be so. Muirhead had arrived to-day easily confident, believing in his own power to make himself agreeable to any one; the boy (who believed in no one) had warned him to be careful where so much was concerned, and he had not been careful and things had gone wrong. There was a change for the better before Muirhead left the house, but the visit, Gerald told himself, had not been a success.

# CHAPTER V

The number of signs and omens which prophesy disaster (after the disaster has occurred) to "every one with eyes in his head" is truly remarkable. When an engagement is broken off half the friends of the lady appear to have "known from the first" by certain symptoms that it would never last. When a man takes to gambling or drinking and finally uses (or misuses) his razor to his throat, his relatives have mostly "seen it in his eye" (horses, brandy-bottle and razor complete) from infancy. Thus when at a subsequent date the newspapers were full of the names of Messrs. Gerald Franklin and Sampson Muirhead more than one of their Staffordshire neighbours declared on their conscience that they felt quite queer and even shivered on first seeing a certain brass plate with the name of "Mr. Sampson Muirhead, Agent for the Merton Insurance Company," on a door in the High Street of Newcastle-under-Lyme. Yet 'twas quite a modest little plate marking two modest little first-floor rooms, nearly opposite

to the town-hall, where on police-court days
you might see the prisoners being brought in
and out by staid policemen, and next door to
the shop of Mr. Briggs, unto whom resort all the
rank and fashion of North Staffordshire when
they require dresses, ribbons, laces, and other
matters of adornment and use.   Upstairs there
was even less cause for shivering.   In the outer
room sat Gerald with a ledger or two in front
of him and a pen in his hand: in the inner
room sat Muirhead writing letters; two more
guileless persons you could not wish to see.
Business came in slowly but steadily, policies
multiplied, commissions swelled, another clerk
was engaged, before a year was over the High
Street office was too small for Muirhead's
work.   He and his young partner sat together
in the outer room one morning before business
hours discussing a move into larger premises,
and debating whether they were justified in
recommending the Company to take a whole
house and engage two more clerks and canvassers.   It was a certain Wednesday morning,
Gerald's sixteenth birthday—how well he
remembered it in after years!—and he had
promised to go home for the afternoon; not
that he had much feeling about birthdays himself but that Miss Bertram and Monica had
made a great appeal for the half-holiday and

Muirhead, for his own purposes, had insisted on according it. At nine o'clock the second clerk arrived, a young man five years older than Gerald in years and about fifty years younger in most other respects. The youth, Nicholson by name, hung up his coat and hat and came to the fire to warm his hands, for it was snowing slightly, an east wind was blowing cuttingly and other genial signs of an English spring were to be seen and felt outside. Gerald saluted the new-comer with a grave good-morning, Muirhead gave him a nod and went on talking, while Nicholson, after leaning over the fire for a moment, went up to his desk and stood looking down on it as if he were a swimmer about to plunge boldly into a sea of figures.

There was a knock at the door, and in response to Muirhead's "come in" there entered a man of middle height, with short black beard, moustache and whiskers, and hair of the dull shadowless black which suggests hair-dye not very skilfully applied. His face was so overpowered by this black framework that no man after talking to Mr. Joshua Marshall for an hour could tell you whether his nose was straight or crooked, whether his eyes were blue or green, honest or shifty; they only knew that he was very black.

"Mr. Muirhead?" said the new-comer interrogatively. It was curious that though there could hardly be much mistake as to which was the elder man of the two, Marshall turned first to Gerald, as if recognising something of the leader in the lad's face, but he was quick to see his mistake.

"I have come down from London to speak to you about a new building society for which we want agents in this part of the world. May I speak to you privately?"

Muirhead led the way into the inner room and Gerald and the stranger followed, the latter seeming to take for granted that the boy would come too. Marshall explained to them that several small building societies in different parts of England had recently amalgamated into one big society which had established some headquarters in London and proposed to extend itself all over England. They wanted help of two kinds; first some local clergy, schoolmasters and such like people who could influence money, but in their own unbusiness-like fashion; secondly, some smart business men to reduce the proceedings of these miscellaneous canvassers to order. The pay for this latter work would be good. Would Muirhead and Franklin undertake it?

The matter was discussed at length, and finally the partners agreed to Marshall's proposals. The man himself filled them with respect, especially Gerald, who was making his first acquaintance with London city smartness. Marshall seemed to know everybody in their neighbourhood, his or her income, prospects and capacities. He knew ten times more about the Merton Insurance Company as a whole than they did themselves, and quite as much as they did about the Staffordshire branch of it. His explanation of the work required by his own society was a model of clearness, and though he held papers in his hand, he rarely looked at them, whether mentioning sums of thousands of pounds or explaining how fifteen shillings could be saved by drawing up building contracts in one way rather than another. Gerald looked on in ever-growing admiration, and Marshall on his side seemed almost as much impressed by the boy, and spoke to him instead of to Muirhead with increasing frequency. Indeed it was the boy who decided the matter at last, agreeing to Marshall's proposals and finally inviting Marshall to come and dine with himself and his family. The visitor knew Miss Bertram's name, apparently, as he did that of everybody in the district with money to invest, and accepted the invitation, for which indeed it might have struck some persons that he had been angling, so that at one o'clock the three men walked down to Hartshill chatting amiably as they went.

Two of them were expected, and Miss Bertram, on being told privately by Gerald of the business on which the stranger had come, did her best to make him welcome. She had an acute suspicion and mistrust of all these financial folk with sharp eyes and incomprehensible talk who were collecting round her young kinsman, but she was obliged to think that it was all right. Gerald, at any rate, seemed to be prospering, to be keeping regular hours and decent company and earning good money. Certainly she ought to be content—and even more, for the lad came to church with them on Sunday morning and evening, talked respectfully enough to his elders, had agreed readily to be confirmed when Mr. Lowe asked him, and even went to three or four of the Vicar's classes before that event, and conducted himself, when there, with perfect propriety. Miss Bertram professed satisfaction with her lips, and, if she did not feel it, could not have told even herself why. One has a vague idea about certain things and people which can only be summed up in the words that they are too good to be true, and, if Miss Bertram had put into words her exact feeling about Gerald, she would have used some such expression. For Muirhead she had a more pronounced dislike and mistrust; though hardly seeing how to prevent them, she objected to his visits here, especially now that Monica was growing up, and she could see—or thought that she could see—his eyes already resting with pleasure on the fair young face of her ward.

Monica Franklin, at the age of seventeen, had the grave sober look common to children who have lived alone with an elder for many years. Her hair was done up, her dresses were long and a little old-fashioned, but the quaint seriousness of dress and manner seemed to suit marvellously well with the grave, beautiful young face of the child. Withal, she was not always to all men a very pleasant companion. While you were admiring the steady grey eyes, you became conscious that they were looking through you, judging and condemning what they saw. As you watched the soft, mobile mouth with its red lips, it suddenly opened and asked an awkward question, or spoke some quiet, half-conscious disapproval of what you were saying. With very few people did Monica drop her reserve and coldly judicial attitude; certainly not with her brother or his friends. Gerald talked freely to her about his likes and dislikes, his plans, hopes, judgments, and work;

he had made no concealment of them from her in the past, and, finding it difficult to begin to do so, he continued his revelations, which squared so little with any of Monica's principles and ideals that she began after a time to merely study her brother and his friends as types of humanity—and very unpleasing types she thought them. To-day, when she came into the room, it was with the intention of keeping perfectly quiet and leaving all the conversation to her aunt and Muirhead. But her intention received a curious check.

# CHAPTER VI

White, nervous and silent, with restless hands and trembling lips, staring blankly alike at Monica when she came in to speak to Muirhead, and at the servant who came in to announce the mid-day dinner—what was the matter with Miss Christina Bertram?  She had been introduced to Marshall, had sat down opposite to him and talked to him in her usual quiet, reserved manner for a minute or two, and then her face had slowly frozen, and her eyes dilated with bewilderment and fear.  He sat opposite to her talking easily about the neighbourhood, which he seemed to have visited before, and to know slightly apart from business matters; and if he looked a trifle whiter than usual, well, no one who knew him was perhaps present to notice it.  He glanced admiringly at Monica as she came in, and flashed an amused look at Muirhead, who started up in eager greeting.  At dinner he talked fluently—rather too much so, praising everything in a slightly condescending fashion.

"English meat is so good," he began once,

"I have passed much of my time in Southern Europe, where everything is so nasty that I am greedy over English meals. I spent a month once in an inn kept by Italians; the only servants were the son and daughter of the landlady. The son waited on us;—a very handsome young man he was, I assure you, Miss Franklin;—his name was Orestes, and after dinner he played the mandolin in the garden. The girl was very good-looking, and a great friend of mine—very great. I should hardly like to tell you all that passed between us, Miss Franklin, I assure you." He laughed across at the girl with bold, coarse eyes, and she coloured angrily. "Then our peace was disturbed by the arrival of some more visitors for whom a chef had to be engaged. The chef quarrelled with Orestes, and as he kept a knife in his belt and a revolver in his pocket, we feared every day that we should be left without a waiter. If I begged Orestes to get me some food he would be sure to come back saying that it was cooked and ready, but that he dare not get it because the chef was guarding it with his pistols loaded and cocked, and his knife sharpened in his hand."

"How very Italian!" laughed Muirhead. "You said it was in Italy, didn't you?"

"It was in Southern Europe," said Marshall

curtly. "The people were Italians, yes. Have you ever been abroad, Miss Franklin?"

It was odd that the man never addressed himself to Miss Bertram, always to Monica. As the girl shook her head he went on talking to her with the expansive smile and voice growing continually louder of a man who thinks that he is the object of every one's admiration.

"I know most of the world pretty well," he said. "My friends tell me that I have been into every country in the world, and brought away a little additional wickedness from each of them. Friends say these kind things to us, Miss Franklin! At any rate I know the four continents well; or are there five, Miss Franklin? I am always willing to receive corrections from you. I shall write my adventures one day. All the books of travel which I have ever read are the most shocking nonsense; one closes the book and one's left eye together. I remember somewhere or other in some part of Europe where I was once in my youth there was a man who used to tell travel stories and to write them too. Every one hung on his words, and no one paid any attention to me. He was the idol of the neighbourhood, you understand, and I was the idler, ha, ha! You must excuse my little jokes, Miss Franklin;

but one day he began to tell . . . Can I help you, Miss Franklin? Is your aunt ill?"

Miss Bertram's face had turned to such an ashen grey during the progress of this narrative that Monica jumped up and ran round to the head of the table, asking whether she should get some brandy or sal-volatile. But by an immense effort the woman recovered speech and movement; with forced calm she made some small excuse for her attack and went on playing with the food on her plate. Marshall did not resume his story, but sat silent for nearly a minute with the vexed puzzled look of a man who knows that he has been guilty of some indiscretion, but cannot settle exactly what it is. A little talk went on between Monica, Muirhead and Gerald, during the interval; then Marshall's loud voice began again, and put a stop to all further conversation by keeping all the task to itself.

Shortly after dinner Nicholson arrived with his sister.

"We are at a birthday party. It is Gerald Franklin's sixteenth birthday," said Muirhead to Marshall, and the latter's stare of surprise amused his companion.

"Sixteen!" muttered the Londoner. "Sixteen! Oh, Lord! Yes, we want that young man for our work. Decidedly we want him."

The afternoon dragged by a little heavily. Marshall's booming voice got on every one's nerves, and all the inmates of the little drawing-room except one were wondering why he did not go. Presently it appeared that he wanted to catch the 6:30 train from Stoke to London, and Muirhead explained the way to the station with elaborate plans. "You can see the whole road from the dining-room window," said Miss Bertram, suddenly rising from her chair and leading the way into the dining-room. Marshall followed and the two stood by the window looking down on to Stoke. Then without looking round or moving, and in a scared shaking voice, Miss Bertram asked abruptly:—

"What are you doing here? Why have you come back?"

# CHAPTER VII

A great friend of mine who had gained a precarious livelihood between the ages of twenty and forty by stealing horses in Texas, "holding up" stage-coaches in California, robbing gold-convoys in West Australia, slave-dealing and illicit-diamond-buying in Africa, piracy on the high seas, and other methods on which Society has placed its irrational ban, told me once that nothing in his career had ever irritated him more than the discovery of those varied and artistic disguises which circumstances (and by circumstances he of course meant the police) forced him to adopt. He was not clever at disguising himself; it was the weak point in his otherwise admirable intelligence; but to the end of his life (which regrettable event took place on a gallows in Sydney, New South Wales) he could never be convinced of this fact, and not only would he recount to me with genuine amazement and vexation how the police found him out again and again, but on one occasion when I met him in the streets of Buenos Ayres disguised as an Argentine police-

man (certainly his most brilliant effort of imagination), and went up to him with a delighted,
"My dear C——, how are you?" the proceeding on my part nearly cost me his friendship.
"Take my word for it," he said, frowning and
working his mouth about so that his wig got
away and one of his whiskers fell off; "take
my word for it you can't annoy a man in my
position more than by recognising him even if
you are his friend, and it is done in private.
Not only does he realise that much time and
money have been wasted, but fancy the fool
that he feels walking about with his discoverer
in the outrageous clothes and false hair, and
high heels and false stomach, which his friend
has seen through and is laughing at!"

Mr. Marshall's annoyance at being recognised by his sister was a reproduction of the
complex feelings so eloquently described by
poor C——. He looked at her first in angry
astonishment, then with a semblance of polite
amazement as if minded to deny that he was
her brother, the ex-secretary of the North
Staffordshire Infirmary; then evidently giving
up this idea as a bad job he looked out of the
window with sullen wrath in his eyes and a
very miserable skeleton of a smile on the rest
of his face.

"I have been trying all afternoon for a

chance to see you alone and tell you who I am," he said, wondering whether the woman believed him, and very easily perceiving that she did not.

"What are you doing here?" she insisted. "Why have you come back?"

"I wanted to make some money," he said at last; "and one can only do that in England. Are you so very unhappy at seeing me again?" he added sentimentally.

The woman turned and looked full at him for the first time since she had sat opposite to him before lunch and realised who he was. She studied the white, slightly-puffed cheeks; the coarse, bold eyes; the profusion of black hair, curled and oiled and scented. The fellow looked like a prosperous provincial money-lender. Miss Christina shuddered slightly and turned away. Above all the other thoughts caused by this return—above the certainty that Marshall was living dishonestly, that he would worry her by demanding her money, making friends with Monica and influencing Gerald, and would generally make her life in Staffordshire intolerable—rose a feeling of pure personal dislike for the man himself. Her brother had filled her with anxiety all his life; now he disgusted her.

Marshall thought that she was overpowered

by emotion and threw more pathos into his face and voice, which looked and sounded like those of a melodramatic actor playing the persecuted curate in a small country theatre.

"It has saddened me," he went on, "to come back to these scenes of my youth, and to think that I shall never be able to visit them again under my own name. At least I suppose not. Did they—tell me, Chris," he dropped his voice still lower and moved nearer to her, "did they issue a warrant against me directly I had gone off? Are they still looking for me, eh? I haven't liked to make any inquiries."

Miss Bertram stood silent. In a second it flashed across her how easy it would be to keep the man in check by fear of arrest if he thought that a warrant had been issued for his apprehension and was still out. Gerald's future, Monica's happiness, her own peace, might depend on her having some hold over him. She could not lie about it, but answered coldly:—

"I suppose a warrant holds good until you are caught, however long a time it may be afterwards. Are you staying on in England?"

"Yes, I am quite safe. Smart chap that youngster of yours. And his sister is a very pretty girl, too. Where did they come from, and what are they doing here?"

"As you will never see or speak to either of them again after to-day, I do not think that I need tell you their story."

The fellow looked at her, stroking his black whiskers and considering. He did not mean to defy her, partly because he anticipated wanting her money, partly because he was not quite sure how far she would go in defence of her young charges. She was clearly very fond of them. Equally clearly, he regretted to notice, she was not at all fond of him, and had no sentimental recollection of the days when they were young and played (or, as he would have preferred to call it in his present mood, sported) together, and were whipped one after another for playing truant from school, and were sent to bed equally hungry in adjoining bedrooms. So Marshall answered her mildly:—

"Of course not; of course not; just as you will. I might have helped the boy, but it shall be as you please. And for his sister . . . she is really a very pretty girl. How old is she? Twenty, perhaps?"

"She is seventeen," said Miss Bertram, stiffly, "and the boy is sixteen. He could be no possible use to you in any business. He is a mere boy, just out of school, and knows nothing of any money-matters, though, of course, Mr. Muirhead is teaching him something."

"Muirhead teach that youth . . . !" muttered Marshall with a laugh. "What he doesn't know about money-matters isn't worth knowing. Muirhead couldn't teach him much. He's forgotten more than Muirhead ever knew. Gerald Franklin . . . that would be a son of that head clerk in the railway office, I suppose?"

"Yes," said Miss Bertram unwillingly.

"I think I remember him. And Monica . . . Monica . . ." The man dwelt on the name with a slight smile on his lips, and Miss Christina glanced at him in angry amazement. At last he turned abruptly away and went into the next room.

"I must catch the 6:30 from Stoke," he was saying when she followed him in, "and must go at once. Good-bye, Miss Franklin. I shall be indeed vexed if I cannot find an excuse to come here again soon, and call on your aunt and you. Good-bye, Mr. Franklin. You will hear from us in London very soon. You are coming part of the way to the station with me, Mr. Muirhead? That is very good of you. Thank you. Good-bye, Miss Bertram." The man looked at her with much show of deprecatory humility, but she shook her head wrath-

fully, and when they were close together for a
moment near the front door, she muttered to
him: "You will not come here again . . .
never, or you know the consequences!"  He
looked at her with a smile, gently and humbly
defiant, and departed.

The swagger and bravado left Marshall as he
turned with his companion out of the gate and
walked along the crest of the hill.  He hardly
heard Muirhead's remarks, and answered at
random, looking down the while, with scoffings
at his own sentiment, but with eyes full of
regret and pain and half-formed impotent
remorse, over the home-scene in the sunset-
tinted valley below.  Which of us can quite
kill the delicate far-reaching fibres of that love
for scenes with which our youth has been
bound up for long, happy years—our youth—
that white dawn which vice, and folly, and passion, have at worst as yet only smirched for a
few moments?  The faith in God, in His for-
giveness, and help and love, in the possibility
of a new life beginning daily, with courage and
hope for its ministers and Heaven for its end:
how many men have lost these through long,
wandering years to find them again in some
wet, scented woods, spring-tinted and silent,
where years ago they used to go a-maying with
the friends whom they have now defrauded or

forgotten, and picked white boughs of cherry-
blossom for a small sister who was too small to
reach them?  How many?  .  .  .  and some,
after the finding, have struggled back through
repentance and restitution, through tears and
retribution, and borne the burden of their
years to the light; while others have sighed
and enjoyed for a spell this new subtle pain
of memory, and stretched out feeble hands
towards the lost innocence; and so come back
to the life of the moment, to an express to
London, a city office, a money-getting or
pleasure-hunting machine, which must go forward at all costs.

# CHAPTER VIII

There is more reality, more intense emotion, a keener pleasure and a bitterer pain in the backwaters of life than in its main stream. Hurry, noise, money-getting, the type-writer and the electric light, are not real life.

On the main stream of the Amazons you fly by on fast steamers, you pass boats bringing turtles from Ega, timber from the Madeira forests, india-rubber from all parts to Para. You stop at Macapa, Santarem, Barra, Manaos; drive bargains in india-rubber; exchange remedies for mosquito-bites; and then hurry along as you voyage to St. Paolo. The river is wide, busy, ugly: you do not stop to think, but hurry on.

But on the backwaters of the Amazons you rest and think, and feel your own emotions, recognising the true value of everything. Sitting under a tree, 200 feet high and 50 feet in girth and 1000 years old, in a forest 3000 miles long and 500 miles across, you see what it really means to be 5 feet 10 inches in height, and to live for four score years. All around you Nature is free to develop herself.  The forest glades are a vast fernery; orchids and lianas hang from the great assai palms; scarlet and green tanagers, red and yellow macaws, bright-coloured butterflies, flit to and fro; down the slow-moving stream floats a great boa-constrictor curled round the branch of a tree, which he steers with his tail.  Big pumice-stones which have been made round as balls by being washed about in the shallow streams at the foot of the Andes volcanoes drift ashore, bearing eggs and seeds of insects and plants from 1200 miles away which are seized upon and propagated in a thousand variations by the insects and plants round you.  And sitting in the midst of this rioting nature you see that you are a small, not so very important part of it all.  You can, it is true, pick the orchids, catch or shoot the parrots, and trample over the ferns; but, man alive! what happens to you if you pass under a branch from which a snake is hanging looking out for something to eat?  And did seeds travel 1000 miles to unite with others in pro-ducing you?  You are not so very wonderful after all.  .  .  .  The truths and realities of life are only seen in life's backwaters.

There was a backwater at Hartshill on the banks of which Mr. Reginald Nicholson, clerk to Messrs. Muirhead & Franklin, wandered, and saw clearly that money-making was so small a part of life as hardly to be worth calling life at all, and that love mattered everything. Anon he meditated on this discovery alone, and anon he told the story of his love to an audience of one. I do not mean to suggest that he ever said to Monica in words, "I love you, please marry me," for this, as he well knew, would have been the signal for his immediate ejection from the house by Monica's aunt; but he said it in a thousand other ways. Indeed, when eyes and mute lips can tell tales so much more clearly than words, it hath always seemed to me remarkable that parents and guardians should attach so much importance to the escape of such second-rate messengers. "Will you give me your word, if I let you remain here, not to speak to my daughter about this for another two years?" Oh, foolish father! to think such a pledge when given worth twopence; when the young man that very morning will look such love and hopes into his mistress' eyes as no words or kisses, or a diamond engagement-ring itself could tell of!

Nicholson was the eldest son of a pottery manufacturer in Stoke who, having a great admiration for Muirhead, had sent his son to

him to be taught book-keeping and other such
business matters as might be picked up in the
branch of a big insurance office.  He did certain work for Muirhead in return for this
instruction, coming into Newcastle every morning at nine, and returning to his home just
outside Stoke (when he could find no excuse
for going to Hartshill, which was not often) at
six.  He was a happy-minded, easy-going
youngster, well educated, contented with life
(except when Monica was angry), unsuspicious,
and clean in mind and body.  His years numbered twenty-one, and he loved Monica Franklin with the single-hearted unselfishness and
purity which you may see sometimes in lovers
of his age.  I do not mean to say that he would
have given her up to some one else if he saw
that she preferred his rival, or that he would
not have sulked for an afternoon if she had
permitted some audacious pretender to button
her glove or give her a new carnation for her
garden; Nicholson would on the contrary have
cuffed the head of such a man, or cheerfully
helped to do him any reasonable injury; but
when Monica wanted something which did not
square with Nicholson's recreations or pleasure
or happiness, the something in question was
always given to her.  The girl watched her
admirer with a little bewilderment (for he was

her first lover), a little wonder and doubt, sometimes with a touch of amusement, and just now and again with a little inclination to return his love. It is only in the back-waters, you know, that two lives like these can be noticed drifting down stream and coming nearer and nearer together as they sweep along. I do not know that their story—it is so old!—is really very interesting. It is stale rather, is it not, this history of young love, this book of innocence written in white on white? But we will get back soon to the main stream. After all, however much more interesting and real the tranquillity of the back-water may be to the philosopher, one must have hurry and noise in a story.

The little house in Hartshill had a garden, and the garden had a summer-house, built by some friendly architect who knew that people occasionally had something to say which entailed sitting close together, touching one another's hands, and other proceedings which cannot be carried on in view of drawing-room windows. On a bench in this summer-house sat Reggie Nicholson and Monica watching the friendly April sun which had come out for a few moments before he went to bed, to dry up the rain and warm the damp air.

"Who is this man Marshall, Mr. Nicholson?"

They had not reached the stage of Christian names yet, even in the summer-house, though now and then Reggie slipped out a "Monica," and pretended to look very much annoyed by his mistake.

"He came down from London this morning," answered the young man. "I don't know what about. Miss Bertram didn't seem to take to him exactly."

"He was detestable," said Monica, which settled the estimate of Marshall for both of them.

"Yet you talked to him all afternoon," said Nicholson, relieved to find that his lady-love had not returned Marshall's too evident admiration, yet willing to air his grievance in case she should think it one worthy of compensation.

"You mean he talked to me," said Monica with a laugh. "I would have been just thankful to any one who had saved me. I looked across at you and your sister a dozen times wishing you would come."

"I suppose then that Franklin or Muirhead or Martha would have done just as well?"

Martha was Miss Bertram's housemaid, and Mr. Nicholson, you perceive, was in a huff because Monica had bracketed him with his sister in her last sentence. Some people are never satisfied, and you may be sure that no one ever knew for certain at what a lover would or would not take offence. Monica did not know, and sat for a moment considering why he spoke in this resentful voice.

"I am sorry that he is coming to see Mr. Muirhead and Gerald again," went on the girl; "he will do them harm: he is not honest."

"I will keep your brother out of his way as much as possible," said the young man, pointedly ignoring her inclusion of Muirhead. And the extent of his acquaintance with his employers may be guessed from the fact that he really believed in his own ability to do what he promised. The girl flashed a grateful little look at him in which was yet a little wonder at the resentment in his voice. She knew her brother about as well as Reggie did, and really believed that he was open to such mild influences as Nicholson could bring to bear on him. Then she stood up and wandered to the front of the summer-house and he stood as close as he dared to her side, happy when a breath of evening wind blew her dress against him, and to think that he must hold her hand in his—for half a minute perhaps if he could talk on and make her forget—when he went. How such evenings hang in the memory when a hundred great triumphs are forgotten! You see, the life of the back-waters, being real, lives on.

It was time to go, long past it really, but even lovers have a parting hour which they recognise as inevitable. It is controlled of course by no such trivial matters as the clock, but mostly by sudden fear lest their mistress should be getting tired of them. Such a suspicion came to Nicholson's mind now, and he rose to go.

"I am afraid your brother means to have a lot to do with this man," he said, being in fact afraid of nothing of the sort and infinitely indifferent to Marshall's proceedings, house building or insurance, honest or dishonest,' in Newcastle; but it was an absorbing topic to Monica, who might therefore forget that her hand was being held all the time; "but I will never miss an opportunity of telling him what I think of the fellow. You must do the same and we will drive him out between us. Good-bye, Miss Franklin. I see my sister coming to look for me. I must go and get the pony-cart and take her home."

The girl stood quite still with her eyes on the ground and a soft flush like the reflection of some pale pink light on her cheeks. He held her hand still, though he could find no further words, could think of nothing except that he loved his young companion and wanted to tell her so, to put his arm round her and whisper his story of love. Then at last she took her hand away and said good-bye in a very low voice, and stood still again for a moment as if waiting for him to say something more. And as he did not say it they both turned and walked slowly homewards. . . . Such an old stale story!—as old as the sunset which was painting the western clouds with gorgeous scarlet and gold, as old as the hills which to-morrow's sunrise would tinge with primrose and rose!—as dull as the little backwater where only the leaves rustle and the waters sweep past bending reeds, and the air sings with the rapid beating of birds' wings! Yet it is a page in the life of the heroine of this tale which must be told if the rest is to be clear, and thus with many apologies I offer it to the readers of Monica's story.

# CHAPTER IX

"No, sir; I am not at all satisfied with Reginald."

The time was about a year after Marshall's first visit to Staffordshire, and the speaker was Reginald Nicholson's father, who after the manner of many of his species was holding forth to a companion about his son's misdeeds. It really never seems to occur to persons of this kind that the knowledge which they obtain about their offspring owing to circumstances (mostly financial) over which the offspring has no control, is private. Most people know the story of Schopenhauer sitting at dinner with a party of men friends round him and a twenty-franc piece by the side of his plate. "There is a louis," said the philosopher, "which I have placed here every night for a month with the intention of giving it to the poor when these gentlemen shall have spoken during dinner of something else than promotion, horses, or women. I still have the louis." It would be safe to make the same promise (though it might be prudent to do it more quietly) with regard to an average party of men at an English club, if you added to your list of subjects their son's school-bills, debts, and other iniquities. This is very improper behaviour on the part of one's father.

Mr. Nicholson's companion was the Rev. Canon Hobart, vicar of Stoke-on-Trent, a middle-aged bachelor with a rich living, nine curates (instead of the nine children which might have been expected from his profession) and a fund of quiet humour which made his parishioners an object of inexhaustible joy to himself, and himself an object of unmitigated terror to his parishioners.

"No; I am not satisfied with him," repeated Nicholson, senior. "My children are all growing up a bit cranky. There is Ethel wanting to ride a bicycle; to dress like a man, Canon; to wear what she calls divided skirts. I said to her, 'Take that thing off, my dear; as a favour to me take it off,' I said. 'I don't object to you trying to look like a man,' I said. 'It's the kind of man you succeed in looking like now that I object to,' I said. That's what I said to her. Then there's Reggie. I began life at his age in Josiah Wedgewood's works with 4s. a week, rising 2s. 6d. every year till I had 31s. at the end of my apprenticeship. What do I offer my son, sir? My own pay, which ought to be good enough for him if it was good enough for me?  Not a bit of it.  I said to him: 'Go and learn figuring with Muirhead and then take a choice.'  I said, 'You can travel for us and then have a hundred a year at once, and two hundred to three hundred later on,' I said; 'or you can stay at home and begin with 30s. a week and go on till you are confidential pricing clerk with £3 a week, and cashier with £250 a year, and then my partner.'  That's what I said.  And what did he say?  Thank me for giving him six months with a clever accountant and for offering him this chance of earning good money afterwards?  No, sir.  He said he was very contented where he was, that Muirhead would pay him a pound a week, which was quite enough for his work, and that he was going to stay where he was!  Now you know, Canon, some fathers would have cut up rough at that, would have said to the chap, 'See here, young man, you go your way and I will go mine, and I will take care that the ways are different.'  That's what my father would have done in my place.  But that's not my style.  I said, 'Take your own way, lad, take your own way.  If it's honest I won't stop you.  You'll come to see the folly of it soon.'  That's what I said.  But it vexed me, sir."

"He prefers to work with that Muirhead lot at a pound a week when you offer him 30s.—to stay among that gang of swindlers with less pay and more work?  That is a programme of such an extremely objectionable character that there must be something more in it than we know.  Is there, I wonder, a young lady in the case?"

"No, sir.  Certainly not.  Why, my son is only just twenty-one!  A pretty age to begin running after the girls!  I was thirty before I thought of such a thing."

"Gerald Franklin, Muirhead's partner, has a sister who is young, pretty, and very charming —ah, Mr. Nicholson, the world begins earlier and goes faster than when we were young!  I have seen her with your son.  I know nothing.  Probably there is nothing to know.  But I can see what may be a reason for your son stopping on in that den of thieves."

"You have your own opinion about Muirhead's office," said Nicholson, in a bewildered tone.  His anxiety about his son was old and permanent and would keep, but Canon Hobart's repeated condemnation of Muirhead required explanation.

"I have a good nose for a rascal," said Hobart coolly, "and I have found out Muirhead long ago.  To be frank, one of the objects

of my visit to you to-day is to remonstrate
about your leaving your son where he is.  You
have authority over him; use it, my friend;
use it vigorously to get him away, I pray you,
unless there is something in the background of
which I know nothing."

"Do you think they are as bad as that?"
asked Nicholson.

"They?  Marshall and Franklin?  Ah, that
is another matter.  Those two are a little
above me.  Muirhead is a scoundrel as clumsy
as he is impudent.  About the other two I can
say nothing."

"But tell me what you think, Canon," said
the other eagerly.  "Every man has an opinion
and may tell it.  I am a bit anxious."

"Well, Reginald has a head on his shoulders."

"Reginald . . . ah, yes."  There was a
sharp impatient tone in Nicholson's voice,
which only one subject can, as a rule, bring to
the front.  "You see the fact is I have £600 in
this Freehold Building Society of theirs.  Six
hundred pounds I have already and was thinking of putting some more in.  Now, what do
you think of it, sir?"

"You should know more of such matters than
I do," said the Rector.

"The Company looks well," said Nicholson,

speaking slowly so as to give his companion
ample opportunity to contradict him by word
or look if he felt inclined; "it has begun down
here in a small cautious way and is doing the
same they tell me everywhere. I know the
properties they have bought down here. A
safe seven or eight per cent. we were promised,
and indeed it looks as if we were going to get
it. Now, you know, sir, that's tempting."

Hobart sat silent for a moment and then
shook his head. "I leave all the business consideration alone," he said. "When you get
eight per cent. for your money you are speculating, but it is no affair of mine to condemn
speculation. What I do say is: keep clear of
Muirhead; take your son out of his office; he
is a scamp."

"It's true he is hand in glove with Luke
Robinson and Fiske and their set," muttered
Nicholson, mentioning the Wesleyan and Bap-
tist ministers and evidently following out a line
of thought not very complimentary to Canon
Hobart's impartiality. The Canon indeed followed the thought and flushed angrily.

"Muirhead's preferences and friendships are
no great concern of mine," he said coldly, "but
I don't think I have ever made myself
notorious by prejudice against non-conformists.
I mostly venture to regard dissent as a family

or even business matter.  Inside my Staffordshire experience it is not a very vital affair.
When a man sets up two horses they mostly
have a habit of stopping at the door of the
Parish Church."

"No offence, sir, no offence to you," said
Nicholson vaguely, but in fact he had spoken
his real thought in suggesting that Hobart was
prejudiced against Muirhead on account of the
latter's friendship with the two non-conformist
ministers.  The Building Society of which he
had spoken was a very taking affair, and had
pleased every one immensely.  During the
eight months in which it had been in existence
in Staffordshire its managers had either by
foresight or good luck put their hand on one
or two thoroughly good bits of property;
shares were being bought eagerly; it was
notorious that the Staffordshire branch of the
Company could have paid a half-yearly dividend at the rate of eight per cent.  And there
was another consideration.  It was and would
be of immense benefit to the working classes
who could by its help gradually acquire possession of the houses in which they lived.  The
Society was a philanthropic work;—a philanthropic work which paid a big dividend.  Small
wonder that Mr. Nicholson invested his £600,
that Mr. Lowe ventured £500 of his last

legacy, and advised Miss Bertram to invest certain savings in the wonderful Company.  To
get a thank-you for some charitable work had
hitherto been a surprise to many of these good
folk.  When they heard charity-managers, who
were their guides, applauding the good work
and business-men on whose judgment they
were used to rely, recommending the investment there was no more to be said or done but
pour money into the ready coffers of the Freehold Building Society.

Canon Hobart encountered another investor
as he left Nicholson's work after his recent
conversation.

"Spare me five minutes, Lowe," he said,
drawing the Vicar of Hartshill on to the ter-
race surrounding the Town Hall.  "I want to
speak to you about a very serious matter.
This building society affair, you know; is it
not a bit out of our line?  Is it exactly our business to recommend it?"

"The amount of good which it will do to all
the working-classes is incalculable," said
Lowe.  "To give a man a chance of buying his
house steadies him, makes him more regular
and hopeful.  And financially the thing is
quite sound, a perfect investment.  But it is
above all a most useful work.  Luke Robinson
says——"

"Luke Robinson!" echoed Canon Hobart.

Vigorously but never too vigorously, often but never too often, doth the wise man preach against the hasty word. So idiotically does the mind of the average man work that seven solid arguments can be pulverised in it by one verbal blunder; or is it that instinct is right, and that your companion's advice is really less valuable if he cannot keep the blunder out of it? I know not; I only know that at this scornful ejaculation of Hobart's, Lowe merely said to.himself, "Oh, that is the reason why you are so strong against the Freehold Society, just because Robinson is for it; well, well!" and so stood silent and indifferent. Maybe also—though I love not to skin my friends, of whom Lowe is certainly one—deep down in the heart of the Vicar of Hartshill was a certain appreciation of a social distance between himself and the Hon. and Rev. Canon Hobart, and of a social kinship with Mr. Robinson, which made this lecture exceptionally unpalatable.

"Robinson understands the needs of his followers very well," said Lowe stiffly after a pause.

"How much commission do you suppose the Society is paying him on the money which he brings in?" asked Hobart scornfully.

Lowe stroked his beard and did not trouble

to conceal his disapproval of this remark, but there was nothing to be said in reply to it. After another moment of silence Canon Hobart went on almost roughly: "But do I understand that you are also recommending the Society?"

"I have spoken in favour of it several times."

"I disapprove of it very strongly, Mr. Lowe. There is disaster in it. I prophesy evil—nothing but disaster and evil from it."

A line of waggons laden with pottery crates went lumbering by, making an amount of noise which justified another silence. Three men came out of the Town Hall one after another, and the big swing-doors swung noisily to and fro. A bell on an opposite factory began to ring for the dinner hour. Lowe noted all these things carefully at the moment because he did not know what to say or do next and was glad of the mental occupation. Years afterwards he saw and heard them all again as vividly as now with Hobart's dark angry form towering over him and Hobart's threatening prophecy in his ears.

Then for a fourth time the doors of the Town Hall swung open and Gerald Franklin appeared. The past year had made no mark whatever on his face or figure, which were those of a boy of fifteen. His manner was a little more assured, but it had been so very

assured before that this was not an improvement. Otherwise he was unchanged. He
came up to the two clergymen and with easy
affability detached Lowe from his superior and
walked with him towards the London and
County Bank.

"My aunt has just had an annoying letter,"
he said, "a notice that the Elvaston mortgage
is to be paid off. It is nearly £5000."

"She will have to find another investment,"
said the parson sympathetically. "Very tiresome for her."

"Very," assented Gerald.

"Why doesn't she . . . what would she
think . . ." Lowe stammered a little, for
the memory of that prophecy was still strong
in him. Then he went on resolutely: "What
could she want better than the Freehold?"

'Well, she will be sure to consult you," said
the boy, looking straight before him and
speaking with apparently complete indifference.
"I can't imagine a better investment myself,
but then of course she would think more of
your advice than of mine. Are you likely
to be coming up to see her to-day or to-
morrow?"

"Very possibly to-morrow afternoon."

"If she mentions the matter to you, then you
will advise the Freehold perhaps? Would you

like to see any of the last papers or other details?"

"Well, thank you, thank you. It is always interesting to know the last news of an affair in which all the neighbourhood is interested as well as oneself. How we are all working for you! Your friend Luke Robinson is bringing in shareholders as if he were paid for it!"

Gerald turned to his companion and for a brief part of a second his eyes rested on him in startled inquiry. After all the boy was only seventeen, when no man has complete command of his features or colour.

Maybe too that in Gerald's mind, as in the mind of many older business folk, there was a touch of superstition or—I would advance no theories about another world, having none which I can defend, but only beliefs—maybe there are really guardians beyond our mortal ken who will not suffer their wards to be injured. But on that night a curious thing happened to Gerald Franklin. He sat late at home over some accounts of the Freehold Building Society; it was midnight when he rose with the sudden satisfied relaxation of a man who has finished his work, and he put away his papers and went to the window for a moment to cool and calm the fever of figures which surged in his brain. The wind flung itself wildly against the branches of two great elms which faced him, swaying them to and fro and tearing down their young leaves and twigs. Through a flying scud of clouds the moon stooped now and again with quick white flashes; and on the cloud-scud there glowed red and yellow and white the reflection of the North Staffordshire furnaces.　Here blazed the fires of the Stafford Coal and Iron works, there the more distant furnaces of the Fenton Collieries, close under him glowed the covered fires of the pottery works, whose tall chimneys, standing up among the flames like giant stokers, seemed to sway to and fro with the fire-shadows.　Gerald looked at them without special notice for a minute, then shivered a little, he knew not why, and re-closing the shutter which he had opened, turned round from the window. . . . Standing by the table where he had been writing, and looking down on the sheets of calculations, was a figure which for a second he did not know and stared at with arrested breath and terrified eyes. Then the figure turned its head and looked at him, and into Gerald's brain there flashed the memory of a morning three years ago, of himself standing by a dying woman's bedside, of the woman's words: "I hear; I will remember."

# CHAPTER X

The first yearly meeting of the Freehold
Building Company—the first, that is to say, in
which North Staffordshire was interested—
received a four-column report and a leading
article in the local papers, and never, sure,
was such universal joy in a neighbourhood.   A
dividend of 12 per cent. had been declared, and
an immense sum carried to the reserve fund.
Among women and men, lay and clerical,
church and non-conformist, rich and poor,
there was but one topic of conversation for the
next few days—the wonderful Company to give
money to which was an act of charity which
brought 12 per cent. in this world as well as
(presumably) 100 per cent. in the next.   Lowe,
Robinson, Nicholson, a score of folk who had
their £500 or £1000 in the Company, and to
whom the difference between 4 and 12 per
cent. on such sums was the difference between
comfort and luxury, could hardly stop talking
about its wonders.   They sang the praises
now of its good works, now of its dividends.
They overbore scoffers, they fairly tumbled
their friends and relations into it.   "My dear

Miss Bertram," said Lowe one day in reply to a remark of hers, "what does it matter whether we do or do not like Muirhead or Marshall? We have only to consider the work of the Company, whose figures tell only one story, that the work is good and successful. Do not let Marshall come to your house if you dislike him, but do not let this prevent you from making yourself comfortable for life by putting your money in his Company." Lowe's ordinarily timid common-sense had been swept away by the excitement of the first financial speculation which he had understood and embarked in, but the reputation of it remained here among folk who had not noticed its wreck, and he fairly forced Miss Bertram to promise to invest her £5000 in the Company. He invested all that he could himself lay hands on; half a hundred ministers of all denominations were doing the same; while the cooler men in the district—Canon Hobart on one side and Luke Robinson on the other—protested angrily or laughed with quiet amusement. To the men who are engineering a boom of this kind there is a quiet humour in it which must be irresistibly charming. You make churches and creeds, finance and newspapers, law and society spin round to your lash as if you were whipping half a dozen tops on a clear floor;

and does any man with a pretence of recollection of his boyhood assert that a more entranc-
ing occupation than that could be found?
Gerald Franklin had never whipped tops, but
the excitement and sport of this game of
intrigue made his eyes shine and his whole face
light up now and again with the joy of it.  The
boy had the whole business at his finger-ends.
He was the real, the only trusted counsellor in
the North Staffordshire department.  I think,
incredible as it may seem—though to be sure
he regarded all men as more or less astute
knaves and all their successful proceedings as
*primâ facie* dishonest—that he saw from top-
most branch to deepest roots the real character
of the Freehold Building Company, and foresaw, dimly, perhaps, but as clearly as any one
could yet do, its disastrous end.

It was an afternoon in May, not very long
after the last yearly meeting of the Company,
and Marshall had come down to discuss with
his confidants the new shareholders who were
coming in.  Muirhead, Gerald, and Luke Robinson lunched with him at the Borough Arms
at Newcastle, and then after an hour's chat at
the offices, the Wesleyan Minister departed,
and Marshall proposed a visit to Hartshill.

"My sister has had rather a surprise since
you saw her last," said Gerald in his quiet,

even voice, unusually quiet this time in order
to hide the fury which was raging below.
"My late aunt, Marian Franklin, who died
three years ago, had an uncle who went out to
South Africa.   He died just before she did and
made a will, of which we have just heard, leaving everything to my Aunt Marian.   My aunt,
just before she died, made a will leaving everything she had to my sister Monica, who so
comes in for this old man's money."

"Is it much?"

His two auditors asked the question in a
breath and then flushed angrily, glaring at one
another.   The boy between them looked
straight before him, and if the corners of his
mouth twitched a little no one saw it.

"His property consisted only of two thousand shares in the Carlton mines in South
Africa.   The shares are only worth about 15s.
each now and are paying no dividend, but the
lawyers who have the will advise us to hold
them because some new machinery is being put
up and a new part of the roof opened, and so
the shares may soon be more valuable."

The two men on each side of the speaker
quickened their pace involuntarily as if the
gold mine shares, even two thousand in a
doubtful mine, were a magnet drawing them to
it faster as they came nearer.

"But it is rather rough on you, Franklin,"
said Marshall at last.

"Oh, I have my own money, as you know,"
said Gerald. "It only pays 4 per cent.; still
it's enough for me."

"Lowe is the trustee of it, isn't he?"

"Yes," was the brief reply.

"He wouldn't make any difficulty about letting you transfer it into the Freehold."

For answer the boy turned his head and
while one might count five looked very quietly
and steadily at Marshall. The elder man
turned away after this momentary understanding and walked on in silence. Astonishment
and alarm were in his mind, with wonder as to
how he should deal with this new development
of affairs. Gerald Franklin knew the finance
of the Freehold and saw something wrong? If
so why not a score of other local managers?
The fellow stroked his perfumed black beard
and stared before him in gloomy perplexity,
wishing that he were alone now with this
youngster. And so they came to Miss Bertram's house.

Monica was alone in the sitting-room and
greeted the party in her usual impassive
manner, a compound of fear lest she should
offend her brother's patrons and suspicion of
the patrons themselves. She listened to Mar-

shall's congratulations on her legacy and explanations about the position of the Carlton mines with polite interest, but asked no questions or advice, while Miss Bertram, who had come in, made attempts to change the conversation. Suddenly a gleam of quiet amusement flashed across Monica's face, and Muirhead noting it, and following the direction of her eyes, saw Canon Hobart walk up the front and ring the door-bell. He leant across and muttered something to Marshall, who answered curtly, "I know it," and then stood up with the rest as the Rector was shown in.

"It is curious that I should not have met you before," said Marshall affably when the two men had been introduced.

"You know a good many people in Stoke now, of course."

"Well, they have put me in charge of their money at any rate. And I know a good many of clients, as one may call them, personally too."

"You have known the neighbourhood before?" asked Hobart.

"Oh, no. I was down here some years ago, but only for a few days. Trade has improved since then. There is plenty of money to invest among all classes now."

"It seems all going into your Company."

"A large amount of it certainly."

"You are in treaty for the Arkhill collieries, I hear."

"We should like the whole Arkhill estate," said Marshall, "if we could get it at our own price, and we don't mind having the colliery as well. It is worth money. Sir Richard Cullamore made a mistake in digging for coal in that particular corner. It was farthest from the house, of course. . . ."

"That was his reason for choosing that spot certainly. And since he died—ten, no eleven years ago, wasn't it?—no one has had money to do any more. You knew him apparently?"

In a French duel between two skilful fencers, you may notice how after reprise of cautious *en garde* fighting, there is a sudden, quick murmur of "*touché*" among the spectators. Before the director or seconds know it, before even the combatant himself feels it, the bystanders seem to guess by instinct that something has gone wrong somewhere. Hobart, Muirhead and Gerald saw with surprise an uneasy look come into Marshall's eyes, heard him begin a long, rapid explanation of how he had come by his knowledge. Then Hobart noted suddenly that he was pronouncing Sir Richard Cullamore's name in Staffordshire fashion — "Culmer"—and he turned and looked straight and fixedly at the man, whose uneasiness, he perceived, increased under the look. Where had he seen Marshall before, where heard this smooth, high-pitched voice? Somewhere, he was certain. Yet likely enough the man had been in Staffordshire ten years ago on very ordinary business: though why in that case should he look so uncomfortable about it, and edge away from all talk about the subject as he now proceeded to do? The Rector bent his mind as he walked home to the problem, but it was no use yet, he could not remember.

In the house which he had left, Miss Bertram drew her brother into the garden:

"Are you mad?" she asked angrily. "Why do you come here if you can't help making blunders like that? Why do you come at all?"

"I am obliged to be in the neighbourhood pretty often," he answered gloomily, "and this is the first time I have made any mistake."

"You will be in prison soon, I can see," said the woman, shaking her finger at him in threatening warning. "But I have to ask you something now"—her voice changed; she hesitated, and then spoke again almost pleadingly—"you are connected with this Company somehow; I don't understand in what position, but I hope you are working honestly; indeed," she added hurriedly, "I daresay you are. But

you know something about it anyhow. I suppose you would not deliberately deceive me''—
she eyed him rather wistfully, and the man did
his best to look honest. "I have got £5000 to
invest, and every one is urging me to put it
into this Company. The loss of it would ruin
me, as you know. Is the Company safe? Tell
me truthfully, Joshua. You don't want to
injure me, I suppose. Tell me if the investment is a safe one." Miss Christina's hands
were being clasped and unclasped in front of
her as she spoke. The lace cap on her head
trembled a little. She stood quite near him,
and once stretched out a mittened hand as if to
put it on his arm.

"Who has spoken to you about it?" he asked,
wanting to gain time.

"Mr. Lowe, Mr. Robinson, every one I meet
in fact."

"You would be quite content with the investment?"

"I feel it would be ridiculous to go against
such advice without any reason."

"Haven't you asked Benson?'' asked her
brother nervously. Benson was the Stoke
lawyer who did Miss Bertram's little bits of
business for her.

"He recommends it too. I met him again
only yesterday in Stoke walking with Mr. Rob-

inson, and they both urged me to buy the shares at once.''

A soft May breeze drifted through the lilac-bush under which they were standing, scattering its scent and brushing off some rain-drops which hung on its vividly-green leaves. The scent from beds of wet yellow daffodils and late primroses and early pinks was carried past them. From the elm-trees, on whose young leaves rain-drops lay gleaming in the sunlight, came the high shrilling of young birds and the answering notes of the parent birds. Spring flowers and greenery, washed by the recent showers from their smoke-covering, flushed out in vivid colours above the smoke-clouds which hung below. Through even these the May afternoon sunlight pierced rainbow paths and turned the chimneys to columns of gold. The familiar home scene, every detail of which seemed to have been burnished up to a degree of beauty which even his exile memories of it had hardly exceeded, worked on Marshall's mind now to such an extent that with a muttered curse on Robinson he turned away, saying aloud: "You should never invest money anywhere in a hurry. Wait till I send you all possible particulars about the company. I will write my own advice too. I don't care to answer any such questions offhand.'' He stood still for a moment looking round the garden, and another great breath of lilac-scent swept across his face; then he came back and stood near his sister.

"I will be more careful, Chris," he said. "You would be sorry, I really believe, if I were nabbed. As for my work now, I am earning money perfectly honestly; you believe that, don't you?"

"I suppose you are," said the woman a little grudgingly. "Everybody speaks well of the work, and I know nothing against it."

# CHAPTER XI

On the "broad road leading to destruction" there is a point, one knows not exactly where, at which it is in effect impossible to turn back; and even as to some persons that text in the Revelation: "He that is unjust let him be unjust still; he that is filthy let him be filthy still," hath always seemed the most terrible ideal of Hell ever conceived, so this house on the road of sin where we may imagine this condemnation to eternal filth and eternal injustice being pronounced is a place of horror unspeakable. A man sits down in it tired of vice, fraud, greed, unsated and knowing himself to be insatiable, sick of self-seeking, tired of the pain and ruin which he has caused, and often euough suffered in the world, horror-stricken at the evil which he has done, is doing and is planning to do. He will repent and reform, he will even restore a little of his ill-gotten gain to mankind; he will retrace his footsteps, enter that other gate, struggle down that other thorny path. But, ah Heaven! where is the road back? There is one, but along it are

scoffing companions and ridicule and shame;
another, but there is suffering and pain for
those who have shared his misdeeds, and the
certainty that to them at least his salvation
means ruin and death; there is another, but it
is very grim, for it leads by confession and
restitution to prison and perhaps even further.
With dim and ever-growing fear the man looks
out and sees that he cannot go back, or even
stay where he is, for retribution is at his heels.
He must go on—on—and his only ambition as
he flies is to outstrip the pursuing vengeance.

"I dare not spare her," muttered Marshall
to himself as he sat in the train speeding back
to London. "Suppose that she and the boy,
both of whom are supposed to be my friends,
refuse to invest money in this, what will people
down here say? I dare not risk it. She must
put her money in, and I will try and save
some of it before the smash comes. That boy!
—how does he know?" . . . The man's
eyes grew dark and furious and his face was
very white—"How can one trust him? Yet
one must; there is no choice." His thoughts
grew more sombre every hour, and when the
express arrived at Euston, late as it was, he
drove to the house of a fellow-director and
asked to see him at once.

Lord Eastney was a peer with a large

country and town house, an army of footmen,
cooks, agents and secretaries, and a considerable estate which produced a nominal rental
known only to readers of the Financial Reform
Almanack and a real income of about £1200 a
year.  He had one valuable asset—an old and
famous name, and on this he lived as comfortably as he desired and as honestly as he could.
He really had no cut and dried desire to
plunder his neighbours, but merely a wish to
get his share of this world's goods; and my
Lord's idea of his share was as much as he
could possibly get without being hanged or sent
to gaol while getting it.

"How are you, Mr. Marshall?  Anything
wrong?"  The Marquis had no great love for
his fellow-director, but regarded his acquaintance—like getting up early, studying figures,
missing two days of Ascot, and lunching in
City restaurants—as one of the evils of an
income which would not cover one's expenditure.  Therefore he shook hands with him,
smiled affably, asked him if he had dined, and
offered him coffee, liqueurs and a cigar.

"I want," began Marshall abruptly, "to say
a few words about that Arkhill property in
Staffordshire before the meeting on Thursday.
You remember the details of it?"

"We were to buy it from the Merton Insur-

ance Company."   The Marquis half-lowered
his eyelids over his eyes and sat straight up in
his chair.  His fingers, which had been twirling
some gold eye-glasses round and round on their
string, stopped working and his face was very
grave.

"I think myself that £85,000 would be a fair
price," said Marshall.

"Yes?" asked the Marquis in a tone which
gave you the impression that the speaker would
have been startled if he had not been Chairman
of the Freehold Building Company, and so past
being startled by anything.

"Yes," went on Marshall aggressively; "the
land round Dently could be let as allotments,
and there is workable coal, I am certain, nearer
the Hall. . . ."

"I know the Arkhill property, Mr. Marshall," said the other a trifle drily.

"Then your lordship must know how it has
increased in value since we bought it for the
Merton."

"Ten months ago that was, wasn't it?  And
we paid £30,000.  Yes, I remember.  Oh, no
doubt it has improved."

"We may consider the price fixed at £85,000
then?" asked Marshall.

"Very good," assented Lord Eastney in a
low voice.

"There is another very small matter. I have been down in Staffordshire several times lately, and there is very little more to be done down there for some time. We have every one in the Company who has any money to invest; we have bought all the property which is worth buying. I want to bring our best man there up here—a man called Franklin. We could send Seymour down into Essex and give his place to young Franklin."

"He is young?"

"Very; but he understands our business thoroughly."

"I see. Yet £400 a year is a big salary for a lad. Don't we want to reserve places of that sort for people who—understand—our business more thoroughly than any lad could?"

"When I find one who knows the whole of it from top to bottom better than this person, he shall have Franklin's place," said Marshall grimly.

"Very good." The pale patrician face was beginning to look very weary. "Is that all, Mr. Marshall? Yes? Then . . ."

With an unusually decisive movement Lord Eastney rose and moved towards the library door, which he held open. Marshall passed out biting his lips, and held out his hand to say good-bye with almost a threatening gesture.

Eastney looked at the hand, hesitated for a moment, then slightly shrugging his shoulders with a "what's the good of it?" air, put his own hand into it for a moment.

Marshall went home frightened and furious; he had never before met with these curt laconic answers, this chilling reception, from the chairman of the Freehold Building Society. Lord Eastney was also a fellow-director of the Merton Insurance Company, and one or two other smaller associations by whose financial jugglings between themselves money flowed into his pocket. He dared not think of what would happen if the Marquis was going to desert him, and Gerald was going to drop hints in Staffordshire about the Freehold finance and its transactions with the Insurance Company. He sat late that night poring over a private investment ledger, and at last wrote instructions for the sale of all his English investments. Then he walked about thinking for another half hour, then sat down again and wrote to his sister, enclosing papers about the Freehold, and advising her strongly to put her £5000 into it. As he finished his letter, and, fearful of his resolution, took it out at once to the post, the sky was yellow and pink and grey, birds twittered in the pearl-grey light and faintly-glimmering stars were dying one by one

in the dawn of day.   For a short time longer a
soft restful silence reigned, and then in far-off
murmurs the life of London began.   As he
reached his own door-step again Marshall stood
for a moment and listened to its rising tide of
sound, half fancied, half real, and wholly awe-
some.   Lives coming and going, pain sighing
gratitude for the daylight, and weariness cursing its recall to toil, dancers coming home from
the ball with music in their ears, and workers
coming out to their labour with the hunger-
spectre at their heels, lovers who have passed
their *nuit blanche* drawing aside curtains to
whisper odes to the rose-tinted sunrise, men
who have blundered frightfully, and spent the
night searching for remedies, and finding none,
and now stood at open windows, muttering
despair—all added their little whisper to the
murmur which floats under the London dawn.
And Marshall, listening to it, shuddered
slightly and went to his room with a curious
feeling of oppression and fear, as of a multi-
tude waiting for him, to tear him in pieces.

# CHAPTER XII

Unrequited love and sea-sickness are the subjects of universal scoffing, yet while their agony is at its height, the world can hardly show more horrible suffering. Some people say that sea-sickness is the worst, and affect to prove their theory by pointing out that the pain of it swallows up—or let us say absorbs, since to swallow up is not a happy expression under the circumstances—the other. It is too true that an unfortunate love, though it may feed on your damask cheek night and day, will certainly be forgotten during a crossing to the Isle of Man or Dieppe, but it has a bigger record of suicide and crime behind it, and therefore I should award it the first place. Yet it may be said again in reply that this record counts for little, since the sea-sick are, for obvious reasons, incapable of committing crime themselves, and that if all the murders and other injuries done in intention—especially to the steward when he cometh not promptly at call, or to the captain who "lies to" for an hour off Douglas Point—were counted, the record of the sea-sick would be the blackest on earth. But your intention and desire to commit murder, whatever their theological value, have none in the eyes of the police, whereas the unhappy lover, with his dagger, and pistol, and poison, most distinctly has. Therefore his record is the worst, and I count him chief among sufferers.

Mr. Sampson Muirhead could yet experience moments of hope. When he was in good spirits, or when good spirits were in him, he could still see himself the husband of Monica, and, though to do him justice this counted for very little, the part-proprietor of her gold-mine shares, and heir to Miss Bertram's little fortune. But it wanted every day a greater height of exaltation to see this vision, and every day the hours of hopelessness grew longer. With all his heart he loved the girl; for her sake he worked hard and steadily, abjuring many a little amusement which cost money or seemed wrong. So far let us pity him. If his manner of getting rich was not very honest—well, the whole business of the Freehold Building Society and the Merton Insurance Company, of which he was nominally local manager, was dishonest from top to bottom, and he was no worse than a hundred of other men in both of them. A scoundrel you call him, and ask why he did not throw up his business, and denounce it in public and private? Ah! messieurs! do you think that such scrupulous men crowd life's highways, and that every other person you meet in the street is so very anxious about poking his nose into the morals of a business out of which he clears £1000 a year, and so very eager to find and hunt down and expose its faults? Pardieu! it seems to me that nine-tenths of my own acquaintances contentedly leave that to the law, and are only thankful if after a crash they find their own skins whole, and themselves on the right side of the county gaol's wide gates. Yet, remember, I have written down long ago that Muirhead is a villain.

The suspense with regard to Monica became unbearable, yet in his heart he knew that certainty would be worse. His visits to Hartshill grew sometimes frequent till they became a daily occurrence, then he would meet young Nicholson at the house three days running, Monica's patient politeness would give way a little, Miss Bertram's reception grew colder, and he would retire, resolved to stay away for a week. The week ended, he came back with a touch of hope in his mind, having explained away to his own satisfaction all previous repulses; his love flamed back and burnt higher than ever before as Monica, anxious lest she should have been rude to him on his last visit, met him with a little extra politeness, and the man's hopes rose to heaven. How many a poor devil lives and thrives on an occasional kind word like that, and is happy for a week because the young lady has offered him tea with a smile instead of with a merely indifferent gaze! Do not, I pray you, young ladies, believe the books which recommend you to discourage all lovers except the one whom you mean to marry. On the contrary, encourage them, talk to them, flirt with them, let the poor wretches be happy till the last possible moment. You might, even when the proposal comes, accept it for a short time, and afterwards explain to the man that for certain reasons you cannot marry him, but for his sake will remain single all your life. Believe me—though to be sure you may not like this part of the argument—he will have forgotten all about it long before your real engagement is announced.

Monica had no intention of stretching her kindness to Muirhead to this point, but the tradition of his protection of Gerald was strong in the minds of both women, and they treated Muirhead as well as they could. They even invited him to spend an afternoon with them occasionally.  Gerald brought such an invitation to the Newcastle office with him one Friday morning, and laughed a little at the quick flush and stammering words of gratitude with which Muirhead accepted it.  Reggie Nicholson heard it too, and a fury of jealousy sprang up in his mind.  She wanted Muirhead, she desired his company for a whole afternoon, she loved him, she was going to marry him.  And by "she" Reggie did not mean Miss Christina, although the invitation came nominally from her.  Mr. Nicholson resolved to give up his post in Muirhead's office, to seek work in a distant part of the country, or even to try tea-planting in Ceylon, and above all never to see or speak to Monica Franklin again.

The three men were soon deep in work, and only the turning of ledger-leaves, the scratching of pens or a murmur of conversation from Muirhead's room broke the silence of the big office.  Presently among some figures, referring to the transfer of shares, which Nicholson was checking and entering on the register of shareholders, were some which he did not understand, and he went into Muirhead's office to ask for an explanation.  Muirhead answered at random; perhaps he was really busy, or more probably he did not understand the transaction very clearly himself, but at last he said impatiently, "Ask Franklin to explain how the entry is to be made."

Gerald took the sheet of figures, glanced through it, put aside a letter which he was writing to study the paper more closely, finally asked abruptly, "Where did you get this?"

"Mr. Muirhead gave it to me this morning. The paper is marked, you see, 'entries for the North Staffordshire share-register.'"

"It came in a bundle of others from London this morning," said Muirhead, looking up.

Gerald picked up the big envelope in which the documents from headquarters had arrived that morning; it was marked "Private and Confidential" in large letters, and, young Nicholson's eyes being directed again for a moment on to the sheet which he had brought, Gerald held up the envelope with his fingers on the words for Muirhead to see. The elder man flushed angrily and Gerald turned back with an impassive stare to the sheet of figures, pretending to study them, but in reality considering what to do. The sheet was to his eyes so simple and straight-forward that he could only suppose that Nicholson had in fact come to know whether he was to enter it as it stood or not. That being so, attempts at disguise would be a blunder.

"These five sums," he said quietly, "make up five-hundred ten-pound shares which Mr. Luke Robinson has sold, and Miss Bertram has bought.  I will attend to the register entries. There is no hurry about them."

"Mr. Robinson has sold all his shares then?"

"Apparently."

"But as a director is he not obliged  .  .  ."

"Mr. Robinson's business has nothing to do with you," said Muirhead angrily; "and let me remind you, Mr. Nicholson, by the way, that everything which you hear in this office is private, not for outside discussion."

"I remember your telling me so," was the cool reply, and the young man went back to his work.

Franklin and Muirhead did not exchange another word for the rest of the morning; in the afternoon a little business talk passed and finally, shortly after six o'clock, they left the office together.

"I wanted a few words with you alone," said Gerald at last.  "I got a letter yesterday from Mr. Marshall offering me a clerkship at the headquarters of the Freehold."

Muirhead faced round on him with terror in his eyes: "And you?"

"I have accepted it of course.  I wrote to do so this morning."

"I think you ought to have consulted some one—myself—Robinson—some one here first."

Gerald laughed a cool irritating laugh which meant "Men do not consult their subordinates before taking steps like that."  Aloud he said: "I have told nobody but you and my aunt about the offer, and nobody but you that I have accepted it.  I believe"—the boy laughed again—"you are being invited to-morrow afternoon to consult about whether I shall accept or not."

"And suppose," said Muirhead angrily, "that I tell Miss Bertram that you have said 'yes' already and then advise her very strongly not to let you go?"

"I don't think you will do that," was the quiet response.

"I will.  Why shouldn't I?  There are a score of reasons against your going. . . ."

Gerald was silent.  When men used arguments to which they knew the answer, he believed in holding his tongue as the most impressive method of showing them that he knew the answer too.  And, like many other strong-minded strong-willed persons, he had a curious power of making a silence mean something—a power which fills your adversary with bewildered awe and is therefore worth cultivating.

"But I am not going to do that," added
Muirhead rather hastily, and a faint ironical
smile flitted across Gerald's face; "because—
because—well, to be candid with you, my lad, I
want something from you, something of very
great importance to myself.  It has nothing to
do with business.  I have walked out here with
you this evening to ask you about it.  I—well,
it is difficult to explain."

"If I can be of any help to you in any way
of course I shall be delighted," said Gerald,
repressing one of the very few inclinations to
giggle which he had ever felt.

"I—I love your sister," burst out Muirhead
at last, stopping in the road and looking nervously round him to be sure that no one was
near, and then glancing suspiciously at Gerald
to see if he was going to laugh.  "I have loved
her for years.  I have said nothing to her yet.
I am afraid.  Do you think—do you know—has
she ever spoken to you about me?"

"Very often, of course," said Gerald gravely,
"but not quite in the way you mean."

"Naturally she wouldn't," said the man
hastily; "of course not.' But your aunt; perhaps she has?"

"Oh, no."

"Well, well . . . there is another little
point . . . you yourself . . . of course

Miss Franklin would think much of your opinion. Will you support me?"

"Certainly, most certainly." Promises of this kind cost nothing, and Gerald would have made a score of them quite cheerfully.

"Do you think yourself that I have any chance of success?"

"Really," said the lad, happy to be able to laugh outright, "I know nothing at all. My sister and I talk so little together. I am always busy."

"Yes, you and Marshall have become very close friends lately. And now you are going. I am sorry, my lad."

"I shall be very sorry for many reasons to go," said Gerald, speaking sincerely for once. "I have been happy here and successful. And I owe much of my success to you. I do not forget that."

"I am glad you think of that still. And now one more question, Franklin. Tell me candidly; you will be open with me, won't you? since you recognise that I have done something for you. I ask you—you who are in Marshall's confidence so much more than myself"—the man's sudden humility was horrible to look at—"is anything going wrong with the Freehold? I have everything I possess in it. I have put several very great friends in it. I am not over-particular of course"—the man laughed uneasily—"but one draws the line at deceiving certain people. Pray tell me if you know anything wrong."

"What should be wrong?  Why should you think so?"

"Several little things, and then Robinson's sale of all his shares.  .  .  ."

"He is speculating, I suppose.  He sells now and hopes to get in again at a lower price. There is nothing in the world wrong, I assure you.  Pray don't suggest such a thing by word or look elsewhere.  It is quite a mistake, as we could easily show, but the directors would be very angry."

"Then I will turn back and say good-bye. Thank you for your promises of help.  Of course I will advise your aunt as you wish to-morrow.  Good-bye, lad."

To-morrow afternoon, thought Muirhead, as he walked homewards, he would end the suspense, put his question to Monica, and know the best or worst.  After all there was some hope for him.  He was apparently a trusted adviser at Hartshill, a family friend, and there was hope.  Even from Gerald's assurances he managed to draw encouragement.  To have an only brother, of whom a girl must surely be fond, strongly on your side, mattered much. His heart grew lighter and his step brisker every moment, till by the time he reached his rooms he was almost laughing to himself with delight. If he were accepted, if he returned here to-morrow evening engaged to Monica Franklin, would not life be blissful! He thought of numberless little points, the gold mine shares which were now daily increasing in value, the assured alliance with Gerald who was now in the inner cabinet of the biggest and richest speculation of modern times; but above every such minor gain, in front of the picture of wealth and success which floated before him, rose the vision of Monica's fair grave face. To see those grave grey eyes with love-light in them looking into his! to put his arms round the tall lithe form and whisper love-words into willing ears, and with lips close to his sweetheart's cheek! . . . A passion of love and longing tore the man's soul within him as he thought. The room stifled him, and he went out of doors and walked along country roads with clenched hands and exclamations of tortured doubt and hope, and even prayer. He must succeed to-morrow! he would succeed! For success here he would make all sacrifices, use all means. The far-off boom of St. George's clock striking midnight reached him as he walked. In twenty hours at most he would know his fate!

# CHAPTER XIII

Gerald Franklin was resolved to be rich. When he was twelve years old he had determined to make a fortune, and had begun at once. He studied politics, the money-markets of the world, the problems of taxation, and even the morality of certain trades and peoples. The latter subject interested him peculiarly, and he had argued out the conclusion (in rather remarkable fashion for a boy of his age) that financial credit is necessary for any big success, and that such credit is dependent on strict commercial and national honesty. He was pleased at first to find himself in such a business as the Freehold. Marshall's admiration and confidence flattered him, turned his head so far and for as long a time as such an extremely well-screwed-on young head could be turned. Then came discovery after discovery, and with it disillusion and disgust. The boy had all the commercial instincts developed through generations of trading ancestors, and as the nose of a Perigord pig has an instinct for finding truffles which no amount of modern science can give to a man, so Gerald began life with an hereditary capacity for picking essential facts out of a maze of figures which marked him out for work of his present kind. Lessons given partly by Muirhead, chiefly by himself to himself, had perfected nature's work, and the lad at the age of sixteen had dropped into the middle of Marshall's work with an amount of knowledge which a chartered accountant in the thick of City work might envy, and a judgment whose sound acumen many a hundred members of that profession might desire. He took in the whole business of the Freehold in a year, brushed aside its pretence of philanthropy, glanced down its (intentionally) confused and confusing mass of figures with a contemptuous smile, and so recognising perfectly well where he was and able to make a pretty good guess at what his masters were coming to and when they would arrive, he sat down to consider his position.

The more he considered it the less he liked it. The subordinates in the Company, schoolmasters, clergy of all denominations, insurance-agents, commercial travellers and such-like, who were all paid a commission on the capital which they brought in, were a noisy horde of plunderers, unscrupulous, ignorant and risky to deal with. Their immediate superiors, the men who reduced this mass of work to order, were half-educated men performing a purely mechanical task, understanding very little of that, and doing it for the most part very badly. Of the four or five men at the head of affairs Gerald only knew one, but from certain signs he judged that they were not working together very harmoniously or cleverly. Contrary orders came down to Newcastle very often; papers marked "private and confidential" arrived one day from the Freehold, and their duplicates came by the next post from some allied company without any such mark.' At any rate disaster was a mere matter of a few months.

So thought Gerald, vexedly and doubtingly, as he sat considering Marshall's offer of the London clerkship. Yet he decided to accept it. A foothold in London was worth something. He would go there reckoning that the Company would last a year, that he must plunder it of all that he could safely get during that time and have another situation ready for himself to step into when the crash came. There were probably some very pretty pickings to be had at those offices in Southampton Row during the next twelve months. As for Muirhead, he must take his luck. To warn

one's friends under such circumstances was the
act of a fool.   Clearly Muirhead had better not
marry Monica, but the boy had paid just
enough attention to his sister's talk to have his
own opinion about the probability of such an
event.  It was necessary to encourage and sympathise with Muirhead in order that this family
council about himself might pass off smoothly,
but he believed and hoped that Monica had no
more intention of marrying Muirhead than of
marrying Canon Hobart.

To his own secret amusement Gerald found
that the family council on this Saturday afternoon was a very serious affair.   Mr Lowe and
Dr. Hare had been invited as well as Muirhead.   Miss Christina had put on her best
black silk dress; fresh piclates and a cake had
been ordered for tea.   "Are there any pro-
grammes?" he asked Monica.   "Shall I have
to make a speech? and, I say, old girl, tell me
—if the council decides against my going to
London—how am I to break it to them that I
am going in any case?"   But Monica ran away
to dress.

Dr. Hare arrived at four o'clock, bluff and
kindly as usual.   He was a disbeliever in the
Freehold, and scoffed at it publicly and
privately though he had no better reason for
doing so than a strong personal dislike of Luke

Robinson.  "He is a good preacher, I daresay," said the doctor, "though, from what people tell me, a mere gas-pipe with nothing real to say.  And if you have nothing to say what is the good of saying it well?"

"But in any case what has that got to do with this Company?" asked Lowe.

"Well, if I want an investment for my money I ask a man who deals in money, not a man who spouts bad—or even good—theology. If I wanted some gas-shares now I might think of going to Robinson about them  .  .  . !"

"You don't like his politics, doctor?" said Lowe, while Muirhead looked at the speaker with some alarm.

"Give you my word I don't know what they are," said Hare.  "Well, yes, I do just know. He possesses—or professes—Liberal opinions, I believe."

"He is very active on the Liberal side," said Lowe.

"He is," retorted Hare.  "Now you come to mention it I remember a story about one of his evening meetings in the Hanley Road chapel at the last election.  He was praying and said: 'May the Liberal party all hang together at this great crisis.'  'Amen,' said a voice in the hall very emphatically.  'Not, oh Lord,' went on Robinson, 'in the sense meant by the blasphemous scoffer down there, but in peace and concord and accord.' 'I don't much mind,' said the voice again, 'what kind of a cord it's in so long as it's all together.' After which the prayer passed rather quickly to other subjects!''

''His influence is immense,'' insisted Lowe, with a little sigh, almost of envy; ''and I really believe he means to use it well.''

''Oh, every one swears by him and sings his praises,'' said Hare, ''because he swears by himself and sings his own praises. Old Mother Eardly began the other day, while I was prescribing for her daughter, glorifying him up to the skies. 'I speak so strongly,' she said at last, 'because I know him so well.' I said: 'Madam, I don't know him, but damn him at a venture.' Forgive me, my dear Miss Bertram. Only a quotation from Lamb, you know; I wouldn't dream of using such words myself!''

''I have a little matter of business which I wanted to ask you about,'' said Miss Christina rather severely; and at this opening of the proceedings every one took their seats and listened attentively to the speaker, for whom indeed every one present had a most real affection and respect. ''My nephew, Gerald, has received an offer from Mr. Marshall to come up to the headquarters of the Freehold

Building Society as clerk with £400 a year. He would begin work next month. I want advice about the offer. Mr. Muirhead, who knows Mr. Marshall very well, has a very high opinion of him" (it was curious to see how the poor woman tried at the same time to do justice to Marshall, and yet to dissociate herself from him; while over his name each time that it occurred she hesitated for a moment as if not quite certain how far its pronouncement might involve herself in telling a lie); "but of course to send Gerald alone up to London is a very serious step."

"It is a good position," said Lowe thoughtfully, after a pause; "very good. Four hundred pounds a year! And Gerald only just eighteen!"

"What does the lad himself think about it?" asked Hare.

"I should like to accept it," said Gerald simply. The boy's power of playing the hypocrite was really remarkable. Even Monica thought for a moment that he was a little anxious about the result of the conference, and would recognise its decision as binding.

Miss Bertram looked at Dr. Hare, her glance seeming to say, "I suppose there is an explosion coming. You may blow up now if you like." But to her surprise the doctor sat silent and grave. When at last he spoke it was very quietly.

"I do not like the Company," he said. "I disbelieve in its philanthropy. 'Charity,' said St. Paul, who did not live in the days of newspapers, 'is not puffed up'; and I prefer charities on the Pauline lines. Partly for that reason, and partly because I dislike all its managers, of course except Mr. Muirhead" — the doctor glanced across at Muirhead, and his eyes changed the "except" into "especially"—"I disbelieve in its financial soundness, too. But I recognise with regret—I admit it openly, with regret—that I have no facts or figures to back my opinion. It is therefore worth nothing."

"Whatever you may think it worth I value it very highly," said Miss Bertram, pleased to find a man of the world's opinion at one with her own feminine instinct. "What do you think, Mr. Lowe?"

"Gerald is young, very young indeed, to go up to London by himself, though of course we could minimise the danger by introducing him to friends and finding him a good home. Apart from those dangers—and we must remember that Gerald is not the first who has gone up from a country life to encounter them, nor is he as young as some others who go—apart from these, I cannot imagine a more desirable opening. I cannot see any reason for refusing such an offer, and we really must have solid reasons for doing such a thing."

"And you, Mr. Muirhead?" As Miss Bertram turned to his friend Gerald suddenly thought what an extremely awkward thing it would have been, at any rate for the moment, if he had not succeeded in "squaring" Muirhead yesterday; and the latter had now proceeded to tell about that letter to London accepting the clerkship.

"I can only express my entire agreement with Mr. Lowe," was the answer. "Dr. Hare admits that his distrust of the Company is a mere personal dislike of its managers. I know, and can say positively as regards its financial position, that he has no grounds for his mistrust. I shall be very sorry to part with Gerald, but I certainly think that he should go."

"I confess to sharing some of Dr. Hare's prejudices," said Miss Bertram; "yet I do not think they ought to stand in Gerald's way."

There was a moment's silence, then a little desultory talk about friends in London, and then Miss Bertram gave her decision: "I think I ought to let him go. Yes, we must accept."

There was another and much longer silence.

The room seemed heavy with fatality; the decision was weighing on the minds of all as something of peculiar and uncomprehended importance.　No one seemed willing to speak, till at last Miss Bertram told Monica to order tea.

"Very sorry I can't stay a bit longer, Miss Bertram," said Dr. Hare, jumping up with a deep breath as of relief from some oppression; "but I must be off to a case.　Your piclates—I feel sure you are going to have piclates—would tempt a man to risk his own life, but one can't risk one's neighbours!　Good-bye.　And good-bye and good luck to you, Gerald.　I start on my holiday on Monday, so I shan't see you again before you begin your London work.　Good luck to you—fame and fortune, health, wealth and wisdom!　Good-bye.　We shall meet again sometime.　I wonder when and where?"

When and where!　If those pictures of the future which now and again we conjure so gaily to come before us obeyed us occasionally and came, what a horrible tragedy they would make of these light-hearted moments!

# CHAPTER XIV

Mr. Lowe went away immediately after tea, and with sudden terror Muirhead realised that fate was giving him the opportunity for which yesterday he had professed to be anxious. He was only anxious now to escape, but he knew that he would despise himself to-night if he failed in his resolution; and besides, his passage through this fearful ordeal was now but a matter of a few weeks. After Gerald's departure his excuses for visiting Hartshill would be rare. And now he was alone with Monica in the garden; they were moving towards a summer-house which they could easily enter, and so be out of sight. Muirhead felt first that he would be insane not to make use of such a chance; secondly, that he would give a year's income to see some one appear and interrupt him. But no one appeared, and already he and Monica had turned the corner of some lilac-bushes and were out of sight of the house.

"Gerald's departure will be a great loss to me," he began, and then thought vaguely that he had said that once, twice, three times before during the afternoon. But his head was throbbing violently; he felt as if his brain were turning round and round; he could not think or see, and could hardly speak coherently.

"It will be a loss for him to leave you," said the girl, forcing herself to be cordial, yet meaning what she said too. She quite believed that Muirhead had been her brother's benefactor and best friend. Then the man's agitation made itself perceptible to her by some means, and a nameless indefinable alarm crept into her mind.

"You really think that this appointment of Gerald's is a good thing for him?" she asked, her anxiety at once fixing itself on the topic of the afternoon.

"Oh, yes, yes, certainly. His absence will leave you dull."

"It will not make much difference. Gerald has been so absorbed in his work lately that he has not shared our occupations much."

He had planned the conversation out yesterday evening quite satisfactorily—what he was to say, and what she was to answer; but her answers were all wrong, and what could he do? He had a half-formed irritable desire to reproach her for this, and to ask her how the matter could get any further if she would not give the right cues.

"I thought you would have missed him more," he began, and as he had no idea how bitterly reproachful his voice sounded, he was puzzled by the girl's little laugh and stare of surprise. But seeing them he pulled himself together and went on with more resolution. "However, it was something else I wanted to say to you. His going away makes me fear that I shall not be able to come here so often. My visits lately, for a year or more past"—why did his miserable voice desert him in this hour of need and become loud, husky and monotonous?—"have not been to . . . altogether on his account."

"Haven't they?" she asked in low, frightened tones; but he had meant her to ask that question just here, and did not notice the fear in her voice, and was glad.

"No, indeed, it was you I wanted to see. I do not know how long it is since I have been thinking of you all day, scheming to try and see you, hoping that you cared a little bit to see me. Monica, I love you! I love you!" . . .

He had prepared a much longer speech than that, about sympathy, his own ambitions and prospects, about her aunt and a score of other matters, but it all ended in that cry: "I love you!" To see the girl standing there with her eyes cast down, her long eyelashes lying on the cheeks from which pink glows were coming and going, her lips quivering, and hands clasping and unclasping in front of her, made him mad with sudden hope. He held his breath after those last words, and as the girl kept silence, he at last put out his hand and tried to take hers. But she drew it away immediately and decisively, and his breath came out in a quick "Monica!" wherein was questioning anxiety. She spoke at last in answer to it.

"It is very—kind of you to like me so much. I did not know. . . ."

"Did not know! Oh! I should not have thought you could help knowing!"

"Indeed I did not know, or I would have tried to show you—I would have told you somehow that it was no use."

"No use!"

"I am very sorry."

"I love you, Monica! I could make you happy if you would marry me. You must . . . you surely will. . . ." The man began to stammer and talk wildly.

"I could not marry you, Mr. Muirhead."

"You don't mean that," he said almost roughly. "You have not had time to think. I implore you to think a little. You will see. . . ."

"It would be no good to think. Indeed I could not marry you."

Muirhead stood silent. The beginning of a great despair was dawning in his eyes, which were fixed on the girl with a look which frightened her and made her move away. The movement more than her words seemed to rouse the man to a sense of his repulse. He flung up his hands in a gesture of half-insane misery and turned away.

"I am very sorry," murmured Monica again. Like most girls in her position, she could not let bad alone without some attempt to make it worse.

"Sorry!" The man turned back to her, and she looked with terror at his passion-distorted face. "Why do you say you are sorry? Does it mean . . . . do you mean that you will let me hope a little?"

"Oh, no."

"There is no hope for me?"

"I could not marry you," repeated the girl, half-wishing that she could find some other words which might sound less blankly repelling. After all she could not feel particularly annoyed with the man for being in love with her. Why should she?

"It is absurd to say you could not. Of course you could," answered Muirhead, coming nearer, and his eyes flashed with excitement and anger. "What is the obstacle? There must be some, I know."

Becoming nervous Monica turned and began to walk homewards, but the man put himself in her way. There was a strained smile, horrible to look at, on his face.

"You like some one else better. Who is it?" he asked, and at the question and his interference with her movements the girl grew first more frightened and then angry.

"Let me go home, please," she said, a little flush of angry red coming into her cheeks. "It is"—she stammered over the word, but was evidently trying to deprecate a quarrel—"kind of you to want to marry me, but I have answered no. That must end it, please."

"End it!" he answered, with a tone and gesture of despair which were rather fine in their abandonment of tragedy. "You tell me to 'end' my life coolly indeed. I have won position, money, respect, here, and thought I should be contented, and they are all nothing to me. All my life is nothing to me. . . . Oh, Monica! Monica, dear! they are nothing if I may not have your love too! Give me a little bit of hope!"

She shook her head, shrinking away from him in alarm, and again her movement seemed to fill the man with a fury of despair.

"It is Nicholson!" he cried out suddenly—he had resolved a hundred times yesterday that in no case would he mention his rival's name, but a passion to know the worst was on him—"it is that young Nicholson who has killed my life, who has taken you away. Isn't it so? Oh! but he shall not do it! I came first! You were mine first!"

At the mention of her lover's name Monica grew angrily scarlet, and the pity and fear alike left her eyes.

"We have talked enough about this," she said. "I cannot imagine what . . . . what Mr. Nicholson has got to do with it. Let me pass, please." And as the man, after a second's hesitation, let her go by, she walked up the path with head erect and flaming cheeks. Turning a corner of the path she looked back through a rose-bush which concealed her, and saw Muirhead still standing there, his arms hanging by his side, his face turned towards her, his shoulders bent.

# CHAPTER XV

To hate anybody night and day with all your
heart and soul, to hate him so that the one
desire of your life is to hurt him mind and
body, present and future, pocket, brain, and
flesh, to hate him so that you would be sorry
to hear of his death because it would put an
end to your plans for his torture—this is a
vigorous but unhealthy exercise. It brings
into play all your wits (and sometimes
muscles), but it takes away your appetite, is
bad for your digestion, and is too absorbing a
pastime for a man who is otherwise and busily
occupied. To hate anybody like this is, in
fact, apart from the morality of the thing, a
blunder.

Poor Sampson Muirhead, however, did not
realise this, or perhaps he did not argue about
the matter at all, or perhaps he thought (which
is a great mistake) that love and hate are
beyond one's control; for he consecrated the
next few weeks to a passion of loathing for
Reggie Nicholson which annihilated every
other feeling and faculty in him. A rival and

a successful rival!—the knowledge that Nicholson was in love with Monica and she with him, that they were together constantly and perfectly happy together, and probably only happy when they were together, had lain in a little cell of his brain unrealised, kept back, for weeks past. Now it flamed into life, stared him in the face like a hideous garish picture thrust suddenly before his eyes, and he could think of nothing else. Again and again after his own rejection he saw them together, and each time wondered how he could have been so blind before as not to see that the two were lovers, and happy lovers, united in thoughts, hope, sympathy, love . . . in love! At the recollection he would fling down pens and papers if he were at work, food if he were at meals, books if he were trying to occupy his mind with them, and start up from his chair sick with fury. Presently—it was but three weeks after his own proposal, but to this man living in hell it might have been three hundred years—he heard from Gerald that the two were engaged.

"Awfully sorry she wouldn't have you," said the boy, watching Muirhead with a slightly amused smile; love was not one of humanity's passions of which Mr. Gerald Franklin took much account; "but it's just a matter of a whim with these girls, you know. They never have any sense."

"Miss Bertram has consented?" The man standing at the window could just control his lips sufficiently to ask the question.

"Oh, yes. Old Nicholson came over and saw her, and they have arranged the business quite happily. He is to take his son into his business at once, and into partnership next year. So you will have another vacancy here to fill. I daresay you have forgotten your own admiration for her by this time, so you must come over and congratulate her. Oh, here is the happy youth. Come in, Nicholson, I was just telling Muirhead about you and my sister. He wants to congratulate you."

Work being a little slack, Gerald was not busy and wanted some amusement. From stories which he had heard and by accident read now and again, he understood that a certain amount of such amusement might be extracted from a conversation between a successful and an unsuccessful lover about the young lady who was the object of their joint affections. That the young lady in the present case happened to be his own sister did not occur to him as a reason for foregoing the amusement.

But he was not destined to extract much

from the present situation.   There comes a
point of suffering when an all-merciful nature
says to us: "You cannot bear this any longer;
come away with me; let me take your mind
out of that torture-environment for a while to
a far-off world of sun-lit skies and babbling
water and rest.   .   .   ."   And so another turn
is given to the rack, another twist to the
thumb-screw; muscles writhe, nerves vibrate
with agony before the torturers' smiling faces;
but the writhings and outcries mean nothing,
for the man's mind is elsewhere and perfectly
happy.   It was so now with Muirhead.   Suddenly and for a little while something in his
brain gave a great throb and tear, and then
hung limp and sensationless like a certain kind
of wire which you pull to a strong straining
point at which it suddenly becomes as slack
and tearable as a long thread of glue.   He
glanced round the room with a slight smile,
nodded to Nicholson, murmured something
about going into Stoke for an hour, and so left
the office.

Once outside he walked on and on, he knew
not where or for how long.   Sometimes he sat
down under a tree and picked bits of grass and
bound them together and held up the plait in
front of him with soft pleased laughter.   Once
he noticed two or three passers-by staring at

him, and, considering the cause, found that he
was singing a psalm—the "De Profundis"—
which he had not heard, he supposed, for fifteen years.   Once he heard a station-bell ring,
and stopping to wonder where he was, found
himself at Great Bridgeford, nearing Stafford,
and so mechanically turned back.   Then he
found himself sitting in a church in which
some one was reading prayers, and a few
people began to sing a hymn.   It was not till
then that he really awoke to reality—awoke
with a vague stare round him, and a muttered
exclamation or two, like a man returning to
life after chloroform.   The whole scene was
quite strange to him—church, people, and
clergyman.   He did not know where he was,
or how long he had been there; in his hand he
held a few wild flowers, but had no idea when
or where he had picked them.   He had left
the Freehold offices this morning after reading
certain letters and hearing some news of something; since then the hours were a dreadful
blank, a nothing, a hideous vacuum of which
memory could not fill one single moment.
The thought frightened him horribly; nothing
in his life had ever filled him with so much
fear as this sudden stoppage of memory and
brain-action.   He looked at his watch; it was
past seven o'clock, and he must have left the

office this morning at ten or soon after. Nine hours in a world of which he knew nothing beforehand and could remember nothing now! . . . A short fainting-fit frightens many of us; a sleeping-draught which will plunge us into unconsciousness for several hours is a terror to many people; the chief dread of death lies in our ignorance of what the grim passage is like and whither it leads. What had he done to his brain that it should play him a trick like that? Would it play him another at any time, in any place that it chose? The man's face grew ashen grey, a cold sweat was on it, his eyes were mad with fear as he thought of such a probability. He remembered. now the news of the morning which had given him the shock—the news of Monica's engagement—and it mattered absolutely nothing to him; beside the dread of another such brain-lapse all mortal pain and disappointment seemed mere child-grief. Abruptly, heedless of the fact that it was in the middle of a prayer, and that the congregation looked up at him with scandalised glances, he got up and walked out of church. He glanced anxiously round the church-yard and the road outside, half-doubting whether even this might not be a part of some night-mare. But with a great sigh of relief he recog-nised a stream which ran past there and saw where he was.   Then suddenly he realised that he was fatigued, footsore and hungry to the last limit of endurance; he must have spent nearly all those hours in walking.   There was a good inn in the village, and going there he ordered food and went into the garden while it was being prepared.   Coming back into the dining-room when he had been told that dinner was ready he saw sitting at a table in the corner  .  .  .  Reggie Nicholson and his father.

Nicholson and his father . . . was it these two men really or . . . A ghastly dread which seized him made him move a few steps towards his own table gazing steadily before him the while.   Then he looked furtively round again to see if they were still there.   Even then he dare not be quite sure that they were flesh and blood, but walked up to them in a hesitating manner and spoke to the elder man with a timidity which the latter put down to a very different cause.

"Better join tables," said Mr. Nicholson at last, and Muirhead unwillingly ordered his dinner to be brought across the room.

"I've just seen your friend, Robinson," said Nicholson.   "So he's sold all his shares in the Freehold, eh?   What's that for?"

"He's speculating, I suppose," said Muirhead, utterly unable to think whether he ought or ought not to be talking about the matter.

"Well, that looks to me a very queer transaction; fishy, d—d fishy, I call it. Anything going wrong? My boy says . . . Oh, Lord! he's treading on my toes under the table. What have I said, Reggie? We're all friends here, aren't we?" Nicholson had finished his bottle of claret with very slight aid from his son and was well on his way through one of the bottles of port for which the inn was famous. "I was only going to say that you didn't like the look of that deal of Robinson's any more than I do. Canon Hobart has a queer story too of Marshall knowing this neighbourhood a d—d sight better than he should do; and here's Robinson selling his shares. It's . . . well, it's" — Nicholson shook his head solemnly, trying to think of a new word, but failing, and his mind drifting for certain reasons to the thought of fresh water, he repeated—"fishy, d—d fishy."

Food and wine were bringing back sense to Muirhead's brain; he took in at last what Nicholson was saying, and then looking at Reggie saw that he was scarlet and playing nervously with some biscuits. Directly his father ceased speaking he began a long explanation of what had brought them there to dinner, but Muirhead did not listen.  So the boy was betraying them!  How much did he know?  With the new life which was throbbing back into Muirhead's nerves came the smart of the old pain.  Monica had gone; this youngster had taken her.  There was no hope now, for an engagement had been announced.  The pain grew, but its sharp stabs were a tonic and Muirhead's thoughts became perfectly coherent.  Reggie would be a relation of Miss Bertram's now.  If he warned her and made her sell her Freehold shares?  If he warned a score of others and it was said at headquarters that his proceedings were Muirhead's fault .  .  .  And what more likely than that he should do so, now that his connection with the Company would soon be at an end?  And what was Canon Hobart's story?  Doubtless some more work of young Nicholson's.  No further word spoke Muirhead that evening except to mutter good-bye as the father and son rose from the table; but he sat there and thought and schemed, and glanced round the room at intervals with a hunted hopeless look, and then thought and schemed again.

# CHAPTER XVI

The Dresden Road Wesleyan Chapel was unusually crowded one Thursday evening in June, the congregation having been attracted by the announcement of a discourse from a favourite and famous local preacher. The yellow glass windows which looked painfully ugly at midday now glowed rather pleasingly in the half-light of a summer sunset. The walls, bare but tiled in one part and soberly painted in another, made the chapel cool and restful to the eyes. Humanity being so much more interesting than architecture the absence of any decorative attraction was rather an advantage than otherwise to a person who wanted to study the audience and their emotions.

The prayer being over Mr. Luke Robinson mounted the pulpit and with his hands folded in front of him and his eyes flashing backwards and forwards among his auditors, stood waiting till the coughing, rustling and settling down of the congregation, was finished. A few persons in the chapel who had not seen

him before peered through the falling light to
try and inspect more closely this man whose
influence in that part of North Staffordshire
was a religious and political power which no
one could disregard.

They saw a man of middle height, square-
shouldered, square-headed, in fact with a
general appearance of (literal) squareness
everywhere. His hands were square (also red
with terribly bitten nails, but of course one
only noticed that on closer inspection), his chin
and forehead were massive and square. His
mouth was that of a man who only spoke to
give orders, and who could enforce obedience
to them by shutting it and looking on. His
eyes were steady grey eyes, a little near
together and rather aggressive under their
dark eyebrows, but always looking straight and
unflinchingly at their object of vision. A fine
face and figure altogether, and one in which
few men found anything wrong. Yet a certain
travelling phrenologist, a total stranger to the
district, once made a curious remark about the
great Wesleyan leader. He gave a lecture in
Stoke and invited some of the audience on to
the platform to have their "bumps" read.
Two or three giggling young men went up one
by one after much persuasion, but the procession was slow and brief; and to encourage

others Luke Robinson, always ready with such good-natured acts, went up and submitted himself to the phrenologist. The man felt him over and made some commonplace but rather apt jokes: "This is what I should call more a wholesale than a retail head"; "our friend here gives orders at twelve o'clock and expects to have them executed by half-past," etc., but his voice grew a little odd at last and the jokes died away. "Say, Jimmy," said a friend afterwards, "that parson chap seemed to puzzle you a bit." "He didn't puzzle me," retorted the phrenologist, "but I was just wondering what he would say if I told him the truth—that his head was the cruellest and selfishest head I ever set hands on!"

"I am going to speak to you this evening about the responsibilities of worldly wealth. . . ." Mr. Robinson could not speak many words without showing you one secret of his influence. His voice was exquisite, strong, clear, perfectly controlled, so that one would have been charmed to sit and listen to the speaker reciting the multiplication-table. Half unconscious of the reason, many of his audience sat back in their seats with a satisfied sigh, ready to take for gospel anything told them by a preacher who had such notes in his voice as this man had.

Besides, the subject was interesting, and Robinson spoke in a strongly authoritative manner. He denounced speculation, especially the turf, and his hearers nodded their heads in approval. "Anything in fact," he went on, "which caused a man to give an undue amount of time and thought to mere increase of money was wrong, but, on the other hand," he said, "anything which increased a man's money without expenditure of time and thought was equally wrong. It was not easy to steer between the two courses, but there were certain rules which, if a man would adopt them, would simplify the difficulties. Money, for instance, could be put into investments which gave no anxiety or thought whatever to their holders, into Government securities, well-established banks or railways and so on. This was good, because it left the holder perfectly free to think of spiritual things, of charity and justice and the duties of his religion. But as such investments only produced a very small interest it was questionable whether a man who put his money into them could really be said to be doing the best for himself and his neighbours. Money again could be invested in the extension and improvement of a man's own existing business, and this was good too, because it employed an increased number of men of whose honesty and welfare the master could directly and constantly assure himself; but such a form of investment was not always possible. Most men had to invest their savings in some business in the management of which they could not have any direct control, and if one wanted more than the very small interest paid by Government securities—and such a desire was perfectly legitimate—one was confronted with innumerable risks and temptations. He, the preacher, thought that that man would not only be occupying a higher moral standpoint, but would actually be more secure from loss who said to himself, 'Is this business in which I want to invest not only a sound money-making concern but of some moral advantage to those with whom it trades? Shall I by investing money in it be helping my neighbours towards justice, morality, righteousness, as well as doing good to myself?' There were such institutions. For instance . . .''

Gerald Franklin, sitting in the body of the chapel amidst the rapt audience, leant forward a little watching the preacher closely. He had listened to this preamble—spread out of course over a much greater length than the above summary, and delivered with frequent interspersion of biblical texts and scraps of worldly philosophy, as well as with much earnestness and eloquence—critically and admiringly, noting with acute approval each well-argued clearly-put premise from which the ultimate conclusion was to be drawn.  He admired the preacher immensely.  Yet—I like when it is possible to put forward a good point or two in my young friend's character; he cannot, I must allow, afford to have the smallest of them passed over—in the lad's heart was a scorn and contempt for Mr. Luke Robinson which not even his far-calculating resolution could always hide.  He despised this man with his greed, humbug, fraud and lies, with a passion of contempt which was almost hatred.  In public, everywhere, even among his most intimate friends, he was obliged to speak in terms of the greatest respect and veneration for Mr. Robinson's opinion, and it was the highest testimony to Gerald's powers of self-control that he was able to do so.  In private he talked and wrote to the preacher with an open scorn and derision under which Mr. Robinson winced and squirmed again; and no higher testimony could be given to Gerald's influence in the Freehold than Robinson's toleration of this insolence.  In his own review of his position in the Society there was nothing which irritated Gerald more than the semi-consciousness that, so far as humbug and hypocrisy were concerned, Robinson and himself would be regarded by the world as in very much the same boat.

The preacher was now well on his way through a strong and emphatic laudation of the Freehold Building Society, its works, managers, finance and prospects. In many places his words would have sounded extravagant and absurd; but Robinson knew his audience, and knew that hints and suggestions would be quite lost on them. The panegyric was straightforward, forcible and consistent. At frequent intervals he recurred to the philanthropic work of the Society, in order to show that his praise of it was not out of place in a religious building, and repeated more than once that the main object of his sermon was to help those who had a proper horror of speculation and yet wanted to do the most possible good with their money. "It is his masterpiece, this sermon," said Gerald to himself, as the peroration came to an end amidst silence, in which every man could hear his neighbour breathe; "the fellow has never done better. I don't wonder he wanted Muirhead to come and hear it. What a glowing report poor old Muirhead would have sent of it to headquarters! Indeed I must take one there myself. The very least one can say about the hypocrite, is that he is worth all the money we pay him. I will go round and see him now."

Mr. Robinson was inclined to regard it as an ill-requital for his labours of the evening, when Mr. Gerald Franklin stepped softly into his room and with an engaging smile congratulated him on his sermon.

"At this moment," said the boy, "when, as you know, things are beginning to look a little queer, we were really in want of a brilliant effort like that. Now I should say that sermon was good for five or six thousand pounds. Quite a little haul of plunder, eh?"

"You will give a proper report of it to Marshall?" asked Robinson, sulky yet anxious.

"Oh, yes; yes, certainly. You shall have all the payment for it which it is our affair to give. And I shouldn't wonder if some of your audience to-night made up the balance one day. You'll have a lively time of it if they do!"

"I do my best for them," said Robinson shamefacedly and hesitatingly. "How can they blame me if something beyond my control goes wrong afterwards?"

"Is anybody listening to us?" asked Gerald in affected alarm.

"Not that I know of."

"Are you keeping up that d—d cant for my benefit? How very funny! However, I hadn't come here to hear a second edition of to-night's sermon. To be honest I find one about as much as I can stomach in a week. There is something I want to speak about before I go up to London. Those shares of yours—did Marshall give you leave to sell them?"

"Are the shares Marshall's or mine?" asked the other with surly bravado.

"Marshall's for all practical purposes. You and Benson have played a trick on us, and we don't choose such tricks to be played."

"Who advised Miss Bertram to buy the shares?" sneered Robinson. "Who talks about plunder after that?"

"Who invited you to share the plunder?" was the cool reply. "Keep clear of our business except when you are told to come forward. Now I am going to speak to Marshall about this affair, and I should think it very likely that he would insist upon the shares being bought back."

"Yes? Insist?" . . . The man's eyes flashed furiously.

"I should think it likely," repeated Mr. Franklin. "We don't choose to have agents without any interest in the undertaking."

"And if I refuse? If I turn round altogether, say I have discovered the truth, and denounce the whole affair here and in a score of chapels all over the Potteries?"

" 'If!' "  . . .  said the boy quietly but derisively. "And 'if' we produce a hundred letters of yours thanking us for money, promising to persuade this, that, and the other person to buy shares, and acknowledging commissions received from us on such new shareholders! Fire away!  Begin your sermons to-morrow! I doubt if you will bring in much more money after to-night.  To-night has about exhausted all that you can do, and for many reasons we should be glad to be rid of you.  I myself for one detest this religious part of the business. I am told that Lord Eastney does too.  So fire away!"

"We could do one another a great deal of mischief, I daresay," said Robinson with an uneasy attempt to pass off the quarrel and resume a lighter tone, "so we need not argue about it.  Neither of us has any intention of beginning.  We both know too much about the other.  Now there is a little matter connected with the Arkhill property.  . . ."

"We will settle about these shares, please. Do I understand I am to tell Marshall that you refuse to buy any more?"

"It is about that very point I am going to speak.  I have seven acres of land at the

corner of the Dently Road and the turn down
to the Hall—a most valuable little lot. Now if
the Freehold would buy that—it rounds off the
Arkhill estate perfectly; Sir Richard Cullamore said so more than once—we might
arrange it. I would take payment in shares,
even with a promise to keep some of them.
Then of course there would be no more talk of
denunciations. If they would give me—say—"
the man, who had been speaking quietly, and
with his eyes half-closed, suddenly changed the
tone of his voice, and looked straight at Gerald,
menacing him—"say five hundred ten-pound
shares for the seven acres, that would satisfy
me."

"You would like five thousand pounds for a
bit of land worth perhaps two hundred, Mr.
Robinson?"—Gerald Franklin was one of those
born rulers of men who, instinctively, and
without stopping to reason, meet threats with
defiances—"I think I will take it on myself to
decline your offer on behalf of the Freehold.
I will speak to Marshall about it, certainly, and
report this conversation to him, but . . ."

"Oh, it was a mere suggestion, Mr. Franklin. Don't make too much of it. Wait a
moment"—Gerald was moving towards the
door—"Pray, Mr. Franklin, do not make mischief between me and Marshall."

"Oh, certainly not," said the boy, drily, "but you see I am just an agent of Mr. Marshall's here, and I must keep him in touch with the Society's business,—with the revolts of its minor agents, and so on."

"But that is nonsense.  Does my sermon to-night, for instance, mean that I am in revolt, as you call it?"

"The sermon in question," was the reply, "is not so very straightforward that I can tell at a glance what it means.  Good-night, Mr. Robinson."

Left alone Luke Robinson sat down, and, I regret to say, swore softly to himself for several minutes.  For about the hundredth time in his life he had met Gerald in open conflict and been badly beaten.  This scheme of his for selling the little plot of ground near Dently to the Freehold for £5000—just fifty times its value—was a pet one which had been maturing for some months, and this evening's sermon was a part of it.  He had meant and invited Muirhead to come and hear the sermon and send a glowing account of it to Marshall, who would thus be in a favourable mood to listen to his plan.  Even when Gerald had appeared instead of Muirhead he had not despaired.  The scheme, in fact, might as well be laid by himself before the boy, whose advice about it

would certainly be asked by Marshall. Then
had come the quarrel, threats, an ill-timed
introduction of the proposal, more threats, and
somehow Gerald had come out of the contest,
as he usually did, victorious. Robinson cursed
him quietly but distinctly for the space of half
a minute more, and then went on thinking. Of
course what the boy said was true, he was in
the Society's power. He could damage them
a little—perhaps: they could annihilate him for
certain in reply. And Gerald had said that his
influence was not wanted much longer: that
to-night's sermon had finished his work. Was
that so really? . . . It chimed in somewhat painfully with certain suspicions of his
own. He had been a fool, ten times a fool, to
preach as he had preached to-night, without
driving his bargain beforehand! There was
little left to hope for if Marshall and Franklin
thought him used up. Gratitude was not a
very conspicuous virtue in gentry of that
description, and fear was apparently an equally
inconspicuous vice. He had already made, it
is true, a moderate fortune out of the Freehold, but moderation is a word of unknown
meaning to men of his breed. Their love of
money becomes gradually absorbed into a passion for money-getting, which is not only the
most unhappy disease upon earth, but nearly

always brings its victims into difficulties, and thence occasionally into gaol, for the simple reason that *there is a limit to the amount of money which you can get honestly.* This latter fact—a discovery of my own and one of the highest importance in political economy—alone prevents certain men absorbing all the available cash of a county or town, or even country into their own pockets, and has been a serious annoyance to many a money-getting machine besides Mr. Luke Robinson.

As he left the chapel he encountered one after another of the auditors of his sermon, and was obliged to listen to their congratulation, approval, and arguments. As he walked up the hill past the Nurses' Home, Canon Hobart overtook him, and the two men nodded to one another. Then the Rector, irritably conscious of certain accusations of intolerance which he had been hearing and which had been gathering volume, to say truth not without cause, during the past eighteen months, joined the Wesleyan minister and they walked on together.

"You have been preaching at the Hanley Road chapel this evening?" said Hobart politely.

"Yes." On any other occasion Robinson would have felt rather gratified at the fame of his sermon having already spread so far.    Now he was simply annoyed.

"About this building society?"

"I mentioned it in my sermon."

"Now, Mr. Robinson, if you won't think me impertinent for mentioning my ideas to you about that affair"—the Rector paused for a disclaimer of such thoughts from his companion, who however maintained a disconcerting silence—"I should like to beg you to re-consider your attitude with regard to it.    I distrust it.    Who is Lord Eastney?    We all know him down here—a poor and not over-scrupulous peer with big expenses and a small income. Who is this man Marshall, the real manager and only apparent business man in the undertaking?    I say who is Marshall?"

"A well-known, perfectly honest financier."

.   .   .   Robinson began a perfunctory defence of Marshall and was in full swing with it; he knew every word by heart, and was sick to death of repeating it; when he suddenly stopped bewildered by his companion's expression.    They had reached the top of the hill and had turned down a short road leading to Robinson's house.    In a valley on one side of them was Stoke: on a table-land opposite to them stood the long line of the North Staffordshire Infirmary buildings just visible in the light of the summer sunset. The buildings had caught Hobart's eye as he asked his question "Who is Marshall?" and the sight seemed suddenly to connect itself with his words. In vivid flashes the train of thought connecting the two ran on. Robinson's words fell on deaf ears. Who was Marshall? What on earth had Marshall to do with the North Staffordshire Infirmary? Was it some mere trifle, a subscription, a speech, a patient? What connection had that face, that smooth silky voice with some one in there? Something he was sure . . . ah! but it was maddening not to be able to remember what! Abruptly wishing the minister good-night Canon Hobart turned back and walked home desperately trying to remember something which eluded him more and more at every step. He had fixed his mind firmly at last upon the patients in the place and was certain that Marshall had been one of them, one who for a reason (probably—certainly—a bad one) had left an impression. But what was the reason? He would ask Marshall the question point-blank, resolved Hobart irritably, on the very next occasion on which he met him.

# CHAPTER XVII

"Mr. Robinson, I believe?"

"Yes, my Lord.  I am pleased to see your lordship down in this neighbourhood."

Lord Eastney motioned to the minister to take a seat.  He had come down from London with Marshall that morning, two days after the now famous sermon in the Hanley Road chapel, and various local lights of the Freehold Building Society had been invited to meet him. The visit, which was in fact a mere business one made in connection with the purchase of the Arkhill estate, caused some commotion. Oddly enough several persons professed at first to view it with suspicion, as indicative of something being wrong.  Then on the following day it was announced in the *Staffordshire Sentinel* that the Marchioness of Eastney and Lady Angela Purvis had come down too.  A report was spread about that the family was looking for a house in the district and once more peace and joy reigned.

"You have done some good work for us here, Mr. Robinson."

"I do what I can, my lord, for my flock in temporal as well as spiritual things."

The marquis looked round at Marshall with a queer glance which seemed to ask: "Am I obliged to keep up this canting nonsense with this fellow?  Can't you tell him to talk openly?" but Marshall took no notice.

"Now we hear—forgive my coming to business rather abruptly; my time is short—that you want to sell a bit of land adjoining this estate which we are buying."

"That is so, my lord.  A very nice bit.  Far more valuable than any other bit on your property.  If there is coal near Dently the seam must run right through my land."

"We will give you £400; that is we will give you forty shares in the Freehold for it."

"Why, my lord, the land is  .  .  ."

"I advise you to accept our offer, Mr. Robinson."

"If you will treble it, my lord!"

"But we won't!"

The door close by Robinson opened and Lady Eastney came in accompanied by a young man and a child; her husband looked up with a slight frown.

"The Harleys have just come," she said, making slight bows to Marshall and Robinson as she walked up the room to the table where her husband sat. "Shall you be able to come and see them?"

"Yes, I will come down shortly. Ask them to wait if they can." He hesitated for a moment and then resolved on a manœuvre which had often enough succeeded before. "Wait one moment," he said as his wife was preparing to move away; "I want to present to you a very good friend of our work down here, Mr. Luke Robinson. Mr. Robinson, my wife, Lady Eastney."

The Marchioness seemed to study her husband for a moment as though to learn something, and then turned to Robinson with a polite smile: "I am most pleased to make acquaintance with Lord Eastney's friends down here," she said. "It is my first visit to the district, and I find it most interesting. Angela and I"—the dark eyes with that infinitely weary smile in them, looked down on the small eight-year-old creature with an odd look of pity—"have been over the Wedgewood works this morning, and we were very much interested. We were given the most charming little vases."

"I suppose Miss Angela will be able to make vases for herself now," said the minister, smiling with embarrassed amiability, and putting his hand on the child's head. He was (self)-celebrated for having "a way with children." The little lady shrank back with a glance of quick proud anger, but the Marchioness with a hand lightly but firmly on her shoulder held her still while Robinson stroked her hair two or three times, and Lady Eastney looked down on her with that curious look of pity still in her eyes.

"We should both love to play with that clay, I am sure," she said. "We should like to go back there every day while we are here; but we want to see something of our friends, and there is not time for everything. Has Lord Eastney asked you to come to lunch with us to-morrow, Mr. Robinson? I know he means to do so, and I hope you will be able to come. Angela and I are so anxious to hear something about the lives and work of all the people we saw in the manufactory this morning, and you must come and tell us."

"His lordship has asked me, and I have been delighted to accept his invitation. I shall be most pleased to tell your ladyship and Miss Angela all you want to know." The man put out his hand again, and with a quick, uncontrollable movement, the little one put up her arms to defend her hair from being stroked. But in response to another warning pressure on her shoulder she dropped them again, though angry tears welled up in her eyes.

"Then we need only say *au revoir* till to-morrow," said the Marchioness, holding out her hand with her most charming smile. "I must go now to some friends who are waiting for me. Bertie!"

The young man who had come in with Lady Eastney, and who had been standing during the interview looking at Robinson as if he were a new and not very pleasing specimen of the ourang-outang tribe of monkey, lounged forward to the door, opened it, and with a long farewell glance at Robinson's coat, as if still doubtful whether it did or did not conceal a tail, went out after the Marchioness.

"Only three days more!" he said cheerfully when they were outside, "and then Scotland and freedom! Hullo, another couple! Women this time! Very nice-looking girl too. Were you looking?" Bertie Alford stopped in front of Miss Bertram and Monica, and addressed the latter with an impertinence which was curious in a man who was usually well-mannered enough. In point of fact he was trying to amuse and distract Lady Eastney, and would have chaffed and insulted half a dozen royalties to bring a laugh to the pale, tired face. "Were you looking for Lord Eastney?"

"We are waiting for my brother who is with him now," said Monica.

"Well, won't you come in here, Miss Robinson?" went on Alford recklessly, and delighted to hear a slight giggle from Angela. He indicated the dining-room of the private suite which Lord Eastney had engaged at the North Stafford Hotel. "Your brother may be some time. He told me . . ."

"That will do, Bertie." Lady Eastney came forward with a vexed look as she saw Monica flush angrily. "But would you like to wait in here?" she went on, turning to Miss Bertram. "My cousin is quite right in saying that Mr. Robinson seemed to be very much occupied with my husband—with Lord Eastney."

"We have nothing to do with Mr. Robinson," was Miss Bertram's chilling reply. "We are waiting for Mr. Franklin. This is my niece, Miss Franklin."

"Oh!—I beg your pardon!" The strangest expressions of sympathy, pity, and something like fear, swept across my lady's face. Her voice, in which also there was an odd touch of fear, made Alford look at her with amazement. "You must be Miss Bertram. I am so glad to make your acquaintance, even in this odd manner." The Marchioness glanced reproachfully at her cousin, who muttered something sounding like, "How the deuce was I to know?" "Please come and wait in this room. Everybody in there looked so very busy that I feel sure you will have a long time to wait."

Miss Christina and Monica followed the tall, graceful young figure into the room, and then sat down and studied her. At first sight Lady Eastney looked younger than her years, which numbered but thirty; on closer inspection she looked as if she were trying to hide the ravages of forty hard-lived years. Her dress of brown holland and white muslin, with diamond brooches holding a lace collar here and a flower or two there, looked too young; a profusion of emerald and diamond jewellery on her wrist, and a long white finger, gave her the appearance to feminine eyes in this particular environment of being slightly over-dressed. There was also something oddly offensive to the eyes of her two present companions in her manner of putting her arms at once round Angela, and holding her tight with an aggressive air of protection. They could hardly, of course, understand that it was an instinctive habit of Lady Eastney's in the presence of any of her husband's clients, or their relations or friends.

"My cousin and I had just been talking to

Mr. Robinson.　This is my cousin, Mr. Alford. Bertie, apologise to Miss Franklin for　.　.　."

"For supposing that she was a relation of Luke Robinson's.　Most willingly," said the young man, but a glance of warning entreaty made him look penitent.

"And you might just go and talk to the Harleys for a few moments.　No, Angela would rather stay with us; you must venture down there alone."

"Does she go about with you everywhere?" asked Miss Bertram, rather at a loss for something to say.

"Yes," said my lady quietly.　"We have been to some pottery works this morning, and she has been carrying about this little vase which they gave her ever since."

Monica held out a hand to the child, who first shrank back a little and then went resolutely forward.　It was dreadful to see how the baby, whose nervousness could be seen in every line of her white blue-veined forehead and black-encircled eyes, had trained herself, or been trained, to obey every such advance; while my Lady's anxious unhappy glances followed her child everywhere.

"Your nephew is coming up to London, I am told?" said Lady Eastney.

"Yes, next Saturday."　There was some

surprise in Miss Bertram's voice, and Lady Eastney answered it with a smile.

"I know a good deal of the Freehold business," she said. "Of course one hears a lot about it. It is a big affair, and my husband, who is much absorbed in it, talks of its business constantly. Are you coming up to London with him?"

"No, he will live with some friends."

"He is very young, is he not?"

"Just eighteen; but his friends, cousins of mine, will take good care of him. My cousin is engaged in some Freehold work too, as well as being a shareholder. We are all interested in the Society now. I have all my money in it too, as perhaps your ladyship knows."

"No, I didn't know. . . . What is it, darling? Something broken in the vase already? Oh, my baby, what fingers!"

"No, but ought that leaf to go like that, mother?"

"I don't quite see why it should. The pattern is funny, isn't it, sweetheart? It is a design which, like some of the designs of Providence, isn't very easy to follow. . . . You know Mr. Lowe, the Vicar of Hartshill, of course, Miss Bertram?"

"Yes, my lady. Another shareholder in the Freehold. He has got everything in it too."

"Everything? . . . Really you are very thorough people down here! Nearly every one I come across seems to have half or all his or her money in the Society!"

"If we can increase our incomes without risk, it is our duty to do so," said Miss Bertram. "There is so much poverty in the world to relieve; so many persons whom a little help will put right for all time; so many who, by sudden accidents or illness, are genuinely incapable for a time of helping themselves."

"And I am sure you are the friend of all of them," said Lady Eastney, studying her companion with very sincere admiration. "How much of the increased income of which your aunt speaks does she spend on herself, Miss Franklin?"

"Not much certainly," said Monica with a smile and a slightly puzzled look at the Marchioness' face, the tired look on which had increased till it gave one the idea of unbearable physical pain. She was very white too, and laid her cheek down on the little head of her daughter with an air of hopeless fatigue. There was silence for a moment or two, and then a door was opened and voices sounded in the passage outside.

"The conference is at an end, apparently," said Lady Eastney, rising from her chair with an arm always round Angela. "Come and find your nephew, Miss Bertram."

She swept out into the passage where Lord Eastney and Marshall were standing talking to Robinson, while Gerald stood a little apart and looked on.

"It is our last offer, on my word," the Marquis was saying; "forty shares and a hundred pounds cash."

"I must take it, my lord, I suppose," was the reply, half-laughing and half-doubtful. "It is a bit of a come-down from the 500 shares which I asked for, though"—he lowered his voice and looked very straight into Lord Eastney's eyes—"perhaps the hundred pounds cash is about the value of the other 460 shares!"

Lord Eastney's face remained perfectly blank and Robinson looked a little foolish. Lady Eastney broke an awkward pause by introducing Miss Bertram and Monica.

"They are waiting for Mr. Franklin," she said. "You really ought not to keep him like this when he is going away from them altogether so soon! Good-bye, Miss Bertram;"— she turned back to the two women—"let me know when you come up to London to see your nephew. Be sure and let me know. I am quite sincere in what I say. If I can ever do anything for you, if I can ever help you in any way at all, I should like to."

"Your ladyship is very good," said Miss Bertram, in some surprise.

"Oh!  One may have one's fancies!" she said, answering Miss Christina's tone rather than her words.  "That is a promise, then! And who knows how soon the time may come for its fulfilment?  Good-bye."

Left alone in the passage with his wife and child the Marquis stared gloomily at a comic hunting picture on the opposite wall for a minute.  Then he asked:—

"What made you talk all that d—d rot to her?  Do you think I want people of that sort hanging about me if ever  .  .  ."

"A whim," answered my lady Marchioness curtly; "one of my whims which I shall gratify whenever and wherever I please.  Come, Angela.  .  .  ."

# CHAPTER XVIII

"How much longer is it to go on? Am I a saint, or rather am I a devil, to look on at such work being done day after day and say nothing? How much longer is it to last?"

Lady Eastney was raving up and down the drawing-room of her suite of rooms in the North Stafford Hotel, while her cousin, councillor and gentleman-in-waiting (self-appointed for life), Herbert Alford, sat on the window-sill beating a devil's tattoo on the windows with his fingers, and on the floor with his heels and toes.

"I suppose," said the councillor grimly, "that the longer it lasts the better it will be for you and your baby."

"The better? . . ."

"I suppose money is coming in from the business. Well, you will have the money."

"When the crash comes he will give every farthing of it back to the wretched people from whom it has been stolen."

"Will he?"

"Well, I shall."

The councillor laughed.

"I would rather go and earn my own living as a shop-woman," exclaimed the woman tragically, "than take a penny of his horrible money after what I have seen for the last six months!"

"And Angela?"

"I will take her away and go and earn my own living."

"Shop-women get about £35 a year rising to £60," said the councillor; "would that keep the baby in stockings?"

"You must be stone, Bertie, to be able to think of those women's faces this afternoon and talk in this fashion, knowing what is going to happen to them!"

"What the deuce do I know about them, or you either, my dear?  They may be the smartest of speculators 'buying for a rise.'  They've got a relation in the business, right inside it, and he will warn them in time.  Come, old girl, there are tragedies enough in the world, even I allow in our own little building society, without working yourself into this state about a half-imaginary one!  We've got a free evening.  Let's enjoy ourselves.  There's a theatre at Longton and the 'Bells' is being played, probably with a local genius as hero. Let's go there and laugh.  Do you remember when we saw it at the Francaise, and the old

Grayshaw cat insisted on coming into our box?"
Alford came over to where Lady Eastney had
flung herself into a chair and put a hand on to
her shoulder: she shook it off petulantly, and
he laughed good-naturedly. He was a young
man who laughed at everything, at his cousin's
tantrums out of which he tried to coax her,
at gambling "wins" which he mostly spent
within twenty-four hours, at gambling losses
which he was rarely able to pay, at the admiration of women for whom he did not care and
the coldness of women for whom he did, at the
tricks and shiftings of a man trying to postpone
his tailor's bill and at the gigantic tricks and
frauds of which his cousin's husband was daily
guilty. For his cousin herself he had a tame-
cat kind of fondness, passing most of his time
at her house, accompanying her to "at homes"
and dances at which Lord Eastney was already
beginning to be received with doubtful looks
and cold greetings, and finally often coming
with her on business rounds of this description
where Lord Eastney insisted on his wife
accompanying him, and on which Mr. Alford
made himself useful by ordering dinner, teaching (and occasionally helping) the hotel cooks
and beating up the neighbourhood for possible
companions.

A waiter appeared with a message to ask if

Mr. Marshall might speak to Lady Eastney for a moment.

"Bertie! That horror is here again! You talk of a free evening! There is no freedom for me. Oh, show him up."

Marshall came in perfumed, smiling, as usual.

"Your ladyship will excuse me, I know. On these business tours we are all at work from morning to night. Lord Eastney has gone out and no one can tell me when he will be in again. Can you tell me?"

"Do you know, Bertie?" My lady passed on the question, and turning round in her chair stared moodily at the opposite wall.

"Couldn't possibly say," said Mr. Alford laconically.

"Do you know where he is?"

"Haven't the least idea."

Marshall took a seat uninvited near Lady Eastney.

"Your ladyship has been seeing quite a large number of our shareholders this afternoon."

The Marchioness responded by a gesture which might mean "yes" or "no," or that she was certainly seeing one too many of them just now—probably the latter.

"Very pleasant people, Miss Bertram and her niece are; rich too. You had quite a long chat with them."

My lady turned to him with a sort of gloomy interest: "They have everything in the Freehold," she said, half as if contradicting the man's assertion that they were rich.

"Miss Bertram has; her niece has a little money elsewhere: some shares in the Carlton mines in South Africa."

"She has, has she?" said Alford with sudden animation, "that's good business for her."

"The shares are not worth much now. They may be some day."

"Your information is not quite as up to date as usual, Mr. Marshall. The new machinery or something has brought luck there. A reef has been discovered in the Carlton property. I know a fellow who has a few shares and who refused £5 a-piece for them a few days ago."

"You don't say so!" said Marshall with a glow of excitement on his face. "Why, Miss Franklin has 2000 shares! That would give her £10,000 if they were sold at the price you mention! Perhaps it may be double that! It is quite a large fortune for people in their class of life!"

"Has the girl control of her own money? Is she of age?" The Marchioness asked the questions apparently of the fireplace, as she did not turn her head, but Marshall answered.

"She is not of age, but a Mr. Lowe, one of our best friends down here, is trustee of the will under which the money comes to her. Yes, Lowe is a firm believer in the Freehold, and would do anything I told him if Miss Franklin agreed."

"So, of course"—the lady still addressed the fireplace—"you will try and get her money transferred to Freehold shares?"

"Need your ladyship ask?" said Marshall with a self-satisfied smile.

"No, I need not.   Do you know this Mr. Lowe's exact powers in the matter?"

"No, but if your ladyship would like to know I could easily find out.   It is very kind of your ladyship to try and help us in the matter. Perhaps if the aunt and niece were invited to the lunch here to-morrow . . .   I can assure your ladyship that they are perfectly respectable persons."

The fireplace had the benefit of a fine faint smile.   The Marchioness opened a little painted fan and swung it slowly to and fro, apparently considering something.

"Yes," she said at last.   "I think they might be invited to-morrow.   Who has sent out the invitations to all these——" my lady suddenly checked herself in a word which described with some vigour and completeness

the guests of to-morrow, and changed it to
"persons?"

"Well, I drew up the lists and wrote the
letters, and his lordship signed them.  A sort
of division of labour," added Marshall, essay-
ing a little humour.

"I will write this one.  Give me my writing-
case, Bertie."

"It will do just as well after dinner," said
Alford in a low voice.

"Do you mind giving me my writing-case
.  .  .  thanks."

Alford brought the old white and gold case
to her side and held it for a moment, muttering: "Think—please!"  My lady took it on
her knee, put a hand on the worn old strap and
sat hesitating, looking at it.  The white
morocco was yellowing in places; ink-blotches
were scattered over it; in a corner was her
monogram with an ink-blot on it and her
coronet over it—the coronet for which she had
sold love, youth, honour, happiness.  She
noticed each of the little trifles, and as she sat
there with her hand on the buckle, her cousin
standing over her with anxious perturbed face,
a queer thought came to her of the mass of
letters which she had written here, letters to
Angela, dinner-invitations, half-joking love-
letters (not to Lord Eastney), congratulations,

condolences, and lately complaints—complaints of friends growing cold, of society looking askance, of snubs and whispers and half-comprehended questions and remarks. They rose up before her for some queer reason, the ghosts of these letters written here, and she sat looking at them. They stayed in her mind when she at last opened the case, and wrote the commonplace invitation to luncheon, and put it in an envelope, and handed it to Marshall with a curt nod and word of dismissal.

There was a brief silence after Marshall had shut the door.

"You are mad, Frances," said the young man by her side in a sort of frightened whisper. "What are you going to do? You are not really going to warn these people?" There was no answer and he went on in the same frightened voice: "Don't you know that a word is enough now to topple over the whole affair? The women are nothing to you! What are you doing this for?"

"My husband asked me rather the same sort of question a short time ago," said the woman in a low voice, but with her cheeks and lips very white, "and I answered that it was a whim, one of my whims which I mean to gratify whenever and wherever I please. That answer must content you too."

# CHAPTER XIX

"Angela.  .  .  ."

"Yes."

"I have just thought of a story."

"Tell it me, Bertie; go on."

Bertie looked round him with an unusual gravity on his insouciant young face.  It was the morning of the luncheon party to which Miss Bertram had at the last moment been invited, and very near the luncheon hour.  In the room Lady Eastney wandered about restlessly, the diamonds in her laces flashing as she passed across the light.  She had carefully avoided being alone with Alford all the morning, and now Miss Eardly—nominally governess to Angela, in reality companion to herself —sat at the table writing letters.

"It is a funny old Eastern story, a sort of parable; you won't understand it."

"You always say that," said her little ladyship with a frown and a wriggle; "now go on."

"There was a certain man who was a famous mischief-maker, who went about the world making quarrels and rows everywhere.  .  .  ."

Angela settled herself down in a chair with her hands crossed and her eyes fixed raptly on the speaker after the manner of an eight-year-old audience. My lady stopped her rambling walk and stood by the window looking out and swinging a blind-tassel absently to and fro.

" . . . One day he came to a town where no one ever quarrelled, where no one talked slander, and every one was friends with every one else. The people who knew him said: 'It is no good coming here; you can't make any mischief here. If you told the most outrageous stories night and day about us no one would believe you. If you collected witnesses and even appeared to prove one of us guilty of a crime you would only be laughed at. You had better not waste your time here.' The mischief-maker laughed and said nothing; but in the morning he bought some honey, and put a dab of it outside a door." . . .

The young man paused for a moment. Angela was looking very puzzled. The blind-tassel swung steadily to and fro.

"Well, and what happened?" asked the Marchioness with a strained laugh.

"A fly settled on the honey," said Bertie laconically; "a spider settled on the fly and eat him: a chameleon settled on the spider and eat him: a cat attacked the chameleon: a dog attacked the cat: the owner of the cat attacked the dog: the owner of the dog attacked the owner of the cat: then all the town came out and took sides. I forget what happened to the mischief-maker himself."

"As he had no motive but a desire to make mischief," said Lady Eastney, "he deserved a bad end."

"It is too short," said Lady Angela, bewildered by the rapid conclusion. "Can't you make up some more?"

"There is no end at all to it, chicken. The uproar in the town, when it once began, went on and on. No one can guess the end of that story even now."

"Then tell me another," said her little ladyship; but if Mr. Alford had meant to comply he was checked by the entrance of Lord Eastney and Mr. Robinson.

Gracefully and charmingly Lady Eastney greeted the luncheon-guests as they arrived one after another, with a word or two and a smile which put every one at their ease, a deeply interested attitude for any one who claimed her special attention, a quick eye for any one who looked as if he or she wanted to speak to her and dare not begin, and an air of never being pre-occupied or having any other care than to listen to her companion of the moment.   Angela moved about with her, receiving head-pats and hand-shakes with polite resignation.  Bertie did his duty too as far as he could, though a little out of his element, in a company which did not make or understand jokes.  Presently lunch was announced, and the company, some two dozen in number, took their places after a certain amount of shuffling about.  Mr. Robinson, Mr. Nicholson, senior, and one or two others, wanted to be near Lady Eastney, and there was a little scuffling near her end of the table.  Luke Robinson found himself standing near Angela and began an: "Ah, Miss Angela, you are coming to sit next to me.  That's right.  I'll give you plenty of pudding," and Lord Eastney called out: "Oh, she is a great admirer of yours, Robinson; take charge of her if you like by all means."  The Marchioness was passing up the room just then, and the little one turned to her with half-raised arms and a passion of frightened appeal in her eyes; but the woman only stooped and whispered: "It won't be for long, my baby," and went on to her place with her own words echoing oddly in her ears.  "It won't be for long"  .   .   .   she had only meant to assure the scared little mortal that this luncheon and the company of Mr. Robinson would not last long, but as she took her place at the end of the table and looked down it her words seemed to repeat themselves with some wider meaning.   Not for long  .  .  .  ?  Well, she for one did not care how soon it ended.

Thoroughly accustomed to such parties as that over which she was now presiding, Lady Eastney soon had her guests eating and drinking, talking and laughing at their ease, and found herself with leisure to look round. Monica, whose face caught her eye first, was sitting between a good-looking well-groomed young man who evidently was or ought to be her lover, and another whose sullen face was a curious study.   She knew the latter—it was Muirhead — and said to herself, "There is crime in that man's mind; I wonder what is wrong."   Then she watched Miss Bertram for a moment and muttered: "That woman looks like a sort of harbour of refuge from all the ills of life.   I should like to go and stay with her and have a long, long cry, with her to console me through it, and then go to sleep for a week with her sitting by me.   How astonished she would be if I told her so  .  .  .  !"   Then Mrs. Robinson claimed her attention with a narrative of how her husband had got the best of Canon Hobart in an altercation about certain rates.

After lunch she moved away with Miss Bertram and Monica into a corner of the drawing-room.

"We hear that your niece has had a great piece of luck with some South African shares," she began.

"We have heard it this morning. Does your ladyship understand these South African affairs at all?"

"Not in the least. Very few people do. Have you some good advisers?"

"My lawyer is Mr. Benson. He is standing just there talking to Mr. Robinson."

"I see. Have you—please forgive these apparently impertinent questions—have you spoken to him about the matter yet?"

"I saw him this morning and he spoke to me again here just before lunch. He says that such shares go up and down every day for reasons which we down in the country know nothing about, and could not possibly foresee, and that we had better sell these shares at once now that they are up."

"That sounds sensible."

"And he said that he could get us some more shares in the Freehold with the money just now if we liked; and if Mr. Lowe, who is a trustee of Monica's, would consent."

"Yes? . . . Miss Bertram, I want to

give you some advice. I know what I am saying and I mean what I say. You are listening
to me?"

"Naturally, my lady."

"Don't put that money into the Freehold.
You have some shares in it yourself now?"

"A large number."

"Sell them. . . . Shall you accept my
advice?"

"But if your ladyship would only . . ."

"I cannot say any more or argue about the
matter at all. It is a very serious affair my
having said this. It is so serious that I even"—
the woman hesitated, looked round the room
with a look of infinite scorn, began another
sentence, caught sight of Angela, and then
began the first again—"I even ask you not
to use my name in connection with it if you
can help it. That is rather a painful—
rather a humiliating request to make, and
I cannot possibly force you to promise what
I ask."

"I promise most willingly never to mention
your ladyship's name," said Miss Bertram, "and
I have to thank you sincerely for advising us.
We must think a little, but we shall probably
take your advice."

"Yes. That is all right." Lady Eastney
rose with a smile on her white lips and a look

in her eyes which flashed terror into those of Bertie Alford as he came up to her.

"You have done it after all?" he muttered.

"Yes."

"Then a *sauve qui peut* begins here this afternoon, and ends—where?"

"It is nothing to me."

"Or Angela?"

"Or to Angela, thank you."

"Just wait and see!"

# CHAPTER XX

Gerald Franklin permitted himself a certain amount of enthusiasm on his first visit to London. . . He had never been there before even for a day, and when the night express arrived at Euston on this Saturday evening in August, and he had said good-bye to Lord Eastney and Marshall on the platform and put himself and his luggage into a hansom, he confessed to himself that he felt excited. It was a pity that Great Ormond Street where his cousin lived was so close by, but that again had its advantages, as he was hungry. Next morning he went with the Ethridges, his cousins, to chapel in Red Lion Square, behaving with great propriety as was his wont, and at last found himself free to go out for a walk. A young man of the Ethridge family accompanied him along Holborn, New Oxford Street, and Oxford Street to the Park, pointing out shops, houses, and music-halls, with a list of their occupants and performers and the incomes made by each, and all the current gossip about them. What a young Londoner of this class does not know about London is not worth knowing. In the Park Sydney Ethridge showed various celebrities of a minor order who were in town in spite of the season, but Gerald, who had listened to him in the comparative silence and desertion of a Sunday afternoon in Oxford Street, grew absorbed in the crowds here and hardly heard. A crowd fascinated him always and everywhere: it was the only object which brought his imagination into play and he could have spent days here, simply looking, cataloguing and criticising. Although it was August, numerous carriages were passing up and down the Row, and Sydney pointed out a well-known face or two. Women with the eyes and mouths of English great ladies — (you distinguish English "grandes dames" by their mouths and eyes as you do French by their speech)—sat here and there under the trees daintily dressed, fluttering their lace parasols in lines of shady summer colours. Men sat by them smoking cigarettes, the slight touch of inanity and of general resemblance to one another as of a flock of sheep (whereas in an assembly of Frenchmen you will not notice two alike and will see a hundred different expressions on each face in as many seconds) being redeemed by their fresh healthy cleanliness and generally well-groomed appearance. A man or two rode by on a park hack, glancing right and left with defiance in his eyes as one who would say, "This animal may be almost extinct, but I prefer it to all others and choose to keep it." Victorias full of country folk, some frankly enjoying the spectacle, others trying to look as if they were passing just once more through an old and weary scene, moved slowly by. Lady Eastney drove past with Angela, on her way to Hurlingham, and with that instinctive feeling possessed by certain people that some one is waiting to salute them, she turned to the side path and greeted Gerald with a bow and smile which filled Sydney with respectful astonishment.

"My eye!" he said, "are we in the upper circles already? Shall we dine in Belgrave Square to-night? If I'd known I was coming out walking with such a toff I'd have put on my new pink tie. That's Knightsbridge Barracks, my young swell. Say now, would you like to come down the river? There's time to get down to Richmond. Mother likes some of us to come to chapel with her in the evening, but Susan and Mike can go to-night. I like Richmond myself."

"Have we time for another walk to the other end of the road and back?"

"No, not to go to Richmond afterwards, but I don't care about it," said the other good-naturedly. "Come along, my young lord!"

Pedestrians and vehicles grew more numerous as the afternoon wore on, and Gerald walked along absorbed and fascinated. This London pleasure-crowd seemed much gayer than those to which he was used in the country. Working men and their families, playing games, arranging tea or eating oranges under the trees, laughed, chatted, moved about more gaily than their fellows in Trentham Woods or Clough Hall. If the faces of the society young men were vacuous, their voices and laughter were pleasant and ready: their mothers, sisters and cousins moved past in a flutter of soft silks and laces and rippling laughter which was inspiriting. He remembered a phrase about English folk taking their pleasure sadly, and rather wondered what it meant. The phrase is certainly out of date. Perhaps it is a satiety of ordinary amusements, together with a large increase in their cost, which has made English youth of all classes more ready to be pleased by a walk and a chat and a look at their neighbours, more grateful for mere sunshine, green trees and companionship. But whatever the reason, it is certain that that idly sauntering crowd, asking for nothing but life and sunshine and plenty of neighbours, which used to be characteristic of the Champs Elysées and boulevards of Paris, has come to London.

The Ethridges assembled at supper at nine o'clock, and Sydney detailed the course of their afternoon's walk.

"You'd hardly think it was August," he added, "to see the Row. As full of folk it was as if it was the middle of June."

"Well, I'm glad there was something for you to see, Gerald," said Mr. Ethridge, "though such sights are stupid to go and look at more than once."

"Many pretty girls about?" asked Michael, the elder brother.

"I didn't notice any," said the boy, simply.

"You must be difficult to please," retorted Sydney.

"I don't mean there weren't any. I simply didn't see them. I was thinking of something else—that it was odd how contented people were. Fancy seeing a heap of folk like that richer than yourself every Sunday, and being satisfied!"

"There must always be rich and poor," said Ethridge, sententiously.

"Anybody can get rich who likes to try," said Gerald.

"Do you mean to try?" asked a girl sitting opposite to him.

"Yes," said the boy quietly, but with a certain compression of the lips as if the sight of Hyde Park had given him a new impatience, a new resolve.

Susan Ethridge looked at him with a little touch of admiration in her eyes, which Gerald saw and approved of. The boyish look on his face was rather a pleasant one, until with a succession of considerable shocks the real Gerald revealed himself. The young man's eyes were grey, and clear, and steady, his skin fresh and fair, his mouth and chin strong and well-shaped. If his face was young the assurance of his manner gave some appearance of age, and several women, chiefly older than himself, had before now expressed some liking for him. Susan Ethridge, who loved laughter, cynicism, good-looks, and ambition, had already come to the conclusion that Gerald was a very agreeable addition to their household. She had passed her twenty-five years in a rather sombre round of learning lessons and teaching them, and was beginning to revolt inwardly against it. Her parents disapproved of theatres, dancing, and most other entertainments: especially they disapproved of any amusement on Sunday, which was Susan's only holiday from the small pupils to whom on those dreary week-days she taught scales and sums. She neither complained nor rebelled: the steady gloom of the girl's home life had so eaten into her heart, that she hardly had spirit to wish for any brightness, and under favourable circumstances would probably marry a friend of her father's, and initiate a home and family of her own on exactly similar lines. The father was absorbed in his work and religion, talking and thinking of nothing else. At meal-time, breakfast and supper, he carried on a portentous monologue on one of the two subjects, speaking slowly and impressively, and so giving you the idea that what he was saying was worth listening to—which it was not. Mrs. Ethridge said: "Indeed, Mr. Ethridge, that is quite true," at regular intervals. Sydney and Michael, both clerks in a neighbouring accountant's office, were asked occasionally for an account of how they had spent their day, and gave it obediently, but otherwise no one spoke. The arrival of this cousin to board with them was the most exciting event which had ever taken place in their lives, and for a short time it quite demoralised them. The mother glanced about her, now at her husband, now at her children, a little anxiously as this conversation sprang up, with the inquiring look which a hen might give to the cock and her chickens if a duckling appeared and invited the party to come out swimming. She intervened with a narrative of having been that afternoon to read to some children in the adjacent hospital. Then Mr. Ethridge discoursed on the necessity for, and advantages of suffering, while the others eat their way silently through cold beef and pickles and a cold custard pudding. Gerald looked up once and caught Susan looking at him with pity and apology; he gave her a just perceptible grateful smile in reply. The little understanding brought them together after supper; and the girl spoke to him with a kindly elder-sister air which was rather pretty.

"What used you to do in the evenings at home?"

"Oh, nothing. I very often had work to do."

"Did you and Monica go to theatres or parties much?"

"Not very often. There are some good theatres near us, but really I didn't care for them. I think acting is simply stupid."

"It is so, my dear boy. It is a form of trifling with the stern realities of life and death which I cannot think to be right. I say to my children, 'What would you do if the Last

Trump should sound and call you to judgment as you sat laughing at the fooleries of . . ' "

Another sermon had begun and Gerald sat down with an air of quiet resignation, but the few words with his cousin had left a warm feeling in both hearts which even Mr. Ethridge's Sunday night discourse could not quite kill.

Next morning Gerald went to his work at the head offices of the Freehold Building Society in Southampton Row, and found business there in very much the same condition as in Staffordshire. The officials were mostly simple, ignorant men with money in the Society and very little knowledge of its work. Their tasks were apportioned in such fashion that no man saw the connection between his neighbour's work and his own. Marshall, Lord Eastney and a big house-agent named Margets were the only three who knew what was going on. None of them were present when Franklin arrived, and he was given certain accounts and books on which Seymour, his predecessor, had been engaged, and was asked to finish them. "What a stupid mass of confusion!" he said to Ethridge after an hour's work. "Where do these figures come from? Who paid the bill for these roads being made, and where are the details and the receipt?"

Ethridge looked stupidly at the papers and admitted ignorance: "If they aren't there, you must leave them out," he said; "of course, in a big London business we have not so much time to give to little trifles as you have had in Staffordshire;" and Gerald laughed inwardly. He had obviously been brought here and given this post as a bribe to hold his tongue, and he hardly supposed that the directors wanted work of this sort examined into very closely. Margets came in next day, and Ethridge, with an air of patronage of his cousin which amused the lad considerably, introduced him, and said that he had been showing Gerald the work, and that Gerald would soon understand it. Of course the difference between London and country business made beginning here a little difficult for the boy: these accounts left by young Seymour, for instance, had puzzled him considerably. Margets took up the bundle of papers referring to some South Kensington flats and began some good-natured explanations, while Ethridge left the room. Franklin did not mean to have his position in these offices misunderstood by any of the superiors.

"I quite understand all the points which you refer to," he said, with a slighting laugh; "only this road has apparently been made without payment—at any rate without receipted payment. However . . ." he laughed again, and Margets looked frightened.

Presently Marshall entered with Lord Eastney. He came up to Gerald's desk and put a letter down there—a letter from Benson saying that Miss Bertram had given instructions for the sale of all her shares in the Freehold. "What does that mean?" he asked. "Do you know?"

"I told you that you would have to take the chance of Robinson's meaning mischief," said the boy after reading the letter. "I am rather surprised myself. I doubted his having the courage for a move of this kind. I know nothing about it, but I suppose it is his doing."

"It is a bad business, whoever has done it," said Marshall. "What do you think, my lord?"

"I should say," said Lord Eastney, in a low voice which only Marshall could hear, "that it is the beginning of the end."

# CHAPTER XXI

Muirhead had been passing through a terrible time.  With Nicholson every day in the office as a constant reminder of his failure, with the daily increasing vague suspicions of financial difficulties, and with a new and most unpleasant feeling of responsibility for the management of the Freehold, he was very unhappy.  Gerald's departure revealed to the poor, thick-headed man how dull his wits really were in comparison with the sharpers and clients with whom he had to deal.  He went through the bundles of papers which came down day after day with uneasy wonder, longing to have back by his side the impassive, cynical young face which used to bend over these documents and take in all their contents in one contemptuous glance; the cool, cock-sure voice which used to decree that those figures meant so and so, and were to be entered in such and such a place.  He realised now how completely he had been the subordinate and Gerald the master.

During the weeks which elapsed between

Franklin's departure and young Nicholson's, Muirhead allowed a passion of hatred for his rival to grow upon him which frightened himself. Reggie now took Franklin's seat in the inner office, and Muirhead sat opposite to him, staring at him sometimes with heavy, angry eyes, forgetting all business in wondering when the lad had seen Monica last, what she had said to him, whether they had been talking about himself, whether Reggie knew that he himself had proposed to the girl, and whether even now perhaps there was some chance of the engagement coming to an end. With his eyes fixed on the young man's bent head he would imagine to himself the love words which had passed between them, the whispered tendernesses which he had pictured himself as murmuring to her, the movements of wandering hands, searching for and finding one another. His mind at last settled on this point, and at intervals in the day he would find himself staring furtively at Nicholson's hands, wondering when they had last touched Monica. He watched the long moving fingers with growing fascination, saying to himself, "Yesterday they touched her cheek, were round her neck, stroked her hair; this very evening they will hold her hands while I am sitting in my room reading dull letters of this and that tradesman, or turning the dreary pages of some unreal story.'' Then slowly a feeling would creep over him that he must do some injury to those hands, that he would pay money, would give months of his life, to tear them, to wrench them off and mutilate them. The idea would pass away with a sudden flash of terror lest this should be another symptom of coming insanity, and with a violent effort he would return to his work. Sometimes, when the hatred in him grew very strong, he would attempt by heaping up unnecessary tasks to prevent the lovers from meeting during the afternoon, but from some words dropped by Reggie one day he learnt that the young man merely went to Hartshill in the evening instead. The picture of this meeting in the summer twilight with only the stars to see the lovers, and with only the nightingales to interrupt their whispers, was the keenest torture of all. He loved the girl passionately, furiously; he could not bear to meet her and hated not to meet her; he loathed the sight of Reggie Nicholson and was half wild when he was out of sight because he would of course be with Monica. And above and through and under all these hatreds and fears and imaginations was the daily and hourly terror of another brain failure, of another of those intervals when time had ceased and responsibility finished, and from which he would wake with horrified wonder as to where he was and what he had been doing.

Life became so utterly unendurable to Muirhead by the end of August that he first of all asked for a holiday, although he had taken his usual fortnight's leave of absence, and this request having been refused, looked round eagerly for some local diversion. Evenings at Clough Hall or Trenthan, afternoons at Longton or Hanley afforded him not the slightest interest or amusement. In the former place he, who had so few friends and acquaintances nowadays (since one would as soon court the companionship of the lethargetic but uncertain-tempered python or the lively and certain-tempered mad dog, as that of a love-sick man who has tried for his prize and failed), was as much alone with his thoughts as in his own rooms. In the theatres a dozen scenes would be sure to take place reminding him of his misery. One day, seeing an advertisement on the walls of Stoke announcing a special train to the Manchester Races, he determined to go there, and accordingly one Thursday morning found himself in company with a large number of more or less familiar faces in a train going to Manchester. It occurred to him more than once that this proceeding on the part of the local manager of the Freehold Building Society, so many of whose members and patrons put "Reverend" before their names either by recognized right or by freak of their own playful fancy, might excite some highly unfavourable comment, but he cared very little for that nowadays. Not only was all other thought absorbed by his desire to cure this miserable condition of mind, but he was beginning to feel that the work of the Building Society was beyond his powers, and that he did not care how soon he was freed from it.

Manchester Racecourse, with the approaches thereto, the Stands thereon, and the view therefrom, is about the ugliest place of its kind in Europe, but as few people who go there wish to admire scenery, this is not of great importance. The crowds are large, sporting in looks and language, and sentiments, tolerant of all things except the victories of outsiders, hopeful of better things when they have lost money, and jocularly content when they have won. If it is not quite such a perfect sporting crowd as that of York or Doncaster, it is many degrees better than the languid picnic-assembly of Sandown Park or the army of scamps and roughs who patronise Brighton. Muirhead, however, was paying his first visit to a racecourse, and was not hypercritical, being indeed more occupied in trying to discover what it was all about. He saw numbers and names on a board, horses and jockeys in various colours, a race with a close finish which the onlookers cheered excitedly, and which did not interest him in the least. The contest between the two horses which had finished first and second might or might not have been exciting; he was willing to believe that it was, but he himself was not excited by it. He watched three races, one after another in this fashion, finding some momentary interest in the excited conversations and alternating joy and despair of the men who stood near him, then sighed heavily, and made his way towards the gate, meaning to go home. To watch another of these contests between galloping horses and flogging jockeys, seemed to him the most dreary of prospects. The shouting and excitement of the spectators were totally incomprehensible to him, the result of the race hopelessly uninteresting.

At the gate just before he went out, he met a certain Robert Fairlegh, a tradesman in Newcastle whom he knew slightly—so slightly in fact that he was considerably astonished at Fairlegh's hearty greeting and his: "You look pretty blue, mister! Were you on Cordova?"

Muirhead was not of course aware that among the touches of nature which make the whole world akin, is the backing of an unsuccessful favourite.

"I don't know anything about Cordova," he answered gloomily, "but I am very dull here, and I am going away."

"Oh, you've been hit rather hard, I see!" answered Fairlegh, who had been drowning memory of the treacherous Cordova in whisky, and was indeed in a condition in which one sees either nothing or double. "Come and have another try. I know a really good thing for the next race. Lighter is bound to win,—a stone blind certainty he is. George Hickson says so, and if George Hickson doesn't know what he is talking about, nobody in this world never knew nothing about nothing at all. Come and get your money back on Lighter."

"I haven't lost any money," said Muirhead pettishly, becoming angry at the attention which was being attracted towards him by this loud-voiced sympathy. "I haven't been betting. I haven't come here to bet."

"Then what the —— have you come here for?" asked Fairlegh, sympathetic but puzzled. "When things go wrong, curse them till they go right again," and this Mr. Fairlegh proceeded to do for the space of half a minute,

making up by the wide extent of his expletives
for some slight uncertainty as to what he was
swearing about.

He had however taken Muirhead in such a
firm grip that in order to avoid a row, or at any
rate in order to change the auditors of the
present row, Muirhead moved back with him
towards the ring.  The numbers were going
up for the fourth race as they came back, and
Fairlegh ordered Muirhead in a thick but confident voice to notice that Leslie was riding
Lighter.

"So he's bound to win, old pal," said the
man, who was of course now on such close
terms of intimacy as whisky and "tipping"
combined must produce.  "So you put all
you've got on him.  Here's young Nick Lunn,
a very honest man young Nick Lunn is, just
the man to do your business for you young
Nick Lunn is.  What odds Lighter, Nick?"

"Fives."

"And a —— bad price too, but it is no good
arguing with you.  You can give me fifty to
ten, Nick, and you can give my friend the
same.  Hand over a tenner to Nick, my boy!"

"Stop talking nonsense," said Muirhead,
angrily.  "I haven't got ten pounds, and certainly shouldn't bet them if I had.  I have only
got two pounds with me."

"Only two quid left! You must have dropped a lot over Cordova," said Fairlegh, with almost tearful sympathy. "Well, hand it over! Put him down ten to two, Nick."

Several other men were standing behind Muirhead pushing impatiently, ordering him to make haste; and regarding the transaction merely as an expensive means of escaping from the scene, Muirhead handed over his money to the bookmaker and moved away. Fairlegh, however, stuck to him, and leading him to a stand close by pointed out the horses as they cantered down to the starting post.

"That's Lighter," he said, "in the pink and black cap. A fidgety little devil he is, but you'll see Leslie won't stand any nonsense with him. Now you'll see that with brute Queen Mab dancing about there'll be a breakaway. There you are, you see." Half-a-dozen horses were, in fact, flying along the course, and Mr. Fairlegh, propped up comfortably but insecurely between Muirhead and a post, nearly fell backwards in an endeavour to wave them back with his arms.

"But you see Lighter hardly budged an inch," he went on admiringly. "Now here's another start; that's right this time; off! Leslie's pulled him back, you see, further and further back still. You'd think he wasn't meant, but he is if George Hickson says so. What George Hickson doesn't know isn't worth knowing. Now you see he is creeping up on the rails; see him, don't you? Ah! but that Queen Mab she's coming up too, curse her. That —— Leslie is waiting too long. He has let the —— little mare get such a —— start already that . . ."

As the rest of Mr. Fairlegh's comments on the race would have to be represented in these polite pages by a series of blanks with a few substantives at very long intervals, and as this would therefore take some time to read with understanding, it is sufficient to say that the famous jockey who was riding Lighter proved himself to be a better judge of pace than Mr. Fairlegh. Queen Mab had been rushed to the front a trifle too soon, she began to stop at the half-distance, and with only one or two slight reminders from the whip, Lighter went past her easily and won by a length. In the course of a subsequent conversation in the bar, during which "George Hickson," and "drinks all round," were at first the only comprehensible words, Muirhead grasped the fact that he had won ten pounds, that he had only to go up to Nick Lunn and demand this sum and that he would immediately receive it. From being dull, bored and angry, he suddenly became almost hysterically excited, and when the money was actually in his pocket began himself to talk almost as incoherently as Fairlegh.

"There's plenty more winners where that came from," said Fairlegh. "You've just got to go and put your money on Royal next. You'll have to lay odds on him. Know what that means, old cock? No, of course you don't. Then you come along with me. Some people might tell you that Mirror was going to win this race, but he ain't. George Hickson says he ain't worth a dollar a leg; that's what he says. You put your money down on Royal."

Muirhead rather reluctantly parted with five pounds and could not understand why he was only to win four, knowing only enough about racing to express intelligent doubts about Mr. Fairlegh's "stone-blind certainties." He understood, however, the business of the race rather better on this occasion and said to himself that no two minutes of his life had been fuller of pleasure than these two, when he stood watching the horse Royal, whose jockey he was able to distinguish after instruction, cantering in front of his opponents from start to finish of the race. He declined to make a bet on the last race of the afternoon, and went home almost out of his mind with excitement. To have had an afternoon of rest from work, of absolute forgetfulness of all his troubles, and to come home fourteen pounds the richer for it, struck him as the finest idea of a holiday which could well be imagined.

# CHAPTER XXII

Muirhead never read any racing news; and horses' names, however familiar they might be to his ears from conversations in the district, conveyed nothing to his mind. Therefore when Fairlegh came round to his rooms on Friday evening and began to talk of a certain King John who was to run next day in the Lancashire Plate, Muirhead's chief thought was that by encouraging Fairlegh's intimacy on Thursday he had let himself in for some rather unpleasant subsequent explanations He answered austerely that he had only gone to Manchester on the previous day for a little bit of amusement and had not suddenly become a professional sportsman.

"But what I say is," said Fairlegh, dogmatically, and in the loud monotone of a man who loves to hear himself talk and knows what he is going to say so well and has said it so often without interruption that he has no intention of allowing it to be disputed: "when a man is in luck let him work his luck for all it is worth. When he's out of luck he should lie low.   George Hickson says, 'When luck's with you play up to it; when luck's against you sit in a chair and drink your winnings.'   Now you're a beginner, so of course you're in luck. Come out and make the best of it while it lasts. You can take your Bible oath it won't last long.   Mine never does," and Mr. Fairlegh proceeded to take a good many oaths (not Bible ones) to that effect on his own account.

"Is he quite certain to win this race?" asked Muirhead meekly.

"As sure as I am here with a thirst on me like a —— furnace," said Fairlegh, who was not one of those weak-minded, weak-speaking men full of constant intelligent doubts about the existence of certainties.   When he thought that a horse was going to win he believed the fact and asserted it, as now, in the strongest words which he was capable of using; and to show the strength of his conviction that King John would win he called for whiskey, and demonstrated without any possibility of cavil the reality of his thirst.

Attracted as much by the oblivion which it had brought him as by the desire of making money, Muirhead went down to Manchester again on Saturday.   Throughout the journey he heard the merits of the famous King John being discussed on all sides.   The horse had

won a race at Ascot, of which he could not
catch the name, and then the St. Leger. He
could not, it appeared, lose to-day's race. Not
having Fairlegh at hand to pass on the famous
George Hickson's certainties, Muirhead made
no bets on the minor races, but when the time
arrived for the Lancashire Plate, he sought
out Lunn and with the best imitation which he
could muster of Fairlegh's manner, asked,
"What priceKing John?"

"He's heard me yelling '2 to 1 the field' for
half-an-hour past," said Lunn with blighting
scorn, "and comes and asks me 'what price
King John?' Do you think he is an outsider?
Would you like 100 to 1? Shall I lay you 1000
to 8? Here, hand over that tenner that you're
holding. Put him down 20 to 10, Jack," went
on the bookmaker, seeing that he had a new
hand to deal with. "Here's a ticket for you,
young man, and if King John wins, and half-a-
dozen nice young men come up and say that
they are Sunday school teachers and will help
you to get the money if you'll give them the
ticket, just hold on to it."

The whole of this speech having been totally-
incomprehensible to Muirhead he went back to
the Stands rather uncertain as to whether he
had or not backed St. John to win, and if he
had, for how much. A neighbour in the

Stands good-naturedly explained the meaning of his race-card to him sufficiently to allow of his making out which were King John's colours. He watched the whole business of the parade and canter with a fever of anxiety which was new and rather pleasant, but after the start his spirits sank to a very low point, for King John was running last and making apparently not the slightest effort to get to the front. Some anxiety was expressed even among the more intelligent spectators, and murmurs of "too late"; "Why don't you let him go?" came from the Stands. Then, suddenly, a great shout went up from the enclosures and to Muirhead's amazed eyes King John seemed simply to race past his opponents as if they had all suddenly stopped. One moment he was racing at the tail of a dozen scattered horses; the next he was galloping easily in front of them all, while the other jockeys were spurring and floundering in desperate and futile endeavours to overtake him. A hoarse shout of delight escaped Muirhead's lips as the winning post was passed, and a number was put up on the judge's box, and spectators here and there shouted King John's name. "Has he really won?" asked Muirhead, almost capering with excitement and putting his hand on the shoulder of the man who had explained his race-card to him.

"Won!  Blimey! ain't you got no eyes?  Do you think it's a donkey race, where the last one wins?  Or do you think he will be disqualified for winning by the length of a street?  Lord!" and with this not very clear reply Muirhead had to be content.

He was better satisfied with it when Lunn handed him his own ten pounds and another twenty with it.  He walked up and down the enclosures with his hands clasped behind him, his lips moving slightly, his eyes blazing with excitement.  Gambling success, which affects so many different men in so many different ways (though there is a dreary monotony about its end), had completely intoxicated this man. Every other idea, hope, regret and desire was burnt up by this fever.  He thought of nothing and talked of nothing but the races of Thursday and Saturday.  In spite of all the popular nonsense which is talked about the joy afforded by money properly earned, I cannot imagine any one who has tried the two denying that money won by successful gambling affords ten times more pleasure to the winner than the other.  This fact is unfortunately hidden by the more obvious and better known fact that to win ten pounds is a certain and not very lengthily spun-out prelude to losing a hundred. The loss of these hundred is a black and unpleasant curtain obscuring from the memory the rapture of winning the ten, and the only point in which a hard-earned ten-pound note can favourably compare with one won on the race-course is that it stays longer in one's pocket. But these reflections being very immoral I bring them to an apologetic end.

# CHAPTER XXIII

Muirhead went over to Hartshill on the Sunday after his debut on the turf in order to hear the latest news of Gerald.   Hitherto it had always been with some reluctance and yet with a sense of hopeless attraction that he paid such visits.   The majority of men, I imagine, are not very constant lovers; rejection is to them a bucket of cold water, effectively and after an extremely short time curing them of their passion.   Of course to be liked by a young lady who cannot, nevertheless, quite bring her love up to marrying point, is tantalizing, and one is sorry for a man who finds himself in such a position, and can excuse him if he goes on hoping.   But there must really be something wrong with a man's brain who continues to be violently in love with a woman who is, and confesses herself to be, totally indifferent to him, or even says that she rather dislikes him than otherwise.   To sympathise with such a person, to listen to his outcries and try to soothe his woe, is impossible.   He is not only a public nuisance but a fool, and the kindest of his friends is the one who tells this to him with the most emphasis. The mere fact that there are a great many more women than men in the world is conclusive proof that such lamentations for the obduracy of one of them are preposterous.

Muirhead, however, was one of the idiots in question, and had no kind friend to point out his folly. He hung about Monica constantly, enduring her snubs, which grew more numerous every week, abjectly thankful for a few kind words, and filled day and night with restless craving to see her and speak to her again. He left his rooms every Sunday afternoon with the intention of going over to Hartshill, and though he sometimes turned back he more often went on. These and other visits ended in his having a few moments' conversation with Monica, and an hour's drearily dragging talk with Miss Bertram, and usually ended up with a glimpse of Reggie Nicholson in the garden. But for the sake of those few minutes' talk, for a sight of this girl and a touch of her hand, Muirhead would risk Miss Bertram's open boredom and Monica's more active disapproval day after day, returning each time to his house with fresh heart-ache, fresh fury against fate, fresh hatred of his successful rival. It was of course hard on him that he

had no means or leisure to go to the Himalayas,
the Rocky Mountains or other refuges of disap-
pointed love, and it was unfortunate that he
had not Gerald there to assure him how soon
he would get over it if he would make a little
effort.

Nicholson senior was with Miss Bertram, and
Monica, instead of as usual saying a few words
to Muirhead and then departing, felt obliged
to stop and entertain him. The man had a
feeling that he had better not mention anywhere, especially here, what he had been doing
lately, and so spoke about other matters. To
his own surprise he talked more fluently and
easily than usual; there was less embarrassment and even a little gaiety in his words. He
cared much less than usual when the girl, who
was not a great adept at hiding her feelings,
and to say truth was more than moderately
rude to this visitor on most occasions without
altogether adequate cause, let slip some of her
usual discouraging comments. Even when
Reggie came into the room and Muirhead saw
her face light up with relief and joy, the sight
hardly caused his pulses to beat an atom faster.
He did not exactly realize all this at the time;
the habit of being miserable, the attitude of
disappointment had become so fixed in him
during the last three months that his mind, so

to speak, took for granted that on each of these occasions it was to experience an increase of grief; but as he walked away from the house and as he sat at dinner that evening it suddenly struck him that, instead of brooding over Monica's unkindness, instead of going over all the words which she had spoken to him and he to her, trying to find hope in them and succeeding in finding failure;—instead of doing this he was looking at a mental picture of a race horse with splendid limbs stretched out as it moved across the turf, that he was hearing the cries of an excited and happy crowd: "King John wins!" "The favourite walks in!" He laughed to himself and then shook himself a little impatiently: "I can't go to any more races this month," he said, "but I think I'll try and manage to get down to Newmarket for a day next month. Fairlegh says that's the real place to see it. Yes! I think I'll put in a day, perhaps two, there next month. What did he say that big race was? The . . . the Cesarewitch."

When Nicholson came over next morning, the last day of his work at the Freehold Society, Muirhead was quite polite to him. Indeed, to his own astonishment he found that he was really rather sorry that the lad was going  He had not actually reached the point of liking

him, but some slight regret was certainly
caused by the reflection that he would have to
teach some one else Nicholson's work.   He
himself understood so little of this business,
which was daily growing more complicated,
that he very cordially disliked having to
initiate any one else into it.

Among the letters which he received that
morning was one telling him to address some
fresh remonstrance to Miss Bertram about the
sale of her shares, and he thought it worth
while to say a word to Reggie about it.

"It's really nothing to us," he said, with an
elaborate unconcern which could not have
deceived a child, "but it seems a pity for her
own sake that she should give up what is paying her so well.   If Benson has been instructed
to sell the shares, of course he will, and I do
not suppose that he will find any difficulty in
doing it, but I think I shall ask her again to
change her mind."

"It would not be the slightest use," said
Nicholson curtly.

"Have you asked her yourself?"

"No," said the other, without further
excuses or enlargement.

"Well, she is going to do a very silly thing,
and I think you would do very well to try and
prevent her."

"She has her reasons, and I quite agree with them," said the boy, flushing. Muirhead looked at his face, and in a sudden flash all his former suspicions and anxieties revived. Gerald, he felt certain, had warned Miss Bertram, and this was the result. Nothing else could possibly account for such an unusual action on her part as the making and acting upon her own decision about money matters.

After a minute's silence, Reggie asked, "When will a purchaser be found for the shares?"

"How should I know?" said Muirhead. "People are constantly investing money, but I can't control it. Holiday time is hardly over yet. She must wait a few weeks before any dealings in the shares begin."

"Hadn't Mr. Robinson better preach another sermon?" asked Nicholson; "or is it only when he wants to sell his own shares that he does that?"

"You had better ask him," said Muirhead with a sudden grim laugh, "for here he is."

Luke Robinson in effect walked into the Office at that moment. Since Gerald's departure his visits there had become more frequent, for he felt himself safe in patronising its present occupants. This morning his face looked grave and severe. He bowed severely to Nicholson and Muirhead, took a seat, and crossed his arms with reproof in every gesture. After a few words about some business matters he asked to see Muirhead by himself, and Reggie left the room.

"I extremely regret to hear, Mr. Muirhead," he began, "that you have been to the Manchester Races twice."

Muirhead looked annoyed.   He was not anxious that his recent actions should come to the ears of any of the Freehold people, and certainly Robinson was the last of them whom he desired or expected to hear of it.   Well as he knew Robinson's position as a paid agent of the Society, ready to put his religious work at their disposal, he had none of Gerald's scorn for the man's hypocrisy, and he had, on the other hand, all Gerald's admiration of his talents and influence.   Therefore he answered humbly enough that he had certainly been to Manchester, but saw no harm in it.

"No harm!   I am astonished, Mr. Muirhead! I could not have imagined that any one could deny the wickedness and folly of turf gambling, or that a person in your responsible position could encourage it."

"I think you overrate the wickedness of it," said Muirhead weakly.

"The  matter  is  beyond  all  argument,"

said Robinson.  "Every man connected with racing is a scoundrel.  The jockeys and trainers and owners, as every one knows, rarely mean to win races; they only want to win bets, to swindle the people who go to races out of their money.  I cannot imagine how any man could be such a fool as to let himself be swindled like that, and I have no sympathy at all with the victims of these scoundrels.  You will have no sympathy for your losses from any right-minded man."

"But I happen to have won," said the other quietly.

"You won!  You made bets and won money!" exclaimed Robinson in horrified astonishment; and then paused for a moment, his natural respect and admiration for any man who made money by any means almost causing him to lose his presence of mind, and ask Muirhead to take him too to Manchester.

"This is really a very serious matter indeed," he went on at last.  "I half hoped that you would tell me at any rate that you hadn't made any bets there.  I cannot express to you the horror with which I regard all such gambling. I see on every side among my flock the tragedies of ruin caused by it.  I see men robbing their masters to pay their debts; starving their wives and children to find this gambling

money; neglecting all their business, religious
duties, all their affairs earthly and heavenly, in
order to give themselves up to this disgraceful
gambling. It is a horror to me; and now I
find that one of the leaders of the Freehold
Society, a Society with which I concern myself
so actively because I believe that it is doing
moral as well as material good to all, has taken
to gambling on the turf! It is most painful to
me."

Muirhead sat in silence under this onslaught.
His main idea was fear lest Robinson should do
him mischief with Marshall or Lord Eastney,
but he really could not lower himself by asking
Robinson to keep silence.

"How much did you win?" asked the
Wesleyan minister abruptly.

"Thirty or forty pounds, though really I
don't quite see  .  .  ."

"Oh!" There was a distinct tone of disappointment in Robinson's voice. It would have
suggested to Gerald Franklin that the minister
had been considering the possibility of levying
a little black-mail, of demanding half the winnings as the price of silence. Neither, probably, would Gerald have had much hesitation
in chaffing Robinson about such an intention.
"Are you going to any more of these disgraceful places?"

"I really haven't thought about the matter at all," said Muirhead; but guilty recollections of his plans to see the Cesarewitch made him flush a little and look uneasily at his companion.

"It will be a most painful matter for me," said Robinson, noting the answer of the man's face rather than of his words, "to take any decisive steps about it; but you will readily understand, Mr. Muirhead, that the Freehold cannot afford to allow such wrong-doing. That is to say," he added, feeling that he had put the case with more truth than discretion, "no society, however great and well established, could tolerate such wrong. I must give you distinctly to understand that if I hear of its repetition I shall write at once to Mr. Marshall."

# CHAPTER XXIV

"What would you do if some one called you a liar?" asked a youthful, pugnacious acquaintance of mine, talking to a contemporary.

"To my face?" asked the other.

"Yes."

"Well," was the reply, "about how big a person?"

This unfortunately is a consideration which has to enter into the calculations of all of us. When a man calls us names and we want to make an effective reply, we positively must know how big the man is in mind and influence, in person and body, so as to be quite sure that his answer when he resumes the discussion will not be too crushing.  Now, unfortunately, outside a certain groove, Muirhead knew very little of human nature.  He could judge his own friends and equals fairly well, but he could not sum up a great man.  Robinson was a great man—a great scoundrel, of course, but certainly great—and required a man of equal intellectual size to deal with him.  Gerald Franklin, who knew what was in the man's

mind as well (to use a vulgar phrase) as if he
had been down there with a candle, would have
met this lecture on gambling by a few home
truths of an extremely unpleasant character
about Mr. Robinson's public and private life,
and would have told him more forcibly than
politely to mind his own business; but fortunately for the minister Franklin was not there.
Robinson had an absolute incapacity for mind-
ing his own business (and might indeed have
pleaded that it was his business to mind other
peoples)'; and a restless resolute way of plung-
ing his hand into the affairs of everybody in
the town.   On the plea of forcing the English
Church authorities of the neighbourhood to
recognise the importance of his own sect, he
thrust himself into Town Councils and charities, committees and bazaars, strikes, political
meetings and newspaper controversies on every
conceivable subject.   His powers of work were
immense.   Like the border-lord who killed
fifty Scots at a breakfast, and washed his
hands, and said to his wife: "Fie on this quiet
life, I want work," Robinson simply could not
find enough to do.   Not only did he want to
take the souls and bodies, the work and pleas-
ures of everybody in the Potteries into his own
charge, but he would have liked another
obedient congregation in London as well, and

desired nothing more than an opportunity for showing the London authorities of the Freehold Society a few specimens of his religious zeal and financial skill.  He would have liked at this moment to write a long letter to Lord Eastney on the subject of the iniquities of the turf and the scandal of Muirhead's association with it.  Muirhead had an instinctive suspicion of this fact, though he knew little about the would-be writer's motives; therefore he cowered under Robinson's threats and said to himself that if he was going to indulge in this new amusement, it would have to be done quietly and at a greater distance from Staffordshire. Newmarket answered his purpose very well, and in October he accordingly decided to get himself four days' holiday and go to the Second October Meeting.

But here fortune played him more than one scurvy trick.  The first persons that he met in the High Street on his arrival were Lady Eastney and Bertie Alford, the former of whom, after a slightly puzzled stare, remembered him and bowed with a look of very decided astonishment.  At St. Pancras he had bought various sporting papers and studied them in the train on the way down to Newmarket, finding that there were many people to supply the place of Mr. Fairlegh as a prophet; that in fact there

was almost an embarrassment of tips. He
found further that each paper gave two, three,
or sometimes four selections for the same race
in different columns, and he conceived the
brilliant idea of adding them all up and select-
ing the horse chosen by the majority. This
scheme was again, however, upset by a most
obliging and affable gentleman whom he met
on the racecourse and who, although connected with half the stables in Newmarket
and the possessor of all their information and
all their secrets, and therefore, one would
imagine, in a position to make a fortune once a
day, was willing to take charge of Muirhead,
and for a consideration which was certainly
trifling, considering what he had to offer in
return for it, to tell him what was going to win
every race. But the owners and trainers of the
horses were lamentably inaccurate in the information which they had confided so positively
to Muirhead's new friend, for not a single horse
which he backed won on the first day of the
Meeting, and he lost under the pressure of his
friend's persuasion the whole of the fifty
pounds which he had brought with him.
Angrily resolved to get it back again, he telegraphed to Newcastle for money to be sent to
him, and went up to the course the next day
resolved to follow his own original newspaper

scheme.  But this worked no better than the
other, and the professional tipster turning up
again later in the day and persuading him to
plunge rather heavily on a horse in the last
race, he again lost all the money which he had
in his possession.  Excitedly angry, as much
at his own ill-luck as at the loss of the money,
and with the real gambler's resolve to get it
all back again by any means, he telegraphed to
Newcastle for a hundred pounds to be sent to
him, and began the third day of the Meeting
in that state of mind in which men cheerfully
commit the first crime or folly which comes to
their hands.

He lost £45 of this money over the first
three races, then wandering about in the
Birdcage he heard two men talking of a horse
called Tealeaf, which was running in the
Middle Park Plate.  One man was apparently
the owner, the other had come up to him saying that he had put £200 each way on Tealeaf.
The owner, whom Muirhead recognised from
his photographs as a famous peer and politician
with an income which ran into six figures,
answered very politely: "Yes, I think he will
win.  I have got £10 on him myself;" and the
lad who had spoken blushed a little.  One of
the idiotic resolves which come to gamblers of
Muirhead's type, immediately took possession

of the man, and collecting all the rest of his
money, without leaving himself enough for his
hotel-bill, he went up to Lunn, and the numbers for the Middle Park Plate now being up,
asked: "What price Tealeaf?"    His knowledge of turf-language was now improved, and
he could even bargain a little about the odds.

"Sixes," was the reply.

"But I want sevens to win," said Muirhead,
"and 7 to 4 for a place.  It is only for £30 each
way."

"Go and eat your £30," was the brief and
somewhat inconsequent reply.

"But they are offering sevens over there."

"Here, Jack!"    Lunn turned to his clerk,
"Give this gentleman your book and pencil.
He's come to do our business for us, and he
knows such a ——— about it that he must do it
all his own way too."

"I only asked for 7 to 1 instead of 6," said
Muirhead.    "It's only one point more."

"You see, Jack, the gentleman knows that 7
is 1 more than 6.  I told you he knew all
about this trade.  I saw in his eye from the
first that he wasn't such a ——— fool as he looks.
I take some credit for seeing that too.  Now,
young man! if you want 6 to 1 about Tealeaf
and 5 to 4 for a place, hand your money over.  If
you don't, make room for somebody who does."

Muirhead handed over his money and walked rapidly up and down the ring in a state of wild excitement until the horses came out and cantered down to the starting post.   Then he went and stood on one of the Stands, staring with white face at the horses as they moved about under the starter's orders.   There was a long delay at the post with several breaks-away, during which Muirhead had ample time to realise what a very idiotic act he had recently committed.   He was as certain as if it had already happened that the horse would get beaten, and that the next which he proposed to back, and now would be unable to back for lack of the money, would win.   For a moment a wild idea came into his mind of going up to Lunn and imploring him to cancel the bet, but there was a crowd of persons round the famous bookmaker doing business with him, and he had not the courage to go among them on such an errand.   The flag fell at last.   It was half a minute before Muirhead could distinguish the colours, so much did his hand which held his glasses shake.   He saw Tealeaf at last in the middle of a whole cluster of horses who were apparently shutting him in, and he dropped his glasses and turned away for a moment muttering prayers, entreaties, threats to the horse's jockey, so that his companions turned round and laughed at him. Then he looked again. The little group of horses had parted asunder, and Tealeaf was in front of it with only two horses in front of him. For a moment Muirhead's heart gave a great jump which sent the blood in a scarlet flush to his face. Then the next moment there began a motion of Watts' arms which Muirhead already knew to mean that the horse was tiring and stopping; but with his eyes fixed on Tealeaf he did not notice that the riders of the two horses which were in front of him had picked up their whips and were already desperately trying to keep their places. Slowly but steadily Tealeaf drew up to them. Watts picked up his whip, flourished it once, brought it down once, and then Tealeaf with a final effort drew clear away from his two opponents. Muirhead watched him go past a length in front of the others, he gazed at the picture almost with fear in his face. Surely he could only have won such a sum in order that it might be taken away afterwards—in order that he might rise to the highest point of exultation and have the greatest possible fall. When the winning number went up, he asked one of his neighbours whether that was really Tealeaf's number; then he asked another whether he too thought that Tealeaf had really won; another whether there was likely to be any objection; another whether Lunn was likely to refuse to pay. He had thirty or forty men in Tattersal's Ring laughing at him before the "All right" was called. Two of the most skilful ticket-snatchers on the course stuck to him and made resolute attempts to get hold of his ticket; but the money, a sum of £217 10s. found its way to his pocket safely at last, and the man's elation was pitiful to watch. He was the worst of winners and losers, a gambler as to whose ultimate fate there could be no possible doubt.

He left Newmarket that night and arrived home in time for business on Friday morning. Feeling the absolute necessity of having some one to talk to about his luck, he invited Fairlegh to lunch at his rooms, and told him this history over a bottle and a half of dry Monopole; champagne at unseasonable hours and meals being with such people an inevitable part of successful betting.

A suspicion that he had much better have held his tongue which occurred to him that evening was confirmed next morning by the arrival of Luke Robinson.

"I feel it now my absolute duty to write to Lord Eastney about this," said Robinson. "It is most painful to me, but not only should I feel in any case bound to do all in my power to stop the reckless proceedings which you have begun, but for the sake of the Freehold I am bound to stop them. You will ruin yourself and the Society. I hear wherever I go now stories about your bets and your winnings. Your winnings most have been something enormous"—there was a queer tone in the speaker's voice as he hinted the last question which would have made Gerald Franklin laugh and ask him whether a ten-pound note would be of any good—"I cannot allow such a scandal to go on for a single day longer."

"My winnings only just paid my expenses," said Muirhead uneasily and untruthfully. "I can't stop your writing to Lord Eastney, but I cannot imagine what there is to make such a fuss about.''

''The amount of your winnings or what you did with them matters nothing,'' said Robin-son.  One might have imagined there was a tone of disappointment in his voice.  ''It's the gambling which horrifies me, and which I must have stopped.''

''You had better,'' said Muirhead rather coldly, for his elation at his own success had taken away some of his fear of the Wesleyan minister, ''speak to young Franklin about it. He is coming down here to-morrow for a few days.''

''Is he?''  Robinson's face fell like that of a child who is told that its holidays are over and that the governess is coming back next day. ''Is he?  What is that for?''

''On private family business,'' said Muir-head, who didn't know the reason but thought it would be wholesome for Robinson to believe that he, Muirhead, knew more about Gerald's intentions than the minister himself.

In fact, Muirhead had made a good shot, and Gerald had come home in consequence of a consultation with Marshall in which Marshall had begged the boy to go down and see whether he could first persuade his aunt not to sell her shares, and then persuade Monica to

invest her recently acquired fortune in the
Society. For the Carlton Gold Mine shares
had been sold for a sum of £14,000, and
Monica as an heiress was one of the latest
sensations of the neighbourhood.

Gerald arrived at home with a pretty clear
idea that he would have some difficulty in
carrying out Marshall's orders. His aunt had
clearly been warned by some one. He knew
her previous opinion of the Freehold, saw from
her letter to Marshall that she had received
some additional information to confirm it, and
thought it highly improbable that he would be
able to say anything to change her mind.
Besides this, he had no intention of allowing
either his aunt or his sister to be involved in
the final crash. Even if he had persuaded
them to invest the money he would have made
them sell the shares before anything went
hopelessly wrong, and in that case it struck him
now that they would hold their shares, if
bought, for a very short time. So it was
without desire or expectation of success in his
mission that he arrived at Hartshill.

The current of excitement over the Freehold
Society was still running strong in North
Staffordshire, and Gerald was besieged with
questions on all sides. He went over to see
Muirhead at once, and was amused to notice

the confusion into which the Newcastle Office
had dropped since his departure. Stories
about Muirhead's racing outbreak were told to
him by various people, at which he laughed
and said that Muirhead was a rich man who
could easily afford to amuse himself. The
others should invest all their money in the
Freehold, and then they too would have some
to bet with. He found Lowe in a state of
great exultation, having just bought a carriage
and pair of horses, built a small stable, refur-
nished his vicarage and begun a course of
dinners, garden parties and other country
entertainments which were certainly an
extremely good advertisement for the Freehold. The Vicar of Hartshill talked to Gerald
with a gratitude and affection which rather
touched the boy and made him view this
development with some concern. . . .
Lowe, he resolved, should be one to receive a
word of warning in time, if it were possible.
He asked the Vicar whether he would give his
consent to Monica's money being invested in
the Society, and of course received Lowe's
prompt assent. "What better investment
could anybody possibly want?" said the man,
looking round on his new chairs and rosewood
cabinets and the new Erard piano.

"But you understand of course," said Gerald

a little impatiently and speaking for once on impulse, "that the Society is not a legal investment for trust money, and that you would be liable for the money if anything went wrong."

"If anything went wrong!" repeated the parson with a smile. "I suppose that you know best whether that is likely to happen and would not be here asking me these questions about your own sister's money if it were."

Gerald got up to go, feeling thoroughly annoyed. Lowe's smiling certainty that everything must be right angered him. Remarkable as it may seem, it had really never occurred to him before that he was doing a most infamous thing in even risking the loss of Miss Bertram's and Monica's money. Was he in point of fact perfectly certain to be able to save it at the last moment? Of course not! the odds were rather against his being able to do so than otherwise. The errand on which he had come down here was, he confessed to himself, an outrageous one. He would do his best to persuade the two women to agree to invest their money as proposed, but if they did agree to it, it by no means followed that he would allow it to be done.

Monica was delighted to see her brother again. Since Lady Eastney's conversation with her she had been extremely anxious about him, and had urged Miss Bertram to insist upon withdrawing him from his present business, even if considerable penalties attached to breaking the agreement with Marshall. But the woman did not quite see her way to do this, the fact being that she only half believed what Lady Eastney had told her. The Marchioness' words, however honestly meant at the time, were as likely as not only the outcome of some quarrel with her husband, or with some other principals in the Society. Her quick eyes had seen the relations in which Lady Eastney and Bertie Alford stood to one another, and oddly enough she had more than half made up her mind that this warning was the result of some complication between herself, her husband and her lover. Gerald had therefore been allowed to continue his London work in peace. The boy was pleased to be at home again and once more among the circle of people who regarded him with admiring awe. The flattery of Muirhead and Lowe had pleased him immensely, and he was in a very good humour when he arrived at Hartshill.

"Is Nicholson flourishing?" he asked Monica gaily; "and aren't you very glad to have me out of the way when he is over here? I suppose you have to go into another room, Aunt

Christina, when he is here, and leave them all to themselves?  Are you allowed to come in to tea with them?"

"I believe Reggie likes Aunt Christina better than he does me," said Monica.  "But now you've got to tell us about Susan Ethridge. You are beginning to blush, I see.  Is she very nice, Gerald?"

"Yes, very," said the boy decisively.

"And pretty?"

"I really don't know, I never looked.  I do not know, on my word," he went on, answering Monica's laughter.  "She's the sort of girl whose looks you don't think about when she's talking to you.  I like her very much."

Monica, who had received more than one long and enthusiastic letter about Gerald from her friend Susan, was amused and interested at her brother's admiration.  She had never heard him speak of a girl before, so far as she could recollect; his conversation having been confined entirely to men and money.  She went on thinking of this new development even when the talk had drifted back to Gerald's more usual themes, and when he began to speak to her about the investment she was thinking all the time of the other matter.  She shook her head laughingly at his proposal, and refused at first even to discuss it seriously.

"Reggie wouldn't hear of it," she said.
"Of course you don't understand just yet what
it means to have a masterful person saying to
you that you are to do this and are not to do
that, though perhaps some day you may find
out what it is like. Is Susan very strong-
minded, Gerald?"

"I wish you would talk seriously about the
thing, my good girl. It's the worst of trying
to talk business with any girl that there is sure
to be a young man hanging about and getting
himself mixed up with the affair somewhere.
You know perfectly well that Nicholson has got
nothing to do with it. It's for you and Aunt
Christina and Mr. Lowe to decide, and you can
take my word for it that Nicholson isn't such a
young fool as to refuse £1500 a year interest
on your money instead of £500. What earthly
objection have you to the investment? Money
can't lie in a bank, you know, and must be put
somewhere."

"Reggie is going to consult his father's
lawyers about it."

"But the money isn't his to do what he likes
with," says Gerald, who was getting quite angry
at his sister's resistance, and was now determined
to persuade her into doing what he suggested.

"Aunt Christina asked him to see about it for
us."

"Well, she'd no business to do anything of
the sort," said the boy.  "Lowe is the proper
person to ask, and if she wanted some other
advice, she should have called Marshall.    I
can't understand why she should suddenly turn
round and insult the whole lot of us like this.
It is simply absurd.   Now are you going to be
reasonable, and think of buying some shares?"

"No, I am not," said Monica briefly.

"Do you mean to say that when you have
got the best investment in England offered to
you, with every guarantee that anybody could
possibly want, with all your friends recommending the thing, you are going to chuck all
advice to the winds, because a chap with whom
you happen to be in love, and who knows nothing on earth about the subject, happens to
think differently?"

"If you like to put it like that, you can,"
said Monica; "but the fact remains that I am
not going to let Mr. Marshall or Mr. Lowe
have anything to do with investing my
£14,000."

"Or me either?"

"No, nor you either.   We all know how
clever you are, and I am sure you would get
me very good interest, but I simply don't want
to speculate."

"Speculate, my good girl!   You don't know

what the word means.  You are simply talking preposterous nonsense."

"That is not a thing which Monica often does," said Miss Bertram, who had come into the room just in time to hear this last sentence.

"I was speaking to her about money matters," said Gerald, who had meant to persuade Monica first, and Miss Bertram afterwards, and was rather annoyed by the interruption.

"Gerald wants me to buy shares in the Freehold with my gold mine money," said Monica.

Miss Bertram had more than suspected from the first that this was the object of Gerald's visit, and her voice was more decided than pleasant when she said: "I think I may answer Gerald on your behalf, my dear, better than you can yourself, as I happen to have the power of disposing of your money; and I can say without any hesitation, that I have not the slightest intention of letting you do what he suggests."

"Mr. Lowe, who is one of the trustees, and a man of business, is perfectly willing," said Gerald rather sulkily.  "I don't know why you should object."

"I can't tell you my reasons.  It is really not worth while arguing the matter.  My mind is quite made up."

"You can't tell me your reasons?" repeated Gerald, interrogatively.

"Well, I don't mean to, if you prefer that answer."

"We shall all think it a little  .  .  ."

"Gerald, I do not wish to have any more words about the matter at all.  If you have been asked to make enquiries about our intentions, you have made your enquiries and have had your answer.  The answer is perfectly irrevocable.  I daresay Monica has already told you herself that she did not care for the investment.  Now I add that if she did like it, if Mr. Lowe advocated it as strongly as he could, nothing whatever would make me change my mind.  Monica is not going to buy any shares in the Freehold, and I am going to sell my own shares directly I can find any one to buy them. That, by the way, does not seem to be very easy to do just now."

"Holiday time is only just over," said the boy in a low frightened voice.  "It will be all right when every one comes back to London; but they say that the fine weather has kept people away very late this year."  He muttered the excuse mechanically, as though repeating some lesson which he had learnt by heart, and then left the room.

# CHAPTER XXVI

The report which Gerald sent to Marshall at
the end of forty-eight hours' stay in North
Staffordshire brought that gentleman down in
person by the next train, and some anxious
consultations between himself, Robinson, and
Gerald took place in the Newcastle office.   The
affairs both of the Freehold and the Merton
Insurance Company were in wild disorder.
There had been a great falling off in insurance
policies and share-buying, and it was impossible to gather from the hopelessly entangled
figures what was going wrong or why.   The
purchase of the Arkhill property had been com-
pleted, and the boring for coal had been begun
in several directions; but so far it had not been
found in paying quantities, and the unsuccessful shafts were there for all men to see.   The
talk of failure went on and grew.   A builder
who was concerned with the Freehold in certain new villas and streets which were being
built near Dentley became bankrupt suddenly,
and denounced Marshall for his failure.   Very
irrationally; for these were only small acci-

dents which had happened in twenty different
parts of the Society's properties, and could not
have affected any sound company; people
began to shake their heads, and to talk of
selling shares. One or two indeed tried
to do so, and found that it was difficult, and
told their neighbours about the difficulty.
Paragraphs were put in the local papers under
"London Gossip," asserting that a dividend of
a perfectly phenomenal character would be
declared at the next half-yearly meeting, but
the business folks of the Potteries laughed at it.

"We must have another sermon, Mr. Robinson," said Marshall, hardly able to hide his
uneasiness. "We must have several more.
You must tell these people that when they try
to sell shares in this ridiculous way they
are in fact speculating, and that speculating is
the worst of sins. Couldn't you preach a
course of sermons about it?"

'I could," said Robinson, "and their effect
would be immediate and very beneficial."

'Very good. When will you begin? The
sooner the better."

"I said that I could do it," said the Wesleyan
minister drily. "The thanks I got for doing it
last time were not, however, so warm that I
should care to do it again."

The two speakers looked at one another, with

a grim smile on one side and impatient annoyance on the other.

"Mr. Robinson is, I feel sure, going to demand something perfectly preposterous," said Gerald in his smooth, ironical voice, "but if I were you, Mr. Marshall, I should explain to him, first, that he very much overrates the effect of his sermons, and, secondly, that if they had any high money value to us (which they have not), we simply have not got the money to pay for them.  Why not ask Mr. Lowe to preach for us?"

"You might go and ask him certainly," said Marshall.  "We should like Mr. Robinson's sermons, too, if the price is not too high."

"I object, gentlemen," said the minister, red with passion.  "I object most strongly to these remarks about my sermons being paid for.  It is insolence to suggest that my spiritual instruction to my flock is being bought at a price.  What has it to do with my sermons if I have land which I wish to sell; if I wish to dispose of the rest of that little Dentley estate, a part of which you have already bought of me at a most ludicrously small price; if I have now ten more acres of land, with three houses on it, and want to sell this?"

Gerald laughed rudely.  "We want to understand clearly that a sermon is to go with each

house.   Then I daresay Mr. Marshall will buy.
Now for the price.   Oh! wait a bit; here comes
Mr. Lowe down the street, and there is my
aunt and Canon Hobart.   They've all met, and
look as if they were talking about coming
across here?   Yes!   That's just what they are
going to do.   Now, we might arrange a regular
course of sermons all over the Potteries, though
I am afraid that Canon Hobart would not do us
very much good.''

The three visitors came in as Gerald had
said, and began various explanations of their
arrival.   Miss Bertram, who was in front, said
she had come in to speak to Marshall about the
sale of her shares.   Lowe said that he had
come to help persuade her, even at the last
minute, to abstain from an act which he
genuinely thought to be extremely silly.
Hobart was there, though he did not say so, to
put that inconvenient question to Marshall
about the Hospital.

Standing in the background, awaiting his
turn to speak, the canon took one more good
look at Mr. Joshua Marshall, and then suddenly, as some long-sought recollection will
flash across us at last at the moment when we
least expect it and are least searching for it, the
recollection of this man flashed into Hobart's
brain.   He knew him now.   The last time he

had seen him he was standing before the Board
of Directors of the North Stafford Infirmary
evading questions about some accounts, pro-
fessing his inability to understand certain
points, and promising to have a complete statement ready for the next meeting.  Hobart
remembered how at the time a sudden touch of
suspicion had come to him.  He was the least
astonished of all the committee at Marshall's
flight.  With this memory at last firmly in his
mind, he stared at the man, and only wondered
now why he had not recalled his face, and especially his voice, before.  The man was speaking to his sister—Hobart supposed that she did
not know him and was surprised—assuring her
that the Company was never in a better condition, cajoling her by all means in his power
into keeping her shares.  The canon listened
with quiet amusement, and then detecting, or
thinking that he detected, signs of wavering in
Miss Bertram, he stepped forward and stood in
front of Marshall with his arms folded and a
slight smile on his face.

"You have a great facility in explaining
figures, Mr. Marshall," he said.  "If I remember right, some years ago you promised to give
a certain explanation of the accounts of the
North Stafford Infirmary.  Is the explanation
ready yet?"

# CHAPTER XXVII

Marshall sat down in a chair and looked from Hobart to his sister, and back again to Hobart. He attempted no bluff, no denial or explanation.   If he had been recognised, he had been recognised, and the mischief was done.   If you meet a man in the street, and he says, "Hallo, Jones! how are you?" it is extremely improbable that it will be of the slightest use for you to turn round and say, "I am not Jones; you are really quite mistaken."   The odds are that your friend will argue less about your identity than your sanity.   Epictetus sagely remarked, "I am evidently conscious of my own identity, because when I intend to swallow anything I never carry it to your mouth but to my own;" and so when a man has taken his greetings and hand-shakes to a certain person, that person is not going to convince him by the strongest arguments or the subtlest philosophy that he is talking to some one else.   I believe myself that even when a man addresses some one like this, and is greeted perfectly truthfully with a polite explanation that he is quite mistaken, he goes away in nine cases out of ten with the impression that his supposed friend is either wanted by the police, or that for some nefarious purpose he is making clumsy efforts at disguise.

Marshall at any rate had the wit to see that denial of himself would have no other result than to irritate Hobart; and that was not a thing which he wished to do. Therefore he looked at him in mild deprecation, then looked at Lowe to see if he understood what this accusation meant, and then glanced through an open door into a room where Gerald and Muirhead and Robinson had temporarily retired as if appealing to Hobart not to speak before them just yet. The rector softened a little at Marshall's immediate surrender, as Marshall had judged that he would, and began to think that he wanted some time for reflection before following up his advantage. Therefore when Miss Bertram turned to him in frightened appeal, saying: "Spare him, Canon Hobart, for my sake and Monica's; spare him! You will not do anything just yet, will you?" he answered her reassuringly.

"I don't understand what is the matter," said Lowe. "Had I better not know? If so, of course, I will go away."

"It is simply," said Hobart quietly, "that Mr. Marshall is in point of fact Mr. Joshua

Bertram, Miss Bertram's brother, who was Secretary of the Infirmary some years ago and left suddenly under circumstances of which you have, I believe, heard. He went to Spain, as I understood at the time, and for Miss Bertram's sake we took no further steps in the matter. What we ought to do now is an affair which requires consideration."

"I have been working honestly ever since. I have done my best to remedy the wrong," said Marshall very humbly. "Everybody knows all about the work which I am doing now; it is perfectly straightforward, useful, honest. My sister knows all about my life now and approves of it. Don't you, Christina?"

The woman leant against the table sick with terror and misery. After what Lady Eastney had told her she could not and would not say "yes" in answer to her brother's last question, but to say "no" was like giving Hobart leave to do his worst. Fortunately the rector was puzzling out something else in his own mind.

"I don't quite understand," he said, turning to Miss Bertram. "Did you know who Mr. Marshall was all the time?"

"I knew him the first time he came down here. Before that I did not even know that he was in England."

"You should have told some one who he was.

You should have forbidden him to bring this business down here," said the rector irritably.

"Before Lady Eastney told me . . ." began Miss Bertram and then stopped in confusion.

"She knew all the time, of course, that my business was a perfectly honest one," said Marshall, perceiving that his sister would not make this reply herself. Even in the middle of this nervous business he had time to note and register the fact which he had half suspected already, that it was Lady Eastney who had warned Miss Bertram against the Freehold Society, and advised her to sell her shares. There was silence for half a minute and then Hobart moved towards the door.

"Are you going to have my brother arrested?" muttered Miss Bertram, beginning to cry.

"No," said Hobart, "I don't suppose there is any good in that. Of course I must talk the matter over with one or two others first, and we shall probably make certain conditions with regard to this Society. I cannot tell you what they will be yet. I know too little of the work myself. I should like you to come with me, Mr. Lowe, if you are disengaged."

Left alone with his sister, Marshall got up and shut the door of communication with the inner room; then came back and sat down by Miss Bertram.

"I have no luck," he muttered in sullen anger. "Luck is always against me. Everywhere I go, and whatever I am doing, if a little bit of luck has got to come into my business, it is always bad. Whether I am acting honestly or dishonestly it is always the same. Posts go wrong on just the one particular day in the year when it matters to me more than on any other that I should get some letter. Trains and ships are always over their time if I am in a hurry, and under it if I want delay. If a thousand of my papers which do not matter pass through some man's hands who rarely looks at them, and there happens to be one of the papers which I do not wish him to see, he is sure to see it. I have backed a horse in a steeplechase in Buenos Ayres which had run for five seasons and never fallen, and he fell the time I backed him. The only time I ever played *trente-et-quarante* at Monte Carlo the *un-après* turned up four times running, a thing which, they told me, happened perhaps once a-year. There is no fighting against luck like that. I think that a man who watches his life for ten years and sees that he is dogged by evil fortune like that has only one sensible thing to do, and that is to shoot himself.

When everything was made, there was nothing made viler or more unbearable than bad luck. I would suffer torture, loss, poverty, and death itself, and would mind nothing if I had brought them on myself by mismanagement and stupidity. It is that feeling of being followed by bad luck, that certainty that wherever chance enters into anything it will be against me, which I loathe. I can remedy the stupidity and mismanagement; against the other I can do nothing. It infuriates me; it drives me mad—mad!"

This sort of tirade was more new to Miss Bertram than to the majority of ladies who have the honour to be related to ne'er-do-weels, and she was impressed by it to an extent which gratified its author. Some vague idea of having heard or read the thing before was certainly in her mind, and it did strike her also that if she had set her brain to work she could have found an answer to most of it; but she was not concerned to do so at this moment, and sat in troubled silence.

'I am at Hobart's mercy," said Marshall at last. "What am I to do?"

"I will go and see him. He seems to pay some attention to my appeals," said the woman. "I will beg him to keep silence."

"If he or Lowe talk to any one they might as

well preach about me in the Town Hall at once.  Half a dozen words to anybody and the story will be all over the place."

"I will say so to him.  I will implore him to keep absolute silence."

The man looked slightly relieved and his sister went on.  "You will not leave England again, will you?  It would be unwise, I think, to come down into this neighbourhood any more, as your presence irritates Canon Hobart, but you could find work in London.  And, Joshua, could you not find something else than your present work?"

"Why should I?"

"You know well enough."

"I certainly see well enough that some one has been talking great nonsense to you, and I can pretty well guess who it is.  What on earth do you suppose that Lady Eastney knows about a business like ours?  She is fighting us merely because that little fool Alford who hangs on to her petticoats dislikes her husband, and she is on the youngster's side.  He is her lover.  I should have thought any woman could have seen through an affair of that sort."

"I cannot argue about the matter, but I know everything, and you know that I know."

"A truly feminine remark," said Marshall,

and then suddenly remembering that he was
not exactly in a position to make sarcastic
remarks to his sister, he went on: "Of course,
my dear Chris, every one may think what they
like about the Society, but you might have
trusted me not to let you and Monica come to
any harm in it.   You have given a very severe
blow to its credit down here by trying to sell
those shares, but of course you must do it if
you think right.   Now we had better leave the
office.   I must go back to London to-night, and
you will see Hobart as soon as you can, won't
you?   It is good of you to stand by me, dear
Chris.   You always did, didn't you."

"I haven't done you much good by it, apparently," said the woman with unusual bitterness.

# CHAPTER XXVIII

Canon Hobart having promised to keep silence about Marshall's identity on condition that no more religious pressure was brought to bear to induce the neighbourhood to invest its money in the Freehold, a little more breathing time was given to the officials of that remarkable institution. It was true that business was at an absolute standstill; that shares could not be sold at any price at all, and that a large and increasing number of persons were increasingly anxious to sell them at any price, but such a fact is a long time in becoming known, and has little significance for the class of investors with whom Lord Eastney and his fellow directors were concerned. Local lawyers or bankers might advise the sale of houses or shares belonging to the Freehold at any sacrifice, but so long as the local postmaster and clergyman or itinerant preachers would strongly discountenance such a proceeding, and express unbounded faith in the Society's prospects, such advice was not of any serious consequence. A few persons like Miss Bertram, who had their entire fortune in this Company, and knew more or less the truth about it, grew desperately anxious as time went on and they were told on all sides to wait; but this minority was unimportant. Muirhead was another who was getting anxious about his prospects, but he had discovered, as he supposed, a new and much more interesting and rapid way of making money, and was less concerned to sell his Freehold shares than to find probable winners for the November races at Derby, Warwick, Manchester, and other places within reasonable distance of Newcastle. The first week in November came at last, many of the actors in this little drama having lived half a dozen lives during the anxious previous weeks, and Muirhead began to absent himself regularly three days a week from the office. Money flowed into his pockets steadily at these "back-end" meetings. He appeared able to commit the most outrageous acts of folly and yet win continually. One day he would back a horse because he had dreamt its number, another because he had seen its colours on a scarecrow from the passing train, another because it was the only one not mentioned by any of the sporting papers in their tips, another for a reason more idiotic than all the preceding ones put together, namely, that he liked its

looks.    He heard of people coming to the office
in Newcastle day after day, local persons anxious about their land or houses, officials from
London who had come down to see himself and
urge caution or activity, but he paid no attention to any of them.    He saw Monica half-a-
dozen times, heard that the date of her
wedding had been fixed, and was as absolutely
indifferent to sight or news as if it had concerned Miss Bertram.    Even when he came
back from a certain day at Derby some thirty
or forty pounds to the bad on the day, it did
not very greatly affect him.    He said to himself that it was an accident liable to happen to
any sportsman, that it came of following other
people's advice instead of his own judgment,
that he would make up for it by an extra heavy
bet or two next day.    The extra heavy bet was
made and lost; another was made with the
same result; and Muirhead looked down the
list of runners in the Derby Cup with a slight
touch of anxiety.    These losses had occurred
before, they would come all right by the end of
the day, never had he gone home a loser two
days running.    He shook his shoulders impatiently and walked quickly up and down the
enclosure searching for distraction.    The great
bare Stands were full of a rather sober-looking
crowd, many like himself were severe losers

over this succession of crowded five-furlong
scrambles, where any clever light-weight who
got well away might be victorious, and winners were best guessed by tossing up pennies.
There was hardly a touch of colour among the
Stands excepting in the County enclosure
where a few gay dresses, survivals from the
Cowes week or Scotch castles, were to be seen.
Bets, though small in amount, were unusually
numerous, and the shouting of the bookmakers
had hardly finished when the horses passed the
winning post, and began again directly the first
number was hoisted. The numbers of the
horses in the Derby Cup had not appeared on
the board when betting on the race, which had
been going on continuously all the afternoon,
rose to an indescribable uproar. Men of all
classes, with five-shilling pieces, half-sovereigns
and bank-notes in their hands, surrounded each
bookmaker in a fiercely fighting crowd, scream-
ing, gesticulating, and furiously pushing past
their neighbours to demand the price of this or
that favourite or outsider. From half-a-dozen
of the smaller bookmakers came cries of "10 to
1 on the field"; even the bigger men were
offering 8 to 1, and making bets faster than
their clerks could write.

Muirhead had a confident feeling that this
was the race on which he was going to retrieve

fortune. It was on races of this sort, with a score of runners and fifteen possible winners, that he had won his great coups hitherto, and he camp up to Goodleigh with £120 in his hand. He asked the prices of various horses. He never made up his mind till the last moment, changing his intention sometimes in speaking. In point of fact, on this occasion, finding that one of his selected horses was a favourite, he chose another, a certain Parmesan, against whom Goodleigh offered him 100 to 6 to win and 4 to 1 for a place. He backed this and The Elf to win and for places, and Table-turner and Chloe for places. He continued putting on money as each new fancy came into his head, and had to take out of his pocket another £15 to add to the £120. It was the biggest sum of money that he had had on a race yet, and his face was white and his lips and hands trembled as he took his place on the steps of the far stand and watched the horses canter down to the starting-post. The field was large and a little unmanageable. There was half-an-hour's delay at the post, and even then the flag fell to a very straggling start. Muirhead, watching them through his glasses, exclaimed at each breakaway, muttered terror, anxiety, relief, and boredom, as the horses one after another ran half the course, were stopped,

brought back, turned into line again and then
again, broke away. As the flag fell at last he
almost ceased to breathe, and as he saw nearly
all his own selections hopeless lengths in the
rear, he felt from the start that his money was
gone. The race was a mere pell-mell scramble
where half the riders were engaged in getting
out of the way of the blundering, swaying
6st.-5 brigade, with young, and small, and
excited stable-boys on their backs. Elf and
Chloe were already entirely out of the race,
being even now hard ridden to make them join
the leaders. Parmesan was sufficiently badly
placed at the start, and suddenly, to his horror
and rage, Muirhead saw him pulled right back
behind the whole of the front division, and
dragged across the course from right to left.
Tableturner, he thought, might get a place.
It was the horse, of course, on which he had
least money of all, and the first touch of the
gambler's feeling that fortune is fighting
against him, the same idea which had been the
text of Marshall's late diatribe, came to this
man too as he looked at the little group of
horses flying up the centre of the difficult
Derby mile. He kept his glasses fixed on
them, especially on Tableturner, till the horses
were almost opposite to him. Then as he
put them down his heart gave a leap which

nearly choked him, and his face flushed scarlet.
It would have occurred to a more intelligent
spectator of the race to wonder why the riders
of the little group which he had been watching
had taken up their whips one by one, and had
sat down to ride for all they were worth.   The
reason was simply that close under the rails,
on the Stand's side of the course, Parmesan had
come up with a rush and was leading by two
lengths.   The result of a race when the winner
is in this position is mostly unperceived by the
majority of the onlookers, and half-a-dozen
names were being shouted.   The shouts confused Muirhead, who kept muttering to himself, "Impossible! impossible!" and could
scarcely believe the result, even when Parmesan's number was hoisted as the winner.
Oakleaf was given second place, and then
another exclamation broke from Muirhead's
lips, for in the third place Tableturner's number appeared.   The man leant against the railings of the stand shaking and almost crying
with excitement.   He did not know how much
he had won; could not remember the calculations which he had made beforehand; knew
nothing, except that he was delirious with
excitement and gratitude.   Presently he found
himself standing opposite Goodleigh with
bank-notes being thrust into his hand.   The

sum which he put away into his pocket-book amounted to nearly £800 (of which £650 were his winnings on the race), and as he stood drinking champagne at the bar he calculated that, in spite of some previous losses, he only wanted another hundred pounds to have won a thousand during his short turf career.  He would win it, he said to himself, on the next race, and then go home and bet no more that year.  Elated by this resolution and the champagne, he came out to find that there were only three runners in the race.  "Gulliver has scared them all away, of course," said a man with whom he had some acquaintance.  "You see the race is a walk over for him, and at this time of the year there is no object in bringing a horse to the race-course, and giving him a training gallop behind something that he can't possibly beat."

"Well, anyhow, I am going to back Gulliver to win a hundred pounds," said Muirhead.

"You are, are you?" said the other, laughing.  "You must have a good sum of money on you to-day to do that.  Listen there!" and Muirhead, listening, heard cries of "I'll take 10 to 1" coming from various quarters of the ring.

"You see, old man, you'll want a pretty stiff sum on to win £100."

"I don't mind having a pretty stiff sum on a certainty," said Muirhead.

"Well, you're right there," was the reply. "I don't much mind buying money myself when I've got anything to buy it with. Look here; lend me a tenner, can't you? I will give it you back after the race. The thing is an absolute certainty, as any one can see, and I want a quid awfully badly. You might make it twenty as you're so flush."

Muirhead pulled out a twenty-pound note and handed it to the man with a good-natured smile, merely saying: "You must bring it me back after the race. I wouldn't mind giving you a couple of quid myself, but there is no reason why you shouldn't get them out of a bookmaker instead. I am going to back the horse myself for a good big sum. As I said, I love a certainty."

Persons who wonder at the acts of folly committed by a gambler, whether on the turf or at a roulette table or elsewhere, forget one important fact, that money loses all "value" in the strict economical sense of the word. Sovereigns and bank-notes are the merest counters which he stakes against other counters for purposes of excitement. A man in whom the desire to make money is genuinely and continuously the uppermost thought does not lose a fortune on the turf, and very probably wins; that is a fact which anti-gambling crusaders might consider, with advantage to the usefulness of their sermons. These sermons, in so far as they are directed against the greed for gain evinced by gamblers, are simply unadulterated nonsense. I am saying nothing against the preachers, whose work, heaven knows, is badly enough wanted in modern Europe; and who for the most part are high-principled, well-intentioned men, saying what they mean and meaning what they say; eager to do work of which there is crying need and lacking only a little more of that detailed knowledge without which their discourses are *magnæ passus extra viam*. Their especially favourite assertion, for instance, that the gambler is trying to acquire his neighbour's money without working for it, is enough to make a whole brilliant series of the most persuasive lectures ridiculous and useless. The gambler cares no more about his neighbour's money than he does about his neighbour's wife. He gambles with bank-notes and sovereigns because they are the counters appointed by convention for the purpose. He would play with bits of wood, or the metal discs which they give you in the cloakroom, or a bundle of old clothes, with almost equal satisfaction; the fact being of course that gambling is as completely a disease as a hundred others which you visit Ems or Homburg to cure; only unfortunately the German baths have not yet been found which will eradicate it. The English turf is divided into three parts; gamblers, business men, who are there to make money, and sportsmen, though of course in a few persons the business and gambling instincts exist together and are constantly fighting for the mastery. No doubt it is because the purely gambling passion does not play a very large part on the English race-course that it is ignored and misunderstood by would-be reformers. It can only be studied and accurately diagnosed at Monte Carlo, where our preachers ought to be sent in a body for a month.

A person who did not know to what a point of insanity this passion will bring a man would have hardly believed it possible that Muirhead would put the whole of his day's winnings, together with all the money which he had brought with him for the day's possible losses, on Gulliver for the next race. A gambler with the slightest shadow of business instinct left in him, or a sportsman who knew the merest elements of racing-business would have refrained from such an act of idiocy, for

the cries of, "I'll take 10 to 1," had died away;
"8 to 1 bar 1" had changed to "7 to 1 bar 1,"
and even that had stopped. "Take 100 to 12:"
"Take 8 to 1:" was echoing round the ring
when Muirhead came forward to make his bet,
and a more experienced hand would have
realised that he had only to wait another ten
minutes to lay 6 to 1. However, he handed
£800 to Goodleigh, who opened his eyes a little
at the bet. So little money was being invested
on the race that this actually had the effect of
making Gulliver rather more steady in the bet-
ting-market for a time. But presently a bet of
"six monkeys" was taken about Goldleaf and
something like a knock-out of the favourite
began. Muirhead heard nothing of it, having
already taken his place on a distant stand
whence he watched the three horses turn into
line and jump off together as the flag dropped.
The outsider was ten lengths in the rear before
half a mile had been covered. At the end of
another half mile backers of Gulliver knew
their fate, for Loates' arms began to swing, his
spurs touched the horse's side, and then as
Goldleaf still swung along at an easy canter
the dismayed plungers saw Loates pick up his
whip, and saw too that it was only with the
utmost exertion that he could keep his mount
level with Goldleaf. From start to finish, in

fact, there had hardly been the slightest doubt
as to the result of the race. At the distance
Kempton Cannon had only to let Goldleaf go
in order to come away and win the race by
three lengths.

Watching a train of men coming home from
the English race-course, it is more difficult than
you would think to tell which are the losers
and which are the winners. A certain number
there are who explain to their companions with
furious voices and adjectives more numerous
than various how some horse had just got
beaten and done them out of a hundred or a
thousand pounds; or how they had "put" some
friend "on" to the winner of a race but had
unfortunately backed something else themselves. But the greater part of each train-load
keeps its woes or its triumphs to itself, and the
average English sportsman, whether he has lost
a fortune or won one, says very little except
that he is thirsty. I think, however, that a
certain craving for company, a very strong
resolution not to be left alone under any circumstances during the next few hours, distin-
guishes the loser. A man who has won
money, if he is an ordinarily amiable person,
would on the whole rather dine with half-a-
dozen jovial companions than otherwise; but
your man who has lost means to have a dinner

companion at any price.  I myself, after having been "discharged of my money by the bookmakers," as a delightful French acquaintance of mine once put it, would dine with a bi-metallist or an impressionist art critic, rather than alone.   But Muirhead, who had to be back in Newcastle that evening, could find no companion except his own thoughts, compared to which the conversation of either of the two gentlemen above mentioned would have been gay and amusing.  The fact was, as he told himself again and again, that he was very nearly ruined.  That afternoon, after the race for the Derby cup, when those bank-notes were bulging out his pockets, he had allowed himself to realise that, but for Parmesan's victory, he would have been in what his racing companions called a tight place.  Previous days' losses had been considerable.  His story of ready money was almost at an end, and all the rest of his fortune was invested in the Freehold —invested in that literal sense of the word which means hemmed round by a good many difficulties about getting it out again.  Unfortunately, now that he had lost those bank-notes, he could not equally quickly lose with them the realisation of his position.  Except for this Freehold money—or rather paper—and for the twenty pounds which he had lent to his acquaintance on the Derby race-course, which was an asset of even less doubtful value, he had barely ten pounds left in the world, and his quarter's pay as local manager of the Society was not due till Christmas. The business instinct which told him that he must find money somewhere; the gambling one which told him that he must get back those losses at all costs, were united in his mind as he at last went to bed muttering: "I will go to Manchester and win it back. If I have to commit robbery and murder to get the money, I will go to Manchester and win those losses back!"

# CHAPTER XXIX

Lady Eastney was driving along Piccadilly in her victoria with Bertie Alford seated by her side and Angela on the small seat in front of her. It was mid-November and bitterly cold, and the Marchioness and her little daughter were wrapped in lace-edged furs. Lady Eastney's face appeared delicately rose-coloured, fretfully angry above her furs. The small person's appeared very white and blue and patient above hers. Mr. Alford, with philosophy on his lips and pity in his soul, was discussing the situation with his companion.

"Fame," he was saying, "is the incredulous surprise shown by a man's friends when he does anything noteworthy. Infamy is the 'I-told-you-so-that's-just-what-I-expected' chorus sung by his friends and relatives when he does anything scandalous. In the nature of things this chorus must be more common than the surprise; therefore your lot is a very common one, and to you who hate to be eccentric that ought to be a consolation."

"I loathe notoriety, and we are notorious!" said the woman.

"Fame and infamy are easy to acquire, but very difficult to keep," said her companion. "In painting and book-writing we demand a celebrated and a new name.  In music we only want a celebrated writer.  Outside these three we want nothing but a new man.  You are, or soon will be, a nine days' wonder; but take it as philosophically as you can during the nine days, and be sure that with any luck they will be reduced to seven.  For myself, if I anticipated such an ill—and even a man who is not a company-director may find himself in the dock at any moment—I should buy an almanack, and mark off the ninth day, and sit down in front of it and say, 'Respice finem.' "

"Is that your idea of consolation?" asked the woman scornfully.

"It is the kind of consolation which I thought you would like best," said the young man with a look of pity and affection at her. "Some women's idea of consolation is to be told that in spite of all affliction their complexion is still perfect and their hat a triumph of genius; but I did not suppose you wanted that.  I say to you what I would like people to say to me when a surgeon was around with a knife, or a dentist with pincers: 'It will soon be over.' "

"It will certainly be over," said the Marchioness bitterly, "when I have every door in London shut in my face and can't have a single guest for a dinner party.  .  .  ."

"The word 'guest' is derived from the Sanscrit 'ghas,' which means 'to eat up.'  One can always get guests."

"Don't talk nonsense.  I say when one can't get a single person of one's own set into one's house, when Eastney has been obliged to sell the houses and has been turned out of every club in London  .  .  ."

"My dear, he will do like Roberts, my tailor, who bought a yacht and said he must have the burgee of the R.T.Y.C. or the R.C.Y.C. or something of the sort to fly on it.  But he couldn't get elected to a single yacht club in England.  At last I found written after the name of his yacht M.O.B.Y.C., and asked him what it meant.  He said it stood for 'My Own Blooming Yacht Club.'  Suggest that to Eastney."

"You are perfectly hateful this afternoon, Bertie.  You would go on with your silly jokes and stories if I told you I was going to poison myself to-night."

"Well, that remains to be seen.  In the meantime you have merely told me that you are going to call on the Duchess of Dovedale. As a matter of courage the visit is superior to poison.   It strikes me that it is also very nearly as foolish.''

"I owe her a call,'' said Lady Eastney, biting her lips.  "Here is Down Street, where you are going to get out.   Come with me?  No, of course you are not coming with me.   You must get out here.   Goodbye.''

Lady Eastney drove into the courtyard of Dovedale House with lips which were a little white in spite of biting, and eyes whose resolute stare could not hide their nervousness. Through the great hall with its powdered footmen standing about, up a small side staircase, through two big saloons and into a small gaily-decorated drawing-room beyond, she passed with Angela's hand held tightly in hers. She waited here for a few minutes and at last the doors were opened again to admit the Duchess of Dovedale, a woman of five or six-and-thirty, tall and rather clumsily made, untidily dressed, and with a slight air of surprise on her face.

"So you are still here,'' said Lady Eastney, after the usual greetings.   "You are beginning to love London as much as I do.''

"We are going away on Tuesday.   Some people are coming to dine to-morrow and Monday, and then we are going.''

"Yes?''   Hostess and visitor had been the

most intimate friends some time ago, meeting
one another every day and knowing all about
one another's friends, entertainments and
guests. Lady Eastney understood the intention of those words, "some people."

"Are you stopping on till Christmas?" asked
the Duchess after a just perceptible pause.

"Probably, or perhaps we may go to Cannes
earlier this year. The winter seems to have
come on so much sooner than usual."

"To Cannes? Really? Shall you go there
again this season?"

"I hope so," said Lady Eastney, who had
nerved herself for this with only a very slight
hope of escaping it; so she went on resolutely
enough: "We shan't be able to afford the same
villa that we had last year, I suppose, so we
shall go to an hotel. It is really more comfortable in hotels in many ways, besides being
so much cheaper. Eastney likes it better in
every way."

"Will Lord Eastney be there this year?"
asked the Duchess, and looked at her visitor
with raised eyebrows and a slight laugh.
When a woman means to insult another nowadays, she does not as a rule trouble to wrap
up the poison in honey. To compose courtly
phrases with a sting in them is too much
trouble.

"It is difficult to be decisive about any arrangements six weeks beforehand, isn't it?" said Lady Eastney with a smile. She had not come here to pick a quarrel but to find out whether the world was going to pick a quarrel. "Have you heard that Sophie Arnold is engaged?"

"Yes, I heard about it."

"They will be married in January. His father has given him Bedford House. They are in luck."

"I heard about it."

There were a few half-whispered words from Angela, and Lady Eastney asked: "May she go up and see Bee and Mary?"

"They have gone out, or they are just going out," said the duchess, with a glance under her eyes, and a slight lifting of the eyebrows, and then a long full stare at Lady Eastney. Only a woman could have thought of hurting another woman through her child like that. .

There was another pause, of longer duration this time, and then Lady Eastney began again resolutely: "I see that Mr. Lightfoot has got a picture into the British Artists' Exhibition. He is painting Frances Hampton's portrait. That ought to be a success for him at the Academy."

"Oh, yes."

"He is very clever and has been very unlucky. I had a good mind to let him paint me. I should like to help him."

"Wouldn't he want to be paid for the picture?" Her Grace's remarks were getting broader as Lady Eastney appeared to be impervious to them.

"I suppose so. I did not exactly mean that I was going to ask him to paint me for nothing."

As she said this Lady Eastney rose to take her leave. She had asked her question and received the answer, and there was nothing more to wait for. The two women stood and looked into one another's eyes for a moment— the two peeresses who to some extent had been rival queens in London for seven or eight years past; who had chatted over every single detail of one another's houses, lovers, dresses, parties and children; who had lorded it together at Sandown, Ascot, Hurlingham, in Scotland, Paris and Homburg, with a crowd of followers, male and female, in their train, with money, credit, wit, admiration, constant change and excitement, and everything which makes life worth living around them. They had been neither friends nor enemies, merely together always, sharers in everything good and bad which Europe had to offer. Now something had gone, or was about to go wrong with one of these chance partners, and the other proceeded to cut the thin cord which bound them together.

Lady Eastney held out her hand and as the other put her limp hand into it, the visitor said very quietly: "Is this a last good-bye?  Is there—is there no pity for me?"

"Pity?" said the other with a cold stare.  "I really do not know what you mean."

Which was quite true.

# CHAPTER XXX

"I am going to ask you a question which of course you will answer or not as you please. I really have no right to an answer, and hardly expect it."

Bertie Alford, dining in Portman Square that evening, was sitting with Lord Eastney after dinner.

"I am not fond of questions and have had rather too many of them lately," was the gloomy reply; "but go on."

"Can you tell me about how much longer the smash of the Freehold will be delayed?"

"Oh, damn the Freehold!"

"That's been done already, hasn't it?" said Alford; "I wanted to know, if you don't mind telling me, when the event is to be announced?"

"Would you think it rude of me, considering the fact that you are my guest here, if I were to ask you to mind your own business?"

"Certainly not,'' said Bertie. "It is a perfectly natural reply to my question."

Each man sipped a whole glass of claret in

silence, then Lord Eastney pushed the decanter towards Mr. Alford with a "help yourself." They both filled their glasses—the claret was Chateau Margaux of 1869, and a man would have been a fool who refused another glass of it because of a woman or a fortune—and then Lord Eastney began again abruptly:—

"I want the news taken to my wife somehow, and you can break it to her, I dare say, as well as anybody. The fact is, it's all over—would you care for some dry biscuits? Frazer has forgotten them—and though I do not know exactly what will come next, I do know that it will be something most infernally unpleasant. I don't suppose that I can be put in prison, though, on my soul and conscience, I don't see why I shouldn't be, quite as much as some of the other chaps who will, but there will be a big scandal. I shall have to give up every penny and we shall practically be paupers. I do not mean that we shall starve on a thousand a year in a house at Brighton or a flat in Paris; I mean that I shall have very considerable difficulty in putting my hands on fifty pounds. I should say that the whole matter will be public property next week, certainly before the end of this month. If you wish to tell Lady Eastney so, I shall be rather obliged to you than otherwise for doing it. She must know somehow sooner or later, and I for one have no wish to tell her.''

''Your confidences are at least complete now they have come,'' said Mr. Alford drily.

''Are they?'' asked Lord Eastney quietly. ''Do you know the whole business now?  If so, then you know a good deal more than I do myself.''

''What will happen to all those men, Marshall, Robinson, and that crew whom we entertained in Stoke last autumn?''

''What the devil do I care?'' was the surly reply.

''Nothing, I feel sure,'' said Mr. Alford; ''but do you know?''

The other shrugged his shoulders: ''Arrest, trial, imprisonment, escape—how can I tell? They deserve all they get.''

''Yes,'' was the meaning answer, ''I can quite believe that,'' and Mr. Alford, having finished his third glass of claret, rose and left the room.

Lord Eastney laughed quietly, and having finished the bottle put on a hat and coat and drove off to Margets' Rooms, where another meeting of the directors had been fixed for 10 o'clock that night.  He sat through the business, weary, absent-minded, smiling occasionally with a far-off tired gaze.  How much did he really care about the scene which he could pretty well guess was going on in his own house? Not very much, he said to himself. Lady Eastney had been resignedly acquiescent, sometimes he admitted to himself almost good-natured, in helping him in his work. She had many good friends of her own and had offered no active opposition to his attempts on their purses. She had helped him actively and ably in robbing his own friends. So said the Marquis to himself now, not caring any longer to mince words about his own proceedings; yet the woman hated and despised him and had been very unhappy with him. Slightly and vaguely her contempt irritated him. He admitted cynically enough that he deserved it, but he knew, and she ought to have known, that but for the circumstances of his poverty and horribly encumbered position, he would have been different. The business of the Freehold Society jarred on himself as much as it could possibly jar on her, and she ought to have recognised this. She had judged and condemned him without mercy, and was now, he supposed, going to abandon him. His pride revolted a little against the idea, but a certain sense of justice, and a feeling that he had lost all right to judge or interfere or make any claim as regards his wife, prevented him from taking any action. Weeks ago, when she had hinted not obscurely what she meant to do—and indeed he had read her intentions himself and needed no such hints—he had resolved not to intervene by word or look or deed; and so now, when he supposed the decisive moment was at hand, he sat in Margets' Rooms listening to sums all of which ended in one answer—ruin; to calculations and forecasts which all ended in one word—disgrace. He kept on signing papers, more than half-conscious all the time that he ought not to be signing nine-tenths of them. He agreed to this and that recommendation, fully aware while he was doing it that he was kicking down one more ladder by which he might possibly have climbed out of dishonour. But it was all done with a shrug of the shoulders, and a bitter laugh, and the thought, "What does a detail more or less matter if there is no one but myself to pay the price." Perhaps after all he did care a little about what was going on in Portman Square.

Mr. Alford had left the dining-room and gone straight to the little boudoir where Lady Eastney went after dinner. He found her there standing by the window, looking out into the November night. A moon was shining out of the dark winter sky on to a little bare black garden at the back of the house, on to the tall unbroken walls which surrounded it and the ugly lines of chimney-pots and stables beyond. One small electric lamp was burning in the room, but its heavy pink shade could not hide the ghastly whiteness of the woman's face. She turned to the young man as he came in and held out both hands. As he took them it was like taking up two bits of ice, and her lips as she held them up to be kissed were almost as cold.

"Have you asked him?" she said.

"Yes, I asked him."

"Bertie! For the love of heaven don't let me drag it all out of you by questions. Pray do tell me the whole story rationally."

"I am going to tell you, my dear. There is nothing the least exciting to tell. We haven't been flinging decanters about, or anything of that sort. I asked him in just so many words when the smash was due. First he told me to mind my own business, then he said in effect that it had come—that it was a matter of days, or hours. That was all."

"That was all? On your honour?"

"Well; almost. He asked me"—the young man laughed nervously—"to come and break it to you."

"Did he?" The woman's eyes flashed with

rage, Bertie could not imagine why. "So that is all he cares! And what are we going to do, you and I? Will you keep your promise? Will you take we away?"

"Of course I am going to keep my promise," answered Alford gravely, and looking at her with eyes in which there was infinite pity but nothing else. "I only want to be quite sure that you want to come with me. We will go now, to-night if you like, and where you like."

"And will you forgive me for ruining your life like this?"

"I have nothing to forgive, dear. It is only kind of you to choose me to save you."

"You will never say anything more than that? You will never change from that?"

"How should I change? What more could I say?"

"If you could say that you love me!" cried the woman passionately. "If you would only just once say that!"

"I love you, dearest. You know that I love you more than anybody on earth."

Lady Eastney stood very still for a moment, crying silently. Then she shook her head slightly and, freeing herself from Alford's arms, moved away to the window. The man stood there with a slightly blank look on his face. He had done his best to persuade his companion that he was in love with her, and she had seen through him perfectly clearly—had seen that he was simply sorry for her and weakly good-natured. Through the long pause he stood there thinking and his thoughts were more clear than pleasant. Lady Eastney was in love with him because he had stood by her with help and sympathy while all other friends were dropping away. She thought that she had only to escape to Italy with him and Angela in order to get a divorce, marry her lover and live happy with him and her child ever afterwards. Bertie knew better, but it sounded horrible to speak out a few facts just now. To spend thirty years making jokes at every good or evil which life brings before you makes the time pass pleasantly enough, but the worst of it is that, when a crisis arrives which refuses to be smoothed away by jokes or epigrams, and demands serious thought, you have no serious thoughts with which to meet the demand. A decision which will merely influence the important but strictly ephemeral question of where you are to dine that night differs of course only in degree, and not in kind, from the decision which will affect the whole of the rest of your life. But somehow or other the numerous dinner decisions are found to be a very inadequate

training for the life decision.   Over this question, as over the question whether he should
order claret or champagne for dinner, Bertie
shut his mental eyes, and shrugged his
shoulders, and said that it would be all the
same a hundred years hence.

"I have sometimes thought" — Lady
Eastney's voice broke in on his desultory and
scattered thoughts, almost making the young
man start—"I have sometimes thought that
the prodigal son was a very lucky person to be
able to say: 'I will arise and go to my Father,'
whenever he pleased.   It seems to me that it
would be easy to live with the swine and eat
the husks if you knew that you could leave
them whenever you chose, at the price of just
a little humiliation.   You and I will not be
able to do that, you know, Bertie.   When we
do this thing that we are talking of, it will be
done for ever.   We may humiliate ourselves
into the dust and cry that we had sinned
against heaven and before the world, till we
can cry no more; but it will be no use.   There
will be no return for us.   It is for all our
lives."

The young man looked at her with wide
startled eyes.   She had put into words so
clearly and suddenly what he had been vaguely
thinking, that he could not hide the effect

which the words had on him. The woman saw this and, with a glance in which love, entreaty and anxiety were mingled, she turned round to the window again, as if wishing to give him time to think over what she had said. But the feeling uppermost now in Alford's mind was one of annoyance that she should have so clearly read his thoughts, and so clearly perceived that his protests of affection were unreal. He came up to her and put his arms round her again, saying eagerly:—

"How often do you want me to tell you that I love you? Apart from all your troubles, apart from every bit of sympathy which I have for you, I love you, dearest. I am thankful for all your troubles because they are going to give you to me. I was thankful when Eastney told me to-night that the smash had come, because I knew it meant that my turn had come at last. I love you, darling! Surely you must believe it."

"Sometimes I do almost," she answered softly, "and then again I feel that I am a fool to believe it. Why should you care for me who do nothing but worry you with my miseries? You like people who laugh, and I never laugh now."

"I love you, my dear, laughing or crying, troubled or happy. It is so ridiculous to doubt that.  You don't doubt it, really?  What more in the world could I do to prove it to you?"

"Nothing! nothing!" she answered with some contentment in her voice for the moment.  "Have we really settled then to go away?  Is everything decided?"

"Everything," said Bertie recklessly, resolved that he would not initiate any more doubts for himself to smooth away afterwards.  "We are going by the eleven o'clock train to-morrow to Paris, you and Angela and I.  Let us go upstairs and tell the baby about it.  Does she know anything?"

"I told her that you might perhaps take me and her away for a few days soon, and she was delighted.  She is quite used to that of course."

"We must tell her not to talk about it this time.  Come along!"

Bertie Alford knew his way very well to the nursery portion of this house, having visited it often enough before with his present companion.  Lady Eastney had one real sentiment left in the world amongst the purely negative sentiments—disenchantment, disappointment, failure, and regrets—which made up her life, and this was a passion of love for her only child. She estimated two-thirds of her friends by what Angela thought of them.  A house or place was dull or pleasant to her chiefly according to whether Angela was unhappy or happy there. She had liked Alford himself at first because Angela approved of him. For people who liked her child and gave her small presents and treats, the Marchioness would do anything. For people who snubbed the little one in any way she had a hatred which was as bitter as it was endless. The whole business was perhaps a trifle ridiculous, but it was the strongest feature in Lady Eastney's life. The child's bedroom was a big front room on the fourth floor. A fire was burning in it, and a great red glow lit up the white wood bed with its muslin curtains and lace pillows and pink ribbons. The little one had been expecting her visitors and greeted them with a low laugh of contentment as they came in. Bertie came forward first, but Lady Eastney brushed by him and took the small white figure in her arms.

"We are going away to-morrow. Bertie is going to take us. Aren't you pleased, my baby?"

"Oh, yes! How long shall we stay?"

"For a very, very long time. Even I don't know how long. Would you rather stay with us, sweetheart, or come home again?"

"Mother, darling!" . . . the small lips

could not so suddenly find words to explain that where her mother was, Angela wanted to be too, and that there all desire ended.

"And you do love Bertie too, don't you?"

"Of course I do.  But, Bertie, you will take Esther too, won't you?"

"Are we going to take her?" asked the young man in a low whisper.

"Oh, I suppose so," said Lady Eastney, who was engaged in tying up a refractory curl of Angela's.  "We had better come and speak to her.  Here she is.  Esther!"

The woman who came in now and came up to Angela's bedside was a tall, quietly-dressed person with a slight stoop, and eyes which drew all children to her like a magnet.

"We are going to Paris to-morrow morning," said Lady Eastney, "Mr. Alford and Angela and I, and we want you to come too; but we must ask you first whether you mind.  Will you come with us?"

"I am going wherever you and my little one go, my lady," answered the woman very gravely.

"And you will stay with us always?"

"Until"—she moved the sheets about with one hand, and put the other on Lady Eastney's arm—"until I am obliged to bring Lady Angela home alone."

"Alone!" echoed the Marchioness, not understanding.

"There will be no resisting certain orders when they come, my lady."

"You talk the same nonsense as Mr. Alford," said Lady Eastney in a low, nervous voice. "Do you think," she went on, pushing the woman aside and holding the child tight in her arms, "that anybody or anything could take her away? I would simply kill the person who tried. You are talking nonsense."

"I am saying what I know, my lady, and what you know. Mr. Seaton told you so when you went to see him. You argued with him, and he told it you again and again."

"There is no argument about it," answered Lady Eastney, "I simply tell you that I would kill the person who tried. But, Bertie . . ."

"Well?"

"I think I would rather put off the start till to-morrow evening. It would be better in a good many ways to go at night, and I want to see that lawyer again. We must come away now and leave the chicken to go to sleep. You must tell nobody about our journey, do you hear, baby darling? You mustn't say a word to anybody. Yes; we will go to-morrow evening instead of in the morning. I must know when and where to be on my guard about the child."

# CHAPTER XXXI

Gerald Franklin was for the moment extremely pleased with himself. For a year or two past he had been chafing at the fact that none of the big dividends being paid by the Freehold Building Society could come to him, and that he was obliged to take 4 per cent. for his £3000. Of course he had no faith in the stability of the Society, but he had a most profound faith in his own ability to make the most of a speculation, and he was entirely certain that if he had that £3000 in his own hands he could get 10 per cent. for the money in one quarter or another, and keep the capital perfectly secure. Now, at last, with Marshall's assistance, he had managed to get hold of the capital. It was not to be invested in the Freehold; neither Lowe nor Miss Bertram would have allowed that; but they had agreed to the purchase of certain shares in the Carlton Gold Mines. Gerald had been extremely anxious to buy them, Marshall had strongly backed up his request, and the Railway stock, which had been standing in Lowe's name in a very casual fashion for the past three years, had been sold.

Marshall had represented during a flying visit to Staffordshire that, as the shares were still fluctuating in price, it would be rational to buy them as cheaply as possible, and accordingly, without the slightest demur, Lowe had handed him the £3000 to be expended in the purchase of the Carlton shares whenever he thought proper. This confiding transaction had taken place on a certain Tuesday, and on the Friday evening, after business hours, Gerald, seeing that the shares had fallen very slightly, and judging that Marshall might have selected that occasion to purchase some, decided to go round to his rooms and make inquiries. He walked down Great Ormond Street and across Queen's Square and Russell Square with a certain amount of elation in his soul, for things had been going well with him lately, not only financially but in new and curious directions about which he understood much less. Sympathy of any kind with his schemes and hopes was new to him. Sympathy of the kind which Sophie Ethridge gave was a most exciting novelty.

The street lamps gleamed in long yellow lines across the wide pavements of Queen's Square and Russell Square as he crossed them. A man with his head bandaged up, and a nun standing by his side, were looking out of the

window at the Italian Hospital, and Gerald
spared him a glance of pity.  On the ragged
little school children playing around the garden
railings; on the old flower woman standing at
the corner of Southampton Row with her
daughter by her side, he bestowed a benignant
smile.  The rooms of some of the houses in
Russell Square were lighted up, and between
half-drawn curtains he could see here and there
an old-fashioned sombrely-furnished dining-
room, where the maid-servants were laying the
table for dinner.  At the front door of one
house the owner was standing watching a passing omnibus, with his latch-key half inserted in
the key-hole.  A small barrel which looked as
if it might contain oysters was in his other
hand, and contented prosperity was written on
every line of his face and clothes.  Gerald
glanced at him, and recognising a partner of a
well-known firm of accountants to whom he
had once or twice brought messages, took off
his hat.  The old gentleman let go his door-
key to return the salute with a slight wave of
the hand, and Gerald looked at him again, saying to himself: "You've gone far, my friend,
but not far enough.  I will go further than
that."  He went on his way, planning his
future as usual, only that now, to his bewilderment, Sophie Ethridge was constantly appear-

ing in it; and at last found himself at Marshall's house in Gordon Square.

He was told that Marshall was out, but being anxious to see him, and being of course a well-known visitor at the house, he was allowed to go upstairs and wait. He entered a room on the first floor—for some curious reason Marshall did not live in chambers, but had a whole house to himself, and used all the rooms in it very much as if he were a man with a wife and family—without any other notice than simply turning the handle of the door. He was surprised, and not a little startled, to see a man jump up from a table at which he had been sitting and begin to retreat towards an inner room. The man, who was clean shaven, and dressed in a rough grey cloth suit, was unknown to him at first; but in the doorway of the inner room he stopped for a second, facing Gerald, and the vague candle light fell full on two flashing black eyes. The man was Marshall.

A wave of terror and fury and despair swept across Gerald's mind. He had no time to think of details, but he was convinced, hurriedly but completely, that the worst of disasters had overtaken him. He shut the door behind him with a bang, and sprang forward towards Marshall, who, perceiving that he was recognised and that escape was impossible, came forward a few steps and confronted him. The lad stared for half-a-dozen moments with quick-coming breath and flashing eyes, seeming to be measuring his own strength against Marshall's in case it came to an open fight. Perhaps Marshall had been doing the same, and had come to the conclusion that the fight was too equal to be altogether desirable, for a conciliatory smile suddenly appeared on his face, and in a very low but amiable voice, he said:—

'The game is up, my dear boy, and I am off. I have just sent a note round to your place advising you to leave, too."

"I have got nothing to escape from," said Gerald, trembling; "and I should have thought that you would have done much better to stop and brazen it out; but that is your own affair. Before you go, however I want my money."

"Your money is in my bank all right, and in my note to you this evening I have sent you a cheque for it, so that you will be able to draw it out to-morrow."

For an instant Gerald had almost believed this assertion, so coolly and decisively was it made; but a glance at Marshall's altered face, a sudden recollection of the man's eagerness to get hold of this money, brought him back to reason.

"I have not got the note or the cheque," he said. "I went to Great Ormond Street before I came here, and there was nothing for me."

"I sent it by post this afternoon," said Marshall, "and you would not get it till this evening." But even as he spoke he felt that the boy did not believe a word of what he was saying, and that this pretence would not serve him for much longer.

"Very likely," said Gerald; "but I do not mean to lose sight of you till I have got it."

"I will cancel the cheque I sent you and write you another now," said Marshall.

"You can if you like," was the cool reply, "but you will not go till it is cashed."

"It could not be cashed to-night."

"Then you will have to wait till to-morrow morning."

"I can't!'

"You must!"

"Must I, you little devil?"

For the last half minute the two men had both been preparing for a contest. Marshall pulled a revolver out of his pocket, but Gerald had calculated, and calculated rightly, that he would not choose to shoot, and so bring the household into the room. The fellow had his

finger on the trigger for a second, but suddenly
recollecting himself, he made a rush at the boy
and struck at him with the butt-end of the
weapon.   Gerald was as little anxious as Marshall to bring the servants on to the scene.
He merely wanted his own money, and beyond
that was rather desirous than otherwise that
Marshall should escape from the country.
Therefore he did not call for help, but trusting
to his youth and agility, first dodged his
opponent, and then, tackling him, tried to hold
him.   The elder man, however, was not only
by far the stronger, but he had a weapon.   As
the boy tried to seize him he held him easily
at arms-length with his left hand, and with his
right struck at him with the butt-end of the
revolver.   The first blow fell painfully enough
but harmlessly on the lad's shoulder.   As
Gerald flung his head backwards and on one
side to avoid the second blow, the heavy
jagged handle of the revolver came down with
frightful force on his throat, cutting open some
veins, and inflicting a horrible bruise.   He fell
back fainting from the pain of the blow, and
Marshall, having stood over him for a moment
to make sure that he was not likely to recover
immediately, took up his hat, blew out the
candles on the tables, stuffed some papers into
his pocket, and then went to the head of the

stairs. Here he listened for a short time to make sure that there was no one moving about in the hall or dining-room, then creeping downstairs he opened the street door, shut it noiselessly with the help of his latch-key, walked up to Euston, and got into an omnibus going to Waterloo Station. Here he took a ticket for Winchester, and having arrived there shortly before ten o'clock, chartered a dog-cart and drove over to Southampton, where he got safely on board the boat for St. Malo.

# CHAPTER XXXII

"Now, Sister!  You said I might have this iron thing off this very evening."

"Robin!  I told you that if you used one single one of those words again, I would put the sheet over your face and keep it there for an hour."

The young gentleman who had made this remark had prefixed to the substantives "thing" and "evening" a string of adjectives, of which a Billingsgate fishmonger might be proud.

"Oh, Sister!  I forgot; forgive me just this once.  It's my birthday to-morrow, so you might let me off "

"You are the very naughtiest boy I ever had here.  How old will you be to-morrow?"

"Six, Sister.  I can swear pretty tidy for that, can't I?  Old Hicks taught me, him as keeps the parrot shop near us.  He taught me and the parrots, too.  You should have just heard us all swear together, him and me and the parrots.  You wouldn't have thought much of me after that."

"It isn't at all clever to swear, Robin; anybody can do it.  I could do it; nurse could do it.  It is only a silly and horrid kind of talk.  It isn't at all funny."

"Why do those doctors laugh, then, every morning when they hurt me and I swear?"

The Sister was spared from answering this embarrassing question by a nurse who brought tea to the small patient.  She got up and passed down the ward towards a bed which was screened off from the rest.  A nurse came out from behind the screens as she approached them saying: "We had better ask Mr. Thornton to come in.  The throat is swelling again on the left side, and I don't like the looks of it at all."

"Send for him, then," said the Sister, and went herself behind the screens.

A curious stillness seemed to rest here, as if something more than cloth and cardboard screens were separating this bed from the rest of the ward.  A murmur of conversation, a rustle of nurses' dresses and dragging of patients' feet as they moved about with tea-trays, the laughter of three or four convalescents who were grouped round the fire, the shrill voices of Robin and a certain young person called Tom-Tit, with whom he had picked a quarrel, seemed to come here, as it were, from a distance. On the bed lay a young man with his eyes closed and a face as white as the bandages which encircled his throat, while by the side of the bed sat another man, with his hands before him, and a certain severe martial air which left little doubt as to his profession.

"I think you may go away, policeman, if you want to smoke or anything of the kind," said the Sister. "One of the doctors is just coming and I shall be staying here for some time."

"Well, thank you, miss. I should like a pipe. It's rather dull work here."

A nurse came in and whispered something.

"I am afraid you won't be able to go after all," said the Sister. "Some friends of the patient have just come, and have been given leave to see him. You would not be allowed to leave them with him, I suppose?"

"No, miss, my orders are very strict about that."

"What's it all about?" asked the recently-arrived nurse in a whisper.

"A financial swindle, miss. Our chaps at Scotland Yard have had their eye on the gang for a long time past, but they haven't been able to do anything till to-day. Unluckily the worst of them, a fellow called Marshall, had reckoned his time pretty accurately and escaped last night. We can't quite make out whether this youngster has tried to commit suicide, or has been having a row with some one. We were told last night that this might have been a queer bungling attempt to cut his own throat. To-day we are told it looks more like a fight. Anyhow, he's under arrest, and half-a-dozen others with him.''

''What rubbish! Of course it couldn't have been attempted suicide,'' said the Sister. ''Well, here's Mr. Thornton, and afterwards, I suppose, his friends will be allowed to come in.''

At these last words, added in a louder voice, Gerald Franklin slowly opened his eyes and looked round. He had been conscious once or twice before, and knew where he was, but a new anxiety seemed to have taken hold of him this time. After thinking for a little he signed that he wanted to ask something, and, being given the slate which was by his bedside, wrote on it: ''Shall I get well?'' As he turned the slate towards the Sister, his eyes looking across her shoulder suddenly clouded with a new look of pain. Thornton, the young surgeon, had just come in, and with him was Dr. Hare, who came up to him and took his hand with tears in his own eyes. One of those trivial memories which come to us at such moments passed into Gerald's mind now;—the memory of the afternoon in his aunt's house, when Dr. Hare had said good-bye and wished him luck, with kindly hope for the future and light-hearted wonder as to when and where they would meet again. This dark November afternoon, the crowded hospital ward with nurses standing round and a policeman sitting by the bedside, was certainly not the picture which either of them had in their mind when the words were spoken.

In answer to the question on the slate Thornton muttered a brief technical explanation to Dr. Hare, who, still holding Gerald's hand, answered gently:

"We cannot be quite sure, my poor lad. Mr. Thornton hopes that he will be able to do something now to help you, but he dare not say that you are quite certain to recover. You would like to see your aunt and sister, would you? They are downstairs, and Mr. Thornton will let them come in for a few minutes first, if you like. . . . No one can see you, you know," he went on, noticing how Gerald looked round him with shrinking fear. "No one can hear or see you except this officer, and I am sure he will be good-natured and wait outside for a bit, or at any rate"—as the policeman shook his head—"will keep out of hearing."

"We would have put him in a private ward," said the Sister, beginning to grow a little pitiful in spite of the stories with which the evening papers had been filled, "only every place is so full. The whole hospital is indeed so full that we are being obliged to bring children into these wards, as you see. Here are the two visitors. It must only be for five minutes. Please explain that to them."

Unable to turn his head away, Gerald shut his eyes as Miss Bertram and Monica came in. The woman and girl were both speechless, and could say and do nothing but stand by the bedside touching the boy's hand and asking him to show by some means if he knew them. They were in utter ignorance, like every one else, as to what had happened to him, except that he had been found wounded in Marshall's room. No one could understand how this had occurred, since the story of the servants of the house was that Marshall had left it at three o'clock and had never returned. Gerald Franklin, they said, had come in much later, and had been absolutely alone in the first-floor room throughout the time of his stay there. Nobody had come in or out of the house, and there had been no sound of a quarrel or the slightest sign of anything being wrong, until a housemaid came into the room to bring some

coal, and had found the young man unconscious on the floor. Every bit of circumstantial
evidence pointed to a discovery by Gerald of
Marshall's flight and the collapse of the business, and a subsequent attempt at suicide on
his part;—everything, that is to say, except the
nature of the wound, which argued forcibly,
though not conclusively, against it. Gerald
would write nothing, being of course ignorant
as to how far the collapse had gone and
whether he would be facilitating further
exposure by a confession. As a result of this,
Miss Bertram and Monica could hardly avoid
sharing the belief that he had tried to kill himself.

The two women stood almost in silence, only
murmuring now and then some word of affection, while the moments went by. The promised five minutes had elapsed and the Sister
came up to Miss Bertram and put a hand on
her shoulder, saying gently but decisively:
"You must come away now, I am afraid. The
doctor has something to do."

Hearing the words, a slight tremor passed
across Gerald's face, and for the first time he
opened his eyes.

"I must ask him one question," said Monica,
pushing past Miss Bertram; and flinging herself on her knees by the bedside, she bent her

face, resolute and almost as white as Gerald's own, over her brother and asked in a low whisper: "Did you do it yourself? Oh, Gerald, do tell me!"

A very faint tinge of colour came into her brother's face. He looked as if he were trying to speak, so that the Sister leant forward quickly, giving him the slate and saying: "You must not try to say anything." The boy took the pencil and wrote "No"; then he held it and lay looking alternately at Monica and Miss Bertram. There was a slight bewildered expression on his face as if he were trying to remember something else which he wanted to say and could not for the moment think of it. Inside the screen every one stood motionless, almost holding their breath. From outside came the murmur of voices in the ward, a boy's laugh, the soft voice of a nurse who was standing over the fire reading something out of a newspaper to two or three men. Even sounds from outside came faintly to their ears, a very slight roll of passing traffic and the shrill voices of the newspaper boys running down Gower Street with special editions. One of the chief items of news in each paper was the last bulletin about the patient by whose bedside they were standing, with the last guesses as to whether and when he would be able to appear before the magistrates in Bow Street, or whether his trial would take place before another judge, and in a court beyond mortal sight.

A flash of memory came back to the young face on the bed, and some words were traced very slowly and with light uncertain strokes on the slate.  The Sister looked away while the two other women bent over the wandering hand with wet eyes.  Behind them, also reading, stood the policeman with a murmured word of apology: "It is my duty to see it, ma'am."

"Even if you think what a merciful ending, please do not say so."

When the sentence was finished the pencil still hovered for a moment, and was then lifted once more to underline the word "please"; then it was put down.

Miss Bertram stared at the words with such evident uncomprehension on her face that Gerald saw it and moved the slate impatiently.

"He means," said Monica in a stifled voice, "that if he dies he does not want us to say that it is a good thing.  Of course we shan't, Gerald darling; but you are not going to die.  You will get well and come and live with us and we shall all be happy again together.  I know quite well , , ,"

"I cannot possibly allow another moment," said the Sister. "This will not do at all. Mr. Thornton is waiting and you must come at once, please."

The two doctors came in as she spoke, and with a hurried farewell Miss Bertram and Monica left the ward. As they passed out of the hospital into Gower Street and Euston Road the newspaper boys were crying out the story of the fall of the Freehold, and Marshall's flight. "Attempted suicide of a clerk," screamed one of them running past Miss Bertram, while further on a knot of men whom the two women passed were talking about the crash, and Monica heard her brother's name mingled with curses and talk of penal servitude.

# CHAPTER XXXIII

Muirhead stood on the bleak Manchester race-course on the Saturday which was the last racing day of the year, and on his face was the haggard, horrible stare of a gambler who is going to play his last stake and knows beforehand what will be the result. It was his last in a very desperate sense of the word, for, like a hundred other weak passionate men, he had become demoralized by his losses to the point of saying, "I must and will have these back;" and from saying, "I must have this money back," to saying, "I must have the capital to get this back," there is of course no step at all; while from saying this latter to procuring the capital, first by questionable means, and then by means about which there is no question at all, is only a moderate step. Muirhead had raised money for several days on various securities with which he had at least a certain right to deal. On Friday and to-day he had raised more money, and no inconsiderable sum either, on securities which he had no right to touch. Half the money which he had brought to Manchester with him that morning was already gone; the other half was at that moment invested on West End for the Manchester November Handicap.

A cold soaking rain was driving down on to the course in heavy, hopeless lines. An east wind blew clouds of smoke and grime from the Ship Canal Works, while all over the stands and along the railings stood wet and shivering men and women, discussing their bets in listless voices, and for the most part too miserable to care whether their favourites lost or won. A few men, warmed up by whisky, or champagne, or hope, stamped about the rings with their collars up and their hands in their pockets, whistling and chaffing the book-makers, but the greater part of the spectators rushed back to cover directly they had made their bets.

Parmesan, carrying a ten-pound penalty for his Derby Cup victory, was running in the race, and Muirhead had hesitated for some time as to whether he should or not back him again. Finally he had decided to back him for a place, but had changed his mind at the last moment, and backed Elf for a place instead. He said to himself that one horse had already won him money, and that it was the other's turn now. The race was very late in starting.

There were three break-aways and Muirhead
was in a fretting fever when the flag finally
fell.    West Wind went to the front with a
great rush; his little jockey, being unable to
hold him, let him go, according to wise orders,
and the horse came round the bend with a ten-
lengths lead.    Muirhead, who knew enough
about racing by this time to guess that "cutting down" tactics were not likely to pay over
mile and three-quarters, watched the animal
with despair and fury, yet with a growing spark
of hope as the horse came on up the straight
without appearing to falter.    Too soon, however, he began to see the field closing up like a
telescope.    Parmesan, Amazon and half-a-
dozen other horses rushed up to West Wind,
and already the little jockey had his whip up
and was lurching about in a desperate attempt
to make his tiring horse keep up the pace.
Long before the distance he had dropped back
hopelessly beaten.    Amazon rushed to the
front, followed by Kodak, Elf, and Parmesan.
With passionate exclamations of anger, Muirhead saw the four go past him with scarcely a
length separating them all.    At least, however, he would not lose much money over the
race if Elf were placed, and he heaved a sigh
of relief when the horses swept past the judges'
box, and he heard among the general uproar

cries that Elf had won. But number seven—
Kodak's number—went up first, then in quick
succession Amazon's number was put into the
second place and Parmesan's number into the
third place. Elf was fourth, and Muirhead had
the not uncommon gratification of reflecting
that his first judgment had been correct, and
that if he had followed it and backed Parmesan
for a place, he would not only not have lost
money on the race but, the horse being at much
longer odds, might even have won something.
When fate begins to inflict such reverses of
fortune, she piles them up to an extent which
her victim mostly finds to be seriously annoying.

After the decision of the November Handicap, Muirhead had exactly £2, 10s. left in his
pocket;—it would hardly be correct to say in
his possession, since the money could not be
said in any possible sense to belong to him at
all. Seven and sixpence of this he spent on a
half-bottle of champagne, keeping half a crown
for his cab to the station, and put the rest on
an outsider for the Final Plate. The outsider,
ridden by a gentleman-jockey, took at the com-
mencement of the race, and maintained to its
finish the conspicuous but disappointing position known as "a bad last," so that a little boy
was moved to put his head over the railings

and call out to the aforesaid gentleman-jockey,
"Hi, Captain! What detained you?" and
Muirhead had left the course before the race
could strictly be said to be finished.

The man's mind was a complete blank. He
refused to think of the past, present, or future,
and took his seat in a cab with three other
men without any other feeling or thought
than annoyance at the rain. Once, for a
second, when he put his hand on a certain
empty pocket-book in his breast-pocket, a sudden momentary realisation of what had happened came to him, and he flung up his hands
in a gesture of horror and despair; but a stare
of astonishment from his opposite neighbour
brought back his senses, or to speak more
accurately, distracted them again, and he
looked round him in eager search for something else to think about. The cab was driving
past a stationer's shop at the time, and his eye
caught the contents board of a Manchester
evening paper: "Exposure of the Freehold
Building Society," "Escape of the Secretary,"
"Arrest of the Managers," "Attempted suicide
of a clerk."

If Muirhead had recently had much time or
attention to devote to the affairs of the Society
of which he was the manager in Staffordshire,
this news would not have come to him with

much of a shock. Half a score of letters and telegrams had arrived even during the last forty-eight hours, which would have been enough to show an ordinarily wakeful business man that a crisis was at hand. But Muirhead had not been paying the slightest attention to any of the affairs of the Society. He had tossed this document to one clerk, that to another, telling them to enter the figures in their proper register, or file the paper on its proper file, and that was all.

The news on this contents bill beat its way through the cloud which hung over his brain like a torpedo boat through a heavy sea, and crashed on to his intelligence. As the cab drove up to the London Road Station, he jumped out, and tossing his share of the fare to the driver, rushed to the bookstall and snatched up the first two papers which came to his hand. Half a page of the Staffordshire Sentinel was devoted to the news. Everywhere telegrams in big letters announcing some additional horror met his eye. "Marshall's escape, a warrant out for his arrest, and all the exits from the country being carefully watched." "Gerald Franklin found in Marshall's house with his throat cut, and taken to the hospital and not expected to live." "All the books of the Society in charge of the police."  "Additional arrests being announced every hour, and numerous others expected." Merciful heavens! what if a warrant were out for his own arrest, just at this moment when it was imperatively necessary that he should be at liberty, in order to arrange a certain little matter with a Birmingham money-lender; a little matter, the discovery of which might also mean arrest and some far more serious proceedings? The man stood on the platform completely stupefied, staring at the paper with suspended breath and ashen cheeks. Presently he saw several people running, and seeing that he only just had time to catch the 5:30 Express to Stoke, he ran down the platform with the open newspapers in his hand, and jumped into the nearest compartment just as the train was moving off. Some one in the compartment who knew him nudged his neighbour and whispered who it was, so that Muirhead, looking up, found himself confronted with scowling suspicious faces, the first of the hundreds which afterwards met his eyes everywhere he turned. Every one was reading the news and talking about it. Passengers for Stoke, Rugby and London were there, all of whom knew some one who would be buried under these tumbling ruins. "Is this true, sir?" asked an old man, rapping a newspaper angrily with his stick, and as Muirhead shrugged his shoulders he went on: "I sincerely trust, sir, that all the scoundrels involved in this business will shortly be in gaol, where they deserve to be," and added a great deal more to the same effect which Muirhead did not hear. He was thinking of nothing now but what he would find when he got home.

As the train ran up to Stoke platform Muirhead saw two police officers standing there scanning each carriage as it went by, and with the prescience which belongs to such moments of tragedy, he knew at once why they were there. He got out and stood by the carriage door, waiting quietly, swinging his race glasses in his hand and watching the officers as they walked rapidly down the train. He knew one of them well enough, it was Burton, the head of the Newcastle police. The two men came up to him and Burton said in a low voice: "I fear, Mr. Muirhead, it is my painful duty to arrest you on charges connected with the Freehold Building Society. Do you wish to see the warrant?"

"No," said Muirhead in a whisper. "Let's be off as quickly as possible. You don't want to handcuff me, I suppose?"

"No, if you come quite quietly."

"Of course I will come quietly," muttered the wretched man. "Oh! for God's sake, do let us come out of this. Here's a crowd collecting. Do make haste!"

# CHAPTER XXXIV

Lady Eastney found that between the making of schemes for departure from England with her lover, and carrying them out, various trivial accidents could fix a gulf. She meant to see Mr. Seaton, her lawyer, before leaving, and it chanced that two people came in to lunch next day and afterwards insisted on taking her into the Park. They were of the tiresome class of persons who, having made up their minds to do what they consider a kindness, refuse to consider the possibility of the other person thinking it a bore, and they laughed away all Lady Eastney's protests about having work to do, under the impression that she was merely protesting against their giving themselves trouble for her. She was weak and they were strong, and the journey to Paris was postponed for another twenty-four hours. Next day Seaton himself had to make a journey into the country and could not see her, but promised to come to Portman Square on the following morning. In the morning, however, he telegraphed from a remote village in Norfolk, saying that he could not reach London till late that evening, but would come round to Portman Square about half-past nine if the business was urgent. The Marchioness telegraphed that it was, and shortly before ten o'clock on that Friday evening Seaton made his appearance. Lady Eastney received him in her boudoir.

"You have heard nothing more about the affairs of this horrible Society, I suppose?" she asked.

"I have been out of town for the last thirty-six hours," he said, "and have driven here direct from Liverpool Street Station. I have heard nothing at all and I still think, as I told you some days ago, that the business may perhaps be wound up without any serious loss or great scandal; but of course I know nothing whatever about it. A few of my clients have some small share in it, but only a very small one, and none of them appear to be very anxious about its affairs. At any rate they have not spoken to me about it."

"There will be a scandal, and a very big one, and it will begin within a few hours," said the Marchioness, little knowing that the first scene had already begun; "but I must not detain you here about that. I want to ask you a question about a more private matter. I told you some days ago," the woman walked away to the mantel-piece and spoke in a careless defiant tone which was contradicted by the scarlet which dyed her cheeks and neck, "that I was going to leave the country with Mr. Alford. My mind is quite made up," she went on quickly, seeing that the lawyer was about to speak, "and my question to you has nothing to do with that—otherwise I can quite understand that you would not care to say anything which might assist me. I want you simply to tell me what I can do to keep Angela."

"Absolutely nothing," said the lawyer unhesitatingly.

"But please think. I am going to take her with me and she will of course be left with me until divorce proceedings have been begun and finished. What difference can they make to her?"

"If they are successful you would have no right to keep the child. She would pass to Lord Eastney's charge."

"But he would not claim her," said the woman; "he cares nothing whatever about her."

"Whether he claimed his rights or not, you would cease to be her guardian or to have any legal rights at all in connection with her."

"He would not exercise his rights, I say!"

"That would not matter, as his relatives would come forward and claim the child. Lady Jane Baxter would probably be asked by the others to do so, as she is married."

"What right would they have to interfere?" The woman turned round from the mantelpiece and faced Seaton. The colour had all died out of her face, and her hands were clasped together as if she were begging the man to give her the answers which she desired.

"Simply this. If Lady Angela were with you, a child of Lord Eastney's with whom you have nothing to do would be under illegal guardianship. They would wish to take it away."

"They could not do it without his help."

"I beg your pardon," said the lawyer, more anxious perhaps to avert a family catastrophe than to explain the niceties of the law, "they certainly could, and I may leave you, with your knowledge of Lady Jane Baxter and her opinions, to judge whether they would."

"They would have to find us first."

"My dear lady, do you imagine that you and Mr. Alford with a child and a maid could travel about in Europe or in any other part of the world without leaving any trace of where you had been? I do not flatter myself that I have any great detective skill, but I think that

I would undertake to find Lady Angela within a week without the slightest difficulty.   A detective would probably ask for forty-eight hours."

"I would kill him when he did find her," said the woman.

Looking at his client as she stood there, trembling, with set teeth and flashing eyes, Seaton muttered to himself: "I really believe you would."   Aloud, however, he only remarked: "Forgive me for talking dull common sense, Lady Eastney, but the supply of detectives is not limited, and the next one who came would, I am afraid, come for you as well as your daughter."

"I would kill her and myself," said the woman, who was rapidly working herself into a fit of hysterics.

"You tell me that your mind is made up about leaving the country with Mr. Alford," said Seaton; "otherwise I would suggest that it would save a considerable amount of anxiety and trouble, and apparently crime, if you remained with your husband."

"Yes, yes, but my mind is made up," said the Marchioness distractedly, and in the tone of a person whose mind had been made up and unmade twenty times in as many minutes and was about to take a twenty-first decision.

"Come in!" she said impatiently, as some one knocked at the door. "Bertie! What on earth are you doing here? I thought you were at the Suffolks'. Is anything the matter?"

"Yes," said the young man simply. "Hasn't Mr. Seaton told you?"

"He has told me no news at all."

"Marshall has bolted. That young clerk Franklin has been found in his room stabbed, or something. The whole business has begun."

"Had we better leave? It doesn't matter talking before Mr. Seaton; he knows everything. Had we better leave early to-morrow morning?"

"We had very much better not leave at all," said the young man doggedly. He folded his arms and looked down on the floor resolved not to meet the woman's eyes. "But I am perfectly ready to do what you like. We will go if you like."

"If I like! If I like! How dare you come here and say that to me? What do you mean by coming and saying, If I like?"

But for Seaton's presence Alford would have been obliged to protest that he himself was passionately anxious for the flight, and that he had only meant to ask whether his recent news had made any change in Lady Eastney's own desires. This would have involved him in another long love scene and the fixing of their departure for an early hour next morning. Therefore he was unmitigatedly grateful for Seaton's presence, which enabled him to answer very quietly: "I mean what I say. You know my wishes and I only asked yours."

There was a long silence. Pride and passion, rage against Alford, who had put her to shame before Seaton, and love for the young man, love for her child and the horrible conviction that what Seaton had told her was inevitable, raged together in Lady Eastney's heart as she stood there with her hands clasped in front of her and her eyes flashing fury at Alford.

"I have had one real sincere desire all this time," she said at last in a low measured voice, with a depth of anger and scorn in it which made Mr. Alford squirm, and a ring of truth in it too which made him flush wrathfully, "and that was to take Angela away from this disgrace and trouble. For you, personally, I care absolutely nothing, as little as I do for myself. You came here imploring me to go abroad with you, protesting that you loved me and would help me to escape this trouble, and I believed you"—my Lady looked steadily at the young man, daring him to contradict her before

Seaton—"I believed you and accepted your offer, as I would have accepted the offer of any man whom I knew well and who promised me a method of escape for the child. Now Mr. Seaton tells me that it is not a method of escape for her, that she would be taken from me and brought back, therefore I have no longer the slightest intention of going any-where with you, for whom, as I say, I care nothing at all. Now you can go away. No! I am not going to hear anything that you have to say. Go at once! Do you hear me? Go!"

Feeling very small, and looking, as he well might, extremely bewildered, Mr. Alford went; while Seaton sat on, stroking his beard and saying to himself: "The woman hardly knows it herself, but on my soul and conscience I believe that when she told the chap she cared as little for him as she did for herself, and had planned the whole of this tom-foolery for the sake of the child, she was telling him the exact and literal truth."

# CHAPTER XXXV

Moltke's well-known dictum, that there are eighteen ways of invading England and only one way of getting out again, has a particular and painful significance for a man wanted by the police. It is said sometimes that London is the best place for hiding in, but London is in fact a very small place, as any one who has ever borrowed five pounds from his neighbour and tried to avoid him afterwards will bear witness. To go to a small country town is good for a time, but these places will, of course, not do for anything but a temporary residence. Besides, life here after London is distinctly dull, and a man, even if he has forged cheques, embezzled money or obtained it under other false pretences, does like his amusements as usual. Where to dine the night after you have committed a murder, and what to do afterwards, is a problem which must have presented itself to many persons. For myself I think that, if I were on good terms with the waiters at my club and could feel tolerably confident that they would not give

me up to the police, I should dine there;—
round a corner of course, and out of sight of
any one who was reading an evening paper.
One would be certain to be comfortable there
and at least as safe as anywhere else.

Marshall did not dine at all on the night of
his flight,—which was a mistake, since anxiety
on an empty stomach is a very severe affliction.
He lay in his berth on the St. Malo steamer
considering his present and future, one, as he
said to himself, damnable, the other spec-
ulative.  Having breakfasted in the buffet at
St. Malo Station, which is the one exception
to the rule that all eating-places in France are
good, he took a train for the South and sat in
it shuddering with alarm at every stoppage.
The fastest method of progression in Brittany,
as every one knows, is the bicycle; next to that
comes walking, and, a bad third, the railway.
For my own part the trains here soothe me.  I
like to get out and walk by the engine-driver
and ask him whether his train is still, in the
cautious language of the railway notices, "*se
dirigeant vers Rennes,*" and to feel that for a
very slight consideration he would go somewhere else.  But this mode of progression, I
am aware, drives most English people mad.
Marshall, for instance, was fuming in his carriage, cursing every station at which he

stopped, declaring that the train ought to be prosecuted for furious loitering, and generally conducting himself as one of his countrymen does who is getting late for an appointment by means of a slow train. As the appointment in his case was one involving escape from ten years penal servitude, Marshall had, it must be allowed, some justification for his annoyance.

The train dragged past Rennes and Redon, and into the pretty valley of the Loire, arriving at last at Saint Nazaire. This being the Compagnie Générale Transatlantique's point of departure for South America, the man anticipated, not without some reason, that his arrival here would be looked for, and he jumped out and made his way to the exit with a face of alarm which would have betrayed him ten times over to a detective if one had chanced to be present. He had however got a good start of the police arrangements, and was able to go in peace to the comfortable old Hôtel Bretagne, where he booked a passage under the name of Taylor on the next steamer for Rio Janeiro.

As ill-luck would have it, he had three days to wait here before the steamer sailed, and he began to speculate seriously as to the advisability of spending them somewhere outside Saint Nazaire. His travels had given him that real knowledge of roughing it, which, while it makes most men able to do so, and fluent in talking about its charms, makes most of them also extremely careful to avoid it if possible. Also he had some experience of Breton villages, where you dine on onion soup and veal and cheese, and are compelled to get up early in the morning because the landlady wants the sheets to lay the table for dejeuner; and though he did not mean to risk anything he was not going to plunge into these joys without good and sufficient cause.

An Englishman who sat next to him at the table d'hôte dinner saved him the trouble of making inquiries about such places in the neighbourhood by making them himself, and Marshall, on the look-out for detectives, studied this person furtively and closely. He was a middle-aged man, with brown hair and broad flowing whiskers and a heavy moustache. His clothes, which consisted of a Norfolk jacket, knickerbockers and thick woollen stockings, were considerably too big for him, and his gait, which was rolling and rollicking, gave you the idea of a man who took his brandy and soda regularly but managed as a rule to walk it off afterwards. Marshall eyed him uncomfortably, and he eyed Marshall with at least equal discomfort. At last the late

Secretary of the Freehold Building Society
looked straight into his companion's eyes and
then dropped his fork with a crash on his plate.
In those features, which one cannot disguise
except with more pain than the ordinary person cares to inflict on himself, Marshall recognised something which made him look for a
scar just above the man's left eyebrow, and
this scar he found. This made him look more
closely at the flowing hair, and search for certain signs indicative of its having been bought
in a wig shop, and these signs he also found.
After this he came to the conclusion, not quite
certainly but with a feeling that he would
stake a good deal of his money on it, that he
was sitting next to Mr. Luke Robinson.
Furthermore he concluded from certain signs
that Mr. Luke Robinson was on the way to
recognise him, if he had not already done so.
One is not always certain of recognising anybody, since marks of identification may be
common to several people, or may sometimes
be in a passive state. The man, for instance,
who came to the Morgue in Paris in search of
his father, and was told, on describing him,
that there were three men at present in the
Morgue answering to that description, and that
he must give some other means of identification; and who then added, in a moment of

brilliant inspiration, that his father was dumb;
was obviously doubtful as to what marks of
identification really meant. Robinson and
Marshall, who both knew what they meant,
had forgotten half a dozen of them in their own
cases. After confronting one another for half
an hour neither of them had the least doubt
about who the other was, and they sat during the rest of dinner merely considering
whether it would be good policy to admit the
recognition. Marshall could find no reason
against it in his own mind, and was, besides,
extremely curious to find out why Robinson
had fled at all; therefore, after dinner, he
strolled down towards the docks with a cigar,
and on turning round perceived that Robinson
was coming in the same direction. He waited
for the latter to join him, and then asked
briefly but forcibly:—

"What the devil are you doing here?"

"What are you doing?" was the not unnatural
reply.

"Waiting for the *Normannia*," said Marshall; "that's easy to guess; and I suppose
you're coming to Rio Janeiro, too, but I don't
understand why."

"It's a—a very healthy country," said Robinson, vaguely and dubiously.

"Very," assented Marshall.

The two men walked on in silence for a space, both debating whether they had better not let matters rest where they were. Marshall made up his mind first. Like the boy who was continually being asked which of a new litter of kittens he would like to keep and which to drown, and who, on being shown some newly-arrived twin-brothers, pointed unhesitatingly to the ugliest and said: "I should drown that one;" Marshall had been engaged all his life in deciding difficult questions, and could therefore do it faster than most people. So he said amiably:—

"My departure from London was rather hurried, and was dictated by motives of prudence as much as health. In fact, the police are looking for me. You are doubtless aware, my dear Mr. Robinson, that the financial arrangements of this Freehold Society were not always conducted as the law requires."

"No, I believe not."

"The Staffordshire branch — a most admirably managed branch it was—was, I suppose, no exception; but I am rather surprised that you should have been so much involved in its affairs as to make this—this little change of costume necessary;" and Marshall looked at the Wesleyan minister's whiskers and knickerbockers and bicycling cap with an engaging smile.

"I had a good deal of work to do in Staffordshire," said Robinson evasively.

"Certainly you had," replied Marshall; "and most admirably you did it.  Did our friends down there notice anything wrong?"

"Well, partly they did," said the other surlily; "and partly they minded their own business."

"My dear Mr. Robinson," went on Marshall, rather dashed at finding that he had given his own confidences, and was not to have any in return, "I can understand that you are slightly annoyed by this catastrophe, but I can't understand why you shouldn't confide in me.  To be frank, it decreases the chances of safety for both of us to be together like this, and I can't imagine why the devil you are here at all.  Forgive me for swearing in your presence."

"The result of my confidence in you up to the present date has not been very fortunate."

"We are going to be travelling companions for some weeks," said Marshall persuasively. "I really think that you might tell me why you are here.  Also I might point out to you that it is but a matter of twenty-four hours my finding out all about it.  No doubt I shall occupy the most prominent place in the English newspapers of Monday, which will arrive here on

Tuesday; but a space will probably be found for your doings as well."

"I should think they would probably offer a reward for your apprehension, won't they?" said Robinson, meditatively.

"Very likely," said Marshall, "but if anybody in this town is thinking of earning that reward, well, faith! I could put my finger on a town where there is going to be trouble."

"To be candid, as you have been," said Robinson, "I could very well dispense with your company on this voyage, and see no reason at all why, if you persist in coming with me, I shouldn't telegraph to the police to stop you."

"Why, you poor fool, for the simple reason that they would have both of us."

"A man cannot be arrested without a warrant and without cause," said Robinson. "No one will have any desire to arrest me for another three or four days at least."

"I will show you another reason then," said Marshall, springing at the man and seizing him by the throat.

The two were standing on the edge of one of the docks, and Marshall's intention was to choke his quondam friend first and throw him into the water afterwards. Unfortunately, however, Robinson managed to emit one or two gurgling cries for help, and then when he finally lost his footing and tumbled over the edge, he was holding Marshall tightly in his arms. The two men fell into the dock with a mighty splash, and presently a dozen small boys, half-a-dozen men and women, and finally two policemen, appeared on the scene.

The two combatants were dragged out and stood on the edge of the dock for a moment dripping and swearing. Marshall's wig was far at the back of his head, Robinson's over his left eye. The latter had also lost one of his whiskers, while the other had moved down under his chin. The crowd, which had considerably increased by this time, stood staring at the Englishmen in considerable and by no means respectful astonishment, and the two policemen were evidently debating as to the propriety of allowing the incident to terminate here. They were, however, saved the trouble of a decision by two other Englishmen who pushed their way through the spectators, and informed the hesitating French policemen that they were English detectives, with warrants for the arrest of the two gentlemen whose appearance was now causing so much surprise.

# CHAPTER XXXVI

Gerald Franklin's life flickered up and down for forty-eight hours; then he began to recover.

"He has not been guilty of any real wrong, my dear," said Miss Bertram to Monica; "it was my poor wicked brother who devised the whole affair and led him astray and kept him at this dreadful work. I do not suppose he knew himself what he was doing."

Monica shook her head miserably. She knew her brother better than that.

"I am afraid you must have lost money in the Society," said Reggie Nicholson, who had come up to London to be near the pair.

"I have lost nearly everything, my dear boy," said the woman quietly. "I tried to sell my shares, but it was too late. I suppose there is no harm in saying now that Lady Eastney advised me to sell them last August, and also mercifully advised me against letting Monica's money be put into the Company. I tried to sell the shares, but it was too late, and now I have got only a few hundred pounds left in the world. I fear that I am only one of many such sufferers. Probably there are hundreds worse off even than myself as a result of this. I shall have to find some work to do, but it will be time enough to talk about that when Gerald is well."

"You will do nothing of the sort, Aunt Christina," said Monica. "You will live with Reggie and me. I wouldn't marry Reggie unless he agreed to that."

"I was only waiting until Miss Bertram had done speaking to say that myself," said Nicholson.

"I am healthy and strong, children," said the woman in a curiously hard voice. "Reggie's father has lost money by this. Monica herself may also be said to have lost some, since I should of course have left her half of mine, and it is all my brother's doing. How could I possibly ask you two to keep me? I am not speaking about the matter without thinking. I have thought it all over, and I shall ask for a post as housekeeper or matron of some small Home. For one thing, I cannot possibly go on living at Hartshill in the middle of all the people whom my poor brother has ruined. How could I meet the Garths and Wintons and Cartons? And then there is Mr. Lowe. Poor Mr. Lowe! He has lost everything and has nothing but the income from his living, and it is my fault.  Why have we all been trying to be rich like this?  To get money without earning it!  we have all set you a terrible example, dear children, we who are supposed to be your guardians and teachers!  But at any rate you will see how severely and promptly such folly is punished.  I think I am going to leave you here together for a little while.  I want to be by myself to think. Remember that we are going to see Gerald at three o'clock.''

As if resolved to escape from Monica's protests Miss Bertram left the room quickly, and the two lovers sat in silence for a time, wondering whether they would be able to change her intention.  She did not as a rule announce such decisions lightly, or readily abandon them when made, and indeed Reggie saw some reason in what she had said about themselves. Nicholson Senior had lost a big sum, a number of his workmen had lost money by the Society's failure, and he would be expected to help them.  The young man foresaw that his own allowance would have to be reduced to very small proportions.  They would in fact have to live for some time on Monica's money, and out of this she would very probably, so far as could be seen at present, have to support her

brother for some time to come. Gerald would
be unable to work for another three months,
and even then a young man with his record
would not find it easy to get work. Yet the
boy, who had almost as sincere an affection for
Miss Bertram as Monica had, certainly did not
mean to let her do any work if she could be
persuaded to come and live with them. He
said to himself, not without a certain amount
of satisfaction, that the best thing to be done
was for himself and Monica to be married
at once, and ask Miss Bertram to live with
them at some place within reasonable distance
of Stoke, though as far as possible from
Hartshill.

It was Nicholson's self-imposed task to read
the morning and evening newspapers, and to
tell Miss Bertram and Monica all that they
were absolutely obliged to know of the proceedings in connection with the Freehold. Monday morning's papers seemed, as the young
man said to himself, to contain news of the
arrest of everybody they knew in London and
Staffordshire. Tuesday's and Wednesday's
papers announced the first appearance of the
prisoners at Bow Street and their remand.
Day after day the story went on of the havoc
and ruin wrought by the men who had planned
and carried out the Freehold Building Society

and its kindred companies. No trace could be found of any money in the possession of either Margets or Marshall, and they professed to have paid everything in order to settle certain debts. Proof of criminal transactions was found, when the public prosecutor got fairly into his work, to be extremely difficult to obtain. Against Lord Eastney there was absolutely none. He posed successfully as a dupe, though there were certain documents signed at the midnight meeting at Margets' house which came near to being his undoing. There was, however, a certain amount of evidence to corroborate his assertion that he had signed a portion without being shown the whole. His acquittal was a foregone conclusion, and took place accordingly. The man went home to his house on the afternoon of the day when the trial came to an end. There would be a sale there shortly under half a score of bankruptcy notices, and Lady Eastney was superintending the packing of her own private possessions. She was alone in the drawing-room when he entered, and looked up with cold enquiry on her face.

"It is all right," he said, "I have got off. The charge, as I told you, was a ridiculous one. As if I could possibly know what the scoundrels were doing!"

Lady Eastney turned round to the mantel-
piece again, her fingers moving restlessly to
and fro among the small ornaments there.

"I am afraid there is a bad time coming for
us financially," he went on hesitatingly, "but
I hope you won't mind it very much.  Of
course I shall look out for some work, and I
don't suppose there will be any difficulty in
getting some.  We could live in London or
the country, whichever you like.  Of course we
can't go on living in this house, but I don't
think you need be very uncomfortable."

For answer the Marchioness muttered to
herself some words which sounded so like, "I
suppose it doesn't matter much so long as we
are safely together," that the man's face
flushed up to the forehead and he moved
towards her.

"Would you—would you really care about
our being together?" he asked with eyes down-
cast and the beginnings of a look of happiness
on his face.

Lady Eastney turned and stared at him in
amazement; then, as she understood, laughed
slightly.

"I meant Angela!" she said.

Muirhead would perhaps have escaped altogether, though his share in the purchase and
management of the Arkhill Hall property was

difficult to explain away, but during the last
three weeks he had simply, as it appeared,
helped himself to large sums of the Society's
money for betting purposes; and this not only
meant five years penal servitude in itself, but
lent a much blacker aspect to the other shady
transactions in which he had been engaged on
behalf of the Society.  It was pleaded, however, with a certain amount of success, that he
had been the dupe of Marshall throughout, and
some very carefully prepared and cautiously
given evidence of Reggie Nicholson's went to
prove that, even if he had realised dimly that
some of the proceedings of the Society were a
trifle queer, he had always believed the Company itself to be sound and solvent.  The
result, however, was seven years penal servitude, and it was not much satisfaction to him
to hear the judge's opinion that he had got off
very lightly.  He left the Courthouse almost
wishing that the sentence had been for life.
What had he to expect or hope for at the end
of these years?  His life was over, with failure
written at the end of every pathway along
which he had walked.  He loathed failure, and
it had pursued and overtaken him everywhere.
He was a born gambler, with the true
gambler's feeling that, in everything he did,
he was playing a game with fortune, the end

of which would be decided by no merit or judgment, no virtue or effort. Everywhere he had been beaten, and, as is natural in this view of life, he saw no hope for the future because he had no counters with which to recommence the game. He saw immediately before him a long term of years in which time was simply to pass without result, good or bad, and in which the most that one could possibly hope was that it would pass quickly. After that he foresaw merely a struggle to live, without hope or expectation of enjoyment; a long, long fight in which there would be neither victory nor defeat but only fighting. He went away with a last dazed look round the Courthouse, and a dull wonder, characteristic of the man, why fortune should have treated him so ill when it had behaved so kindly to some of his companions.

In Marshall's case defence was, as he coolly told his sister, an entire waste of money. "I never meant to offer any defence," he said, "I simply meant to escape, and I can't think what induced me to put it off so long. It is a blunder which will cost me pretty dear now."

The blunder cost Mr. Marshall twelve years penal servitude, which sentence he heard with a resigned sigh, but a feeling on the whole of relief. "That means eight years," he calculated, "unless I try to escape, or knock the warders down, or complain of the food. Well, I have lived hard at various periods of my life, and I do not suppose that life at Portland will be much worse than the years in Madrid after that last little *contretemps*. And when I come out, I shall, after all, be well on the right side of fifty, and there is the best part of £40,000 put away in that bank at Buenos Ayres which Jackson will look after for me faithfully enough. It will double in these eight years, won't it? Or how long is it that these sums take to double? I must ask for an arithmetic book at Portland and find out. It is a bore, but a man is not moribund at fifty; he has got ten years of enjoyment at least before him, and there is a good deal of spending in £60,000. We will call it £60,000. To get hold of Master Gerald's £3,000 at the last moment was a great *coup*, though I expect that the delay which it caused has helped to land me here. Well, these accidents will happen, and eight years is not eternity."

It must be admitted that Mr. Marshall deserved his sentence, and might be held by the most lenient moralist to have deserved a good deal more.

Gerald Franklin's case was the one on which most doubt existed, and on which much legal debate took place. He was defended with great ability on the lines that he was a subordinate of a subordinate, "the dupe of a dupe," as one counsel remarked, and could not for a moment understand why the explanation was received with general laughter. Much was made of a theory invented for his benefit by Dr. Hare, that the lad had found Marshall on the point of escaping and had received his wounds in a gallant attempt to stop him. The boy's innocent and youthful appearance was of course a great help to the defence, and difficult as it was to combat the statement of the prosecution that somebody in North Staffordshire had thoroughly known and understood the proceedings of the Society, and that that somebody was certainly not Muirhead, Gerald's counsel was finally successful. To his own infinite astonishment the lad heard a verdict of acquittal for himself, and for a moment hardly knew which to do first, to rejoice in his escape or despise the jury for believing in his innocence. It was of course pleasing to be free; but it was very unpleasant to be free because twelve of your fellow countrymen, having deliberated on the matter for some time, had concluded that you were a fool. Liberty, however, was worth having even at this price, and, as Gerald very properly argued, it was the highest triumph of genius to have all the management and all the profit of an undertaking in your own hands, and let somebody else bear all the losses and the blame for all the mistakes.

And so with a sentence of eighteen months imprisonment for Robinson and five years penal servitude for Mr. Margets, the trial of the directors and managers of the Freehold Building Society came to an end.

# CHAPTER XXXVII

The injury to Gerald's throat was sufficient to prevent him from working for many weeks, even after his departure from the hospital and discharge from his trial. He had no money and his prospects were small, for no firm would willingly give employment to any one who had been connected with the recently exposed Building Society, whose clerks were obviously either fools or scoundrels. Re-established in his rooms in the Ethridges' house two days after the conclusion of the trial, it occurred to Gerald, who had hitherto been absorbed by his own danger, to wonder how the weekly bills were being paid. Miss Bertram, he suddenly remembered, must have lost nearly all her money in the crash of the Freehold. It was not likely that Ethridge was keeping him for nothing. He himself was more than penniless, for any money which he had saved had been absorbed ten times over by the expenses of his defence. His real position suddenly occurred to him, that he was penniless, without means or prospects, living on his sister's charity. The unpleasantness of the situation had been dulled by illness and danger. Now it fully confronted him and he writhed under it. Monica was sitting in the room as he lay on the sofa calculating facts and chances. He had been told to talk very little and move very little, and there was therefore nothing for him to do but to sit there and read. Many even of those people who love reading find it a detestable occupation when it suddenly becomes their only one, and Gerald did not love it at the best of times. For the past forty-eight hours he had been reading the newspaper accounts of himself and his friends, with criticisms of the Freehold's finance, and had been considering, as was his wont, how much better he could have written them himself if it had been his business to do so. The articles amused him, chiefly on account of the elaborate theories by which the writers accounted for Marshall's success. The managing director of the Society had, it appeared, made the most wonderful statements and put forth the most wonderful proofs as to the value of the Society. Evidently, muttered Gerald, it takes people a long time to find out that nine people out of ten believe any statement which you make to them about money matters without any proof at all, if you make it three times in a loud voice.

But the newspaper criticisms palled after a time; thought and anxiety followed, and Gerald began asking questions.

"So nothing could be got out of Marshall about my money?" said the lad to his sister this afternoon.

"He said, you know, that he had spent everything he had on bribing people to keep quiet till the last possible moment," said Monica.

"Yes, I know," said Gerald with a laugh, "one believes as much of that as one pleases." Marshall's character was in fact, as the boy knew, very much like his own, and he himself knew a good deal better than to try and bribe people into silence.

"I am afraid however that it is gone," said Monica, on the whole content that her brother was beginning to think again.

"And Aunt Christina's too?"

"Yes," said the girl. "She is talking of accepting a place as matron of a small orphans' home at Chester which has been offered to her. The pay is £40 a year, and I have had great difficulty in making her promise to take another £60 a year out of my money."

Gerald raised himself up on his arm, looking thoroughly horrified and startled: "I did not quite realize that it meant that," he said in a low voice, and, practical young man as he was,

Monica thought it very probable that he was speaking the truth.

"It is very sad," said the girl, "but she has got plenty of courage."

"And I say, old girl, about myself . . . It is a horrible thing to have to ask you, but you know I have got nothing left either. As you see from the trial it is not altogether my fault. Those fellows knew what they were after, and I didn't. You see how they gulled me. . . ."

"Oh, Gerald dear!"

Looking up quickly the boy met his sister's eyes fixed on him with a curious pleading look in them. He flushed scarlet and looked down at the sofa-cushions, picking one of them with nervous fingers. In the silence which followed there flashed back into his memory a score of occasions on which he had told Monica the truth about some transaction in which he was involved, and let her into half a hundred secrets, in looking back upon which she could not fail to see how deeply he himself had been involved in Marshall's roguery.

"I suppose I have been rather mean to you," he said at last, and even such a grudging confession as this made Monica more contented; "but anyhow the others have known so much more than me that they have got the best of me in the end," went on the boy ruefully, "and I have got nothing left at all. Of course I shall soon get some more work to do, but, as you heard old Carter say, I am good for nothing yet. Could you"—the words stuck in his throat again and again—"Could you help me a bit? Could you lend me enough to go on with till I get some work?"

"Of course I will, Gerald, and you needn't surely mind so much about asking me. At any rate," she went on, suddenly mindful of a hundred injunctions which her aunt had given her as to what she was to say when this inevitable moment came, "I will give you whatever is necessary. It wouldn't be fair to Reggie to give you more, though indeed, my dear old boy,"—Monica could not remember her injunctions for more than ten seconds at a time—"of course you come before him. I am going to give you £100"—she had been told to give him £50, but somehow that didn't sound enough—"and that will enable you to pay Dr. Carter and the Ethridges, and will keep you till you are well and can get some more work."

The lad tried to mutter a few words of thanks, but something choked them back. His throat hurt him violently after these few minutes conversation, and the humiliation of the moment was almost more than he could bear.

It was curious that when only a few months
before he had been asking his sister for the
whole of her money to invest in a security
which he knew to be quite worthless,—which
meant a 5 per cent. commission for himself and
absolute ruin for the young investor—he had
had no hesitation and very little shame.
To-day when he was asking for £100 he was
almost crying with the degradation of it.

Monica saw his misery, and, the matter having been settled, tried to turn the conversation
to something more pleasant.

"Of course you will get work easily enough,"
she said, "and then you will begin to settle
down better and save a little for certain purposes, won't you?"

"To pay you back again?" asked the boy
with another great flush of colour. "Yes, of
course I shall."

"Indeed, I wasn't thinking of that," said the
girl with a frown at this misinterpretation of
her words. "I was thinking of—of Sophie."

"Oh!" The flush continued on Gerald's
face, but a slight smile was added to it.

"Shan't you try to save something for her?"
asked the girl.

"How do I know that she would take it
when it was saved?" said Gerald with a shy
laugh.

"I think she would, but you might ask her."

"Very well, I will."

"And then you will have something else to think about besides making money. That has never seemed to me to be the one thing worth thinking about; and all of you who have thought so much about it, and about nothing else, have been very unlucky."

"Well," said Gerald, "whether Sophie likes me or not, I am still resolved to be rich."

"A very nice resolution in its right place," said Monica with the air of some one who knew several resolutions which were better, and a glance up at Reggie Nicholson, who came in and asked her what she was preaching about.

PRINTED BY R. R. DONNELLEY
AND SONS COMPANY AT THE
LAKESIDE PRESS, CHICAGO, ILL.